THE BISTRO BY WATERSMEET BRIDGE

JULIE STOCK

CLUED UP PUBLISHING

Cover Design: Oliphant Publishing Services
Editing: Helena Fairfax
Proofreading: Wendy Janes

*To Sylvia and John who gave me an early
appreciation of good food and wine.*

CHAPTER ONE

Olivia went over what she was going to say to her father one last time as the train rattled its way towards Bristol. Years of habit kept her back straight, her knees pressed together, her ankles crossed and her hands folded lightly in her lap, but her mind was racing with what she was about to do. There would be no coming back from the ultimatum she was going to give, and she was still unsure whether she was doing the right thing. But the job offer from Café Express had come at just the right moment and it was time to put herself first. Her mind returned to her speech and she was soon lost in her thoughts again.

The train finally squealed to a halt and people all around her stood up, impatient to get off the train and on their way to work. Olivia picked up her bag, left the carriage and set off on foot for the short journey to the company offices, leaving the grand old station behind her. She pulled her woollen coat tighter around her and made her way towards the river Avon, resisting all the coffee shops with their glorious early morning smell of roasted beans. The bright March sunshine calmed her and took her mind off the impending showdown with her father. As she approached the white metal bridge across the river, her long ponytail swinging behind her, she wished things hadn't come to this between them.

In no time at all, she found herself on the pavement outside the gleaming windows of the high-rise offices of La Riviera, the restaurant chain her father had spent his life building up. She was soon swept up by all the other employees making their way inside. The automatic doors swooshed open, and a second later she was crossing the sand-coloured marble foyer. Using her ID badge, she passed through the barrier and walked towards the bank of lifts. Several other employees were already waiting there, but even though she recognised some of them, she didn't speak to anyone, and no-one spoke to her. She studiously avoided eye contact, after several years' practice, refusing to let her guard down long enough to let anyone else in.

The lift arrived and she followed everyone else inside, squeezing herself into the back corner. The lift stopped at every floor as people made their way to work, but eventually, she was alone, speeding up to the executive suite of offices. This was where her father dominated the rest of the company, and where she was planning to do battle with him. She drew in a deep breath, trying not to let fear overwhelm her. She had put up with his behaviour for long enough. Now it was time to break free.

'Ah, the lovely Miss Fuller. I trust you had a jolly weekend?' Ryan started badgering her before she'd even taken off her coat.

'I'm sure you've got far more important things to do than annoying me, Ryan.' Olivia busied herself hanging up her coat on the stand in the corner of the office they shared with two other members of the Sales and Acquisitions team, and steadfastly ignored him. His eyes never left her the whole time she was booting up her computer and she willed him, for once, to leave her alone. As Marcus and Jake arrived, Ryan became distracted enough to give up bothering her, and she released a slow breath.

It wasn't long until the start of the Monday morning briefing, so she quickly scanned her emails to see if there was anything important she needed to know beforehand. She planned to speak to her father straight afterwards. He was a stickler for punctuality and if she upset him by being late, she would already have lost her advantage.

'C'mon, gorgeous. Time to go and listen to your old man's pearls of wisdom.' Marcus gave her a salacious wink before turning towards the door.

Olivia worked hard not to roll her eyes at him. She was used to the jibes of her colleagues. She didn't appreciate their taunts, of course, but she'd found it was best to simply ignore them. That way, they usually lost interest fairly quickly. She picked up her notebook and pen and joined the others on the walk to the boardroom. She stayed a few paces behind the rest of the team, who had joined them from adjacent offices. They were all men, hand-picked by her father or his lackeys for their ruthless business approach, and rejected by her, almost every one of them, for their cheesy come-ons. She'd made the mistake of letting one of them in once, but never again. She was still recovering from that experience and the effect it had had on her. Her trust in men had been severely damaged when she'd found out he only saw her as a way of gaining favour with her father. Somehow, though, she still held out some hope. Surely there was a man out there for her somewhere who would respect her for who she was and what she wanted to do with her life, rather than because she was the daughter of their wealthy boss?

She came to a stop, as everyone else had done. They were still in the corridor and clearly unable to enter the boardroom. She stood on her tiptoes and strained to see what was going on. Other people were doing the same, so raising herself up made no difference to her view. Marcus pushed his way to the front and bent his head to study some-thing on the glossy wooden door. Next thing, he walked back to rejoin Ryan and Jake before the three of them turned around and made to go past her.

'That's a first. Who'd have thought old man Fuller had it in him to break with tradition like that?' grumbled Jake.

'What's happening?' Olivia was startled out of her usual silence by the sudden change of plan.

'The meeting's been postponed to this afternoon.'

Finn stared at the silver-haired man sitting opposite him at the table, next to his banker, Mr Stephens. The older man oozed wealth and authority in his crisp, pin-striped grey suit, white shirt and tie, and his cufflinks glittered as he brushed a speck of imaginary lint from his lapel.

Finn stood out in this ancient office in his jeans and his faded t-shirt, the complete opposite of the other two men. He didn't warm to the stranger at all, but he did his best to put his anxiety to one side. He was hoping this meeting might be the answer to his prayers. He fidgeted in his seat, eager for it to start so he could find out what was going on. Mr Stephens spoke first, and Finn swiftly met his gaze.

'Finn, I'd like to introduce you to George Fuller. He runs the La Riviera chain of restaurants down here in Devon and around the south-west. He has a proposition for you, which I would advise you to consider very carefully.'

Finn tried hard not to grimace at the name of the soulless Mediterranean restaurant chain. He sat up straighter in his chair, trying to convey the idea he was every bit the successful restauranteur, despite his casual attire. Mr Fuller leaned back in his chair and crossed his legs gracefully, leaving one foot, clad in a shiny black leather shoe, dangling in the air. 'Mr Anderson – or may I call you Finn?'

Finn nodded and swallowed, wondering what the proposition was going to be but not daring to speak.

'I believe the restaurant you own on the high street in Lynford is in trouble financially?' Mr Fuller's eyebrows rose in query.

'Er, yes. I can't afford the loan repayments any more, so I've put the restaurant up for sale.' Finn reddened at having to admit this to a complete stranger.

'Quite.' Fuller paused and steepled his hands in front of his face, as if considering what he was going to say next. Finn swallowed again and waited, darting a quick look at Mr Stephens to see if he might give him any clues. The banker's face gave nothing away so Finn returned his gaze to the enigmatic Mr Fuller.

'Well, Finn, I think we may be of service to each other. I will take over the restaurant lease for you and I will pay off the £50,000 outstanding on the bank's loan. But I want something in return.'

Finn's jaw dropped at the man's audacity. In the silence that followed, after he'd quickly closed his mouth, the only sound was the clock ticking on Mr Stephens' desk. Meanwhile, Finn tried to control his rising anger towards the arrogant man in front of him. He relaxed his clenched hands and blew out a long breath before speaking again.

'My restaurant is worth much more than the value of the loan on it, Mr Fuller. That's why it's up for £100,000,' he said at last, glancing again at the banker in the hope he would help with the negotiation. But again, Mr Stephens remained silent.

'It probably is worth more than that, but I believe I am the only buyer currently showing an interest. You've had your chance to prove its worth and you've failed miserably. I'm only interested in paying off your loan because it suits my purpose. Otherwise, you'd be on the brink of going bankrupt and losing everything.'

Finn gritted his teeth and gave the man his best steely glare, but Mr Fuller didn't seem remotely bothered. Instead, he sighed and stared at his manicured nails. This ability to stay calm in difficult negotiations was undoubtedly the reason he had a chain of restaurants to his name, Finn thought to himself. That, and the fact he seemed to be a complete bastard. Finn wondered what it was the older man wanted from him, but he was damned if he was going to ask.

'I haven't got time to waste sitting here waiting for you to ask me what it is I want in return, so I'm going to get straight to the point,'

Fuller said. 'In return for paying off your loan, I want you to continue as chef at the restaurant when the new manager I put in place takes over.'

Finn held his breath for a long moment before speaking again. 'And why would you want me to do that?'

Fuller shrugged. 'It's simply a condition of this deal that you agree to stay on as chef for the next six months, so if you want to clear your debt and have a go at restoring your reputation, I need your answer now.'

Finn ran his hands through his hair and stared down at his lap, wracking his brains to see if there was a catch to this deal. If he didn't take up Fuller's offer, the bank would foreclose on the loan, and he'd still owe the best part of fifty grand to them with no prospect of ever paying it back. But if he did take Fuller up on his offer, Finn would still be working at his restaurant, despite all that had happened recently, and maybe there was a chance he could clear his name, rebuild his own reputation and make everything right again. He looked up into Fuller's smug face, and gave a small smile.

Fuller stood, stretched his arms and pulled neatly on each shirt sleeve, as if to emphasise his victory. Finn scraped back his chair and grasped Fuller's extended hand.

'Excellent decision, Finn. Now, let's iron out the details.' Fuller stooped to pick up a small, leather briefcase and rested it on his chair to open it. He pulled out a slim Manila folder and flipped it open to extract a sheaf of papers.

'This is the contract I had my lawyers draw up. It outlines everything I've said to you today, and one or two other minor conditions.' He handed the papers over to Finn along with a pen and sat back down to wait for him to sign it. As Finn read the first clause, all his earlier hopes and dreams drained away in the face of the stark reality of the contract: 'I, Finn Anderson, agree to sell Le Bistro Français and all its assets to La Riviera. I will no longer have any say in the day-to-day running of the restaurant or any authority over operational matters. I will be an employee of La Riviera, nothing more.'

Olivia returned to her desk in a daze. Now, slumped in front of her computer, she pondered what on earth could have prompted this change of plan by her father. He never missed the Monday morning briefing, and woe betide any of his employees who missed it. Where was he? She'd seen him at dinner the previous evening and he hadn't given any indication he wouldn't be in today. She hadn't seen him at breakfast, but then that wasn't as unusual. He'd stolen her thunder, as always, even if he'd done so unwittingly, and she wasn't sure she could summon up the courage now to deliver her speech.

She released a small sigh as she pulled herself up straight and opened the latest company file she'd been working on. At least she'd become an expert in what made restaurants succeed and fail in the three years she'd been left dangling by her father, with nothing better to do than pore over company reports. She didn't mind the theory, but she longed for the practice of managing her own project. She wanted to work in a restaurant and put all she'd learned into action.

She was so focused on her latest report that when her phone rang a little over an hour later, it made her jump. It was her father's PA, and, as always, Mrs Bell came straight to the point.

'Your father would like to see you in his office at once.'

Olivia's palms began to sweat. Her father hardly ever called her into his office. He was determined not to be seen to give her any advantages over her peers. Her instinct was to jump up and follow the order she'd been given, but instead she breathed in, closed her eyes and went over her speech one last time in her head.

'*I've been working here for three years now and you still haven't given me a restaurant of my own to turn into a success. In the beginning, I understood your reasons but now it has gone on too long. I won't be passed over for one of the men in the team one more time. Either you give me a business or I'm leaving. I've been offered another job and I'm not afraid to take it.*'

She opened her eyes to find Marcus, Ryan and Jake all staring at her.

'All right, princess? You looked like you were away with the fairies then,' mocked Jake. The other two snickered in their usual schoolboy way. After years of their sneering, Olivia was almost immune to it. Almost. She stood up, pushed her chair under her desk, turned her back on them and left the office. She worked hard not to ever give them the satisfaction of knowing when they did actually get to her.

On the way to her father's office, she nipped into the ladies to check her appearance and to reassure herself one more time she was doing the right thing. She studied herself in the bank of mirrors, staring critically at her lightly freckled face and trying to tame her curly hair into submission within the ponytail, but failing as always. Her minimal make-up was flawless and although she smoothed down her skirt, there was no need. Her outfits were always pristine and she took confidence in that. A couple of minutes later, she let the door close behind her, lifted her head and walked steadily along the corridor towards the executive suite. She came to a stop in front of Mrs Bell's desk, just outside her father's office.

'I have Miss Fuller here to see you, Mr Fuller,' Mrs Bell said into the phone. 'Yes, sir.' She smiled slightly and nodded at Olivia. 'Go straight in, Miss Fuller.'

Olivia hated the way even Mrs Bell wouldn't let her guard down towards her. She had nothing against Mrs Bell particularly; she was only doing what her father had instructed her to do in addressing staff members so formally, but it still felt as though no-one was ever on her side. She didn't reply, she just turned on her heel and headed towards her father's office, knocking briskly on the solid oak door before going in. Her heels sank into the pile carpet at once and it was an effort to take each step without losing a shoe. She stopped in front of her father's desk and waited while he finished making some hand-written notes on a report he was reading. This was his way of making his employees uncomfortable and she had long since lost hope of him treating her any differently to anyone else. She used the time to look at the photograph he kept of her and her mother on his desk. Olivia was just a baby in the black and white photo, and it was her mother's smile that captivated her. She turned to study her father and suppressed a sigh. In her heart, she believed he loved her, but he seemed incapable of showing her.

Finally, he looked up and gave her a fleeting smile. 'Take a seat, Olivia.'

'I prefer to stand for what I have to say, Father.' She congratulated herself in her head for having made the first move.

His eyes widened. 'You have something you wish to say to me?'

She took a calming breath. 'I do. I've been working here—'

'I asked you to take a seat, Olivia.' His request had been rhetorical. He would not be manipulated in his own office, especially not by his daughter. He glared at her and she lost some of her nerve.

'And I would like you to listen to what I have to say... please,' she said.

'So, you don't want to hear about the restaurant I want you to manage?'

Olivia gasped, despite herself, and sank into the nearest chair.

'I thought that might get your attention.'

'That's wonderful news, Father, thank you.' All thoughts of the job she'd been offered at Café Express went out of her head. This was what she had dreamed of for so long.

'To be honest, Olivia, it's a stroke of luck I hadn't sent you anywhere else before, because now you're free to stand in as manager at the new place I've bought down in Devon. Rupert called this morning to say he was in the hospital with a broken leg. Damn fool for going skiing in the first place, if you ask me. Anyway, you can go in his place until he's fit again. And don't worry about your lack of experience. I've kept the old chef on to give you a hand while you get started.'

Finn returned to his tiny flat above the restaurant after the meeting, his head spinning. He sank down into his one armchair, let his head fall back and closed his eyes, desperate to forget the humiliation he'd endured. He'd had no choice but to sign the contract there and then, selling his beloved restaurant to that awful man and, at the same time, agreeing to go back and work in the place when it no longer belonged to him. Finn had at least had the foresight to push Fuller into paying him a decent salary once the restaurant reopened. He had the feeling Mr Fuller thought he had let the restaurant fail on purpose, but nothing could be further from the truth. He loved the restaurant with every fibre of his being and had done since his first day there as a teenager, when he'd been given the job of washing the dishes.

His moment of wallowing in self-pity was rudely interrupted by a loud knock on his downstairs door. He'd been avoiding his friends for days, so he forced himself to get up to go and see who it was.

'Finn, where the hell have you been? I've been worried about you.' His friend Ed, stood on the doorstep, his rugged face creased in a frown.

'Come in and I'll tell you everything.' Finn held the door back and Ed squeezed his six foot plus frame through the tiny opening before ambling up the stairs into Finn's small living space.

'What's the story, man? Is the restaurant really for sale?' Ed sat down on the sofa, ignoring the armchair, which experience had clearly taught him was nowhere near big enough to take his body.

Finn fetched two beers from the fridge, passing one to Ed, and took a long gulp of his own before facing his friend. 'It *was* for sale, because I couldn't pay the loan on it any more. But it's not for sale as of today. I'm sorry for not filling you in before now. It's been a lot to deal with.'

'Shit, I had no idea things were as bad as that. Do you have a buyer now?'

'Sort of, yeah.' And Finn filled him in on the nightmarish scenario he now found himself in.

'Christ, I don't know what's worse – losing the restaurant or being forced to work in it again when it no longer belongs to you. That's going to be a real bummer for you, and plus, you have no idea what the manager's going to be like. Mind you, looking on the bright side, this is a fresh start.' Ed gave him a wink, ever the optimist.

Finn groaned. 'To tell the truth, I feel like I've let everyone down that ever had faith in me. When Bob and Jen retired, I tried hard to make the restaurant a success. If they knew how badly I'd failed, they'd be ashamed of me, and even more so if they could see what I've agreed to now. I'm not sure I can try as hard to make a go of it on someone else's behalf. That's about the worst thing anyone could ask me to do.'

'On the plus side, your loan will be paid off and you have a clean slate to start as a chef again, without any of the business responsibili-ties.' Ed smiled, and Finn was grateful he'd let his friend in.

'I just have to hope the manager knows what he's doing, and he's not too awful to work for. At least it's only for six months.' Fuller had been very clear about that condition – if he tried to leave before the six months were up, he would find himself saddled with his debt again.

'And then what will you do?'

'I'll have to move on, I suppose. It's not like any other restaurant here is going to give me a job with my track record, is it?' For a moment, Finn was lost in regret, but then he shook himself out of it. 'What I'd like is to make a success of the restaurant again and then to buy it back one day.' Ed gave him a sceptical look. 'I know, I know, it sounds crazy but I love that place and I'd like to give it another try, if only to prove to myself that I can do it.'

'But that sounds impossible when it belongs to this new company. You need a miracle, I reckon.'

'Well, stranger things have happened, you know.'

Ed nodded wisely. 'Does this new freedom mean you'll get out and about more now? I haven't seen you in the village for ages. We need to go out for a few drinks at the pub, before this manager arrives and you have no free time ever.'

'To be honest, I didn't think I could show my face around after having to close the bistro and put Zoe and Jamie out of a job as well. They didn't deserve to suffer because of my failings. And the rest of the community can't have a good word for me, either.'

'Don't be daft. Everyone knows how hard it is to keep a business running in a tourist place like this, and on top of that your mum was ill and your business manager moved away. The whole village knows you did your best to keep on top of everything when you were visiting your mum in the hospice. Zoe's got another job already, and I don't think Jamie minds losing his washing-up job when he's got to concentrate on studying for his A levels anyway. So don't be too hard on yourself about what happened. Now, when are we going for that beer?'

'How about tonight, then? No time like the present.' Finn smiled, but his earlier optimism was fading. Even though Ed was right, he was still burdened by what had happened to the bistro and the way his staff had lost their jobs, through no fault of their own. Still, at least they were well out of the new situation.

'Excellent, let's get to it.' Ed hauled himself off the sofa, deposited his empty bottle in the sink and made his way back down the stairs, with Finn trailing behind him.

CHAPTER TWO

Olivia returned to her office in a state of shock. On the one hand, she was delighted to have been put in charge of a restaurant at long last. But on the other, she was so disappointed she had only been given the job because Rupert was off sick. She pulled a face and shuddered at the thought of her ex. She lifted her burgundy leather satchel out from under her desk and slid her laptop inside it, together with a few folders and some other bits and pieces from her drawer. She cast a quick glance over the desk again to make sure she hadn't forgotten anything. Satisfied, she turned to collect her coat from the stand. When she turned back, the three vultures – otherwise known as her colleagues – were circling. She allowed herself a smile as she guessed where their thoughts were going.

'Oh dear, poor little rich girl couldn't hack it, eh? Has Daddy sent you packing?' Ryan taunted. He'd always been the worst of the three. His constant arrogance never failed to amaze her.

'I bagsy her desk,' cried Jake, pulling her chair towards him, as if he could declare his ownership of the desk by having the chair. He was like a spoilt toddler, grabbing at everything he wanted without thinking about who he might hurt in the process.

'I'll miss you, Olivia, I really will,' said Marcus, his face serious for a moment. Olivia was about to say something pleasant in return when he doubled over laughing. 'Ha, not even I'm that dumb.'

She stood and looked at each of them in disgust, weighing every word she was about to say.

'My father has not sacked me. Quite the opposite in fact. I will be away from my desk and my chair temporarily while I go to manage a new restaurant my father has acquired, something none of you has had the pleasure of being asked to do yet, I believe. I can honestly say I won't miss any of you for one single moment.'

With that she turned on her heel and walked proudly to the lifts, without looking back. She didn't hear a word from them and would have loved to have seen the looks on their faces as her words sunk in. As the lift doors opened, she stepped inside and let loose a single whoop of joy, along with an uncharacteristic fist pump, before regaining her composure and acting as if nothing had happened. She hadn't mentioned she was only filling in for Rupert – she didn't want to give them the satisfaction – and although it wasn't ideal to be covering for him, she was going to do everything in her power to keep him away for as long as possible.

Once in the foyer, she made her way towards the automatic doors that would bring her back onto the street. It was colder now and a brisk wind had built up, so she decided to take the bus back to the station.

Half an hour and a short bus ride later, she was sitting on the train home to Clifton Down, trying to think about what she should pack for her journey. She decided only to take clothes for a couple of weeks, because she didn't see the need to stay down in Devon the whole time. Once she got the business up and running, she'd be able to pop home from time to time to see her father and her friends. Her father hadn't given her a report on the business as yet. She frowned at that oversight on his part. There was always a report, prepared by someone just like her. She would follow that up with him as soon as she had the chance.

She arrived back at the house, ascended the flight of steps and let herself in using her key, something she hardly ever did, because her father preferred her to wait for the housekeeper to open the door. Usually she did, but today was an unusual day and her spirits were high.

'Miss Olivia, is everything quite all right?' The housekeeper looked pained to have missed her arrival at the door.

'Everything is wonderful, Mrs Thomas,' she replied cheerfully as she crossed the marble floor of the wide, open hallway. She removed her shoes, her tired feet groaning their thanks as she did so, and padded her way upstairs.

Once in her bedroom, she packed her compact travel bag in record time, grabbing a handful of her work suits and a couple of pairs of smart jeans and blouses for any leisure time, and was descending the grand staircase a mere fifteen minutes later, just as her father came in through the front door.

'I'm glad you're home early so I can see you before I go,' she said.

Her father pulled a face she found hard to interpret.

'Go where, Olivia?' His clipped words made him sound angry but she had no idea why.

'To Devon, of course. I'm going to book my train ticket now.'

'Absolutely not. Ted will take you by car tomorrow.'

'No, I want to go on the train.' Olivia glared at him, determined to get her own way for once, especially after the way he'd treated her in his office earlier.

Her father's face softened. Olivia knew at once he was going to give in. She lifted her chin and forced herself to wait for him to speak, rather than filling the void. He might be in charge in the office, but it was time she started standing up for herself outside it.

'I thought we could enjoy a last meal together tonight before you go, which is why I've come home early. At least let's do that, and if you insist on travelling by public transport, you can set off early tomorrow.' Olivia suppressed a groan. This was what he always did. He managed to get his own way even though he seemed to be letting her get hers. Well, it wouldn't hurt for her to give into him one last time. Tomorrow would come round soon enough, and then she could get started on this brand new phase of her life and make the most of every single minute.

She smiled indulgently at her father and descended the last few stairs towards him. He looked tired and there was a curious expression on his face, one she'd never seen before. She would have loved to have given him a hug, but her experience, and the way he kept her at arm's length, had taught her not to. Instead, she looped her arm through his and they walked together through to the conservatory, where Mrs Thomas served them both dinner.

'So,' Olivia began, as they were eating their chicken chasseur, 'what made you decide to buy this particular restaurant?'

'It's not really a restaurant, more of a bistro, I suppose you'd call it. It probably has around twenty covers. I don't think it's one we can add to the chain. The location, deep within the village isn't busy enough for that, but it might have potential as an independent. It will take a lot of work to get it to that level, though. The chef has no head for business, but I'm hoping that his cooking's up to scratch. It's bad luck that Rupert is unavailable, but I know you've been keen to take on a business, so this little place has come up at exactly the right time.'

Olivia tried not to think about Rupert. 'Well, I'll find out about the chef's cooking skills soon enough, but what happened to the restaurant business-wise to make it fail?'

'All I know is the chef couldn't pay the loan he has on the place, so he had to close. The bank has forced him to put the place up for sale, which is where we've come in.'

'And will you send me the report on the company once you get more details?'

'There wasn't time to do a report, and I wouldn't normally need to make one if Rupert was managing the place, but I do have the bank's sales details for the business, which includes a picture.' Her father opened the briefcase he'd brought in with him and passed her a sheet of A4.

'Oh, it's gorgeous. A typical French bistro.' Olivia studied the picture, which revealed a burgundy frontage. The old-fashioned gold lettering across the window identified it as *Le Bistro Français*. As much as she loved the look of the place and the reminder it gave her of restaurants she'd visited in Paris in the past, she knew it would need modernising if it were to have any chance of success in a Devon seaside village.

Olivia was surprised her father hadn't investigated the restaurant more fully, but she put it down to his trust in Rupert. However much she disliked the man, she had to admit he was good at his job. She rubbed her hands together with a grin on her face. 'I'm excited to have this opportunity after all this time, and I'll do everything I can to turn the place round. Do I have a budget for refurbishments and suchlike?'

'Yes, I should be able to spare some cash for that, but think carefully before spending too much. I don't want to sink money into it with no chance of a return.'

'Of course not, but we're planning for the longer term, aren't we? So we'll probably need to invest a little in order to get something back.'

Her father nodded and frowned slightly, and that curious expression crossed his face again. It was almost as if he was about to say something but then thought better of it.

'I know you're probably worried about my lack of experience, Father, and that's bound to make this first business a challenge for me, but I'm confident of my ability to do the job. I've gained more insight than you might think from poring over all those restaurant reports for the past three years. I have lots of plans to make this restaurant a success and I can't wait to get started.'

'The thing is, you mustn't worry if it doesn't work out exactly as you plan. These small businesses in seaside towns and villages can be awfully difficult to make a success of. If everything goes wrong, it won't be the end of the world. Rupert will simply take over and you can come home again.' Her father gave her a bright smile.

'What a funny thing to say. I'm going to do my damnedest to make it work, so when I do come home it will be with a successful business to my name. And then you can give me something else to do. I hope this will be the first of many successful businesses in my portfolio.'

'You don't need to build a portfolio if you're working for me. I'll know what you've done, won't I?'

'Well, I might not always be working for you, and it's good practice to have a portfolio to show around when the time comes.'

Her dad frowned but then quickly changed the subject. 'Let's not talk any more about business now. I want our last evening together to be a peaceful one.'

They finished their meal and Olivia cleared everything through to the kitchen and stacked the dishwasher, as the housekeeper had now gone home for the night. She was keen to have an early night to make sure she was well rested for her long journey tomorrow, but as she came back into the hallway she saw the door to her father's study was still open. She moved closer, still hesitant about whether to go in after all these years.

Her father was just visible in the semi-darkness, sitting at his desk with a glass of whisky. He picked up the photo of herself and her mother that he kept on his desk and stared at it. Olivia had been so young when her mother died in the car crash, and it pained her still to think how deeply that loss had affected them both. Over the years, her father had become more and more distant, and the good times they'd shared when her mother was alive were now a hazy memory for her. Her father's policy of keeping her at arm's length at work hadn't helped, and at times he'd been tough on her. But now was her chance to finally prove herself to him and to make him proud of the businesswoman she would become. She just hoped she could pull it off.

Finn was glad Ed had encouraged him to go down the pub. It had been a while since he'd mingled with the rest of the community. In the good days, he'd been so busy with the restaurant he'd never had time to socialise, and he would spend his two days off catching up on sleep. Recently, he'd felt too embarrassed about showing his face around town after letting so many people down.

His old school friend, Ewan, was at the bar when he pushed open the door.

'Hey, Finn, long time no see. How are things?' They'd always got on well and it was good to see his friendly face. Still, that didn't stop Finn feeling embarrassed when he saw him. Ewan and his wife Rosie ran the village bakery and they'd supplied the bistro in the past. Finn still felt ashamed about all the times they'd had to chase him for payment.

'Not great, to be honest, what with the restaurant shutting down.' He signalled the bartender, and after checking Ewan didn't want another, ordered two pints of bitter for himself and Ed, who was chatting to a woman further down the bar.

'Yeah, I was sorry to hear that. What are you going to do now?' Ewan took a sip of his pint.

'Well, the bank has found a buyer and they've asked me to stay on as chef under the new manager.'

'That's great news. At least the restaurant will keep running.'

Finn's face fell. 'Yeah, but it won't feel the same if it isn't mine, you know.'

'Damn, I hadn't thought of it like that. Have you met the new manager?'

'No, but I'm expecting him soon.'

Ewan raised his eyebrows. 'That should be interesting.'

'Hmm, that's one way of putting it. Listen, I'm sorry about taking so long to pay you and Rosie last time. I know how difficult it must have been for you, but I want you to know it wasn't deliberate. I had so much other stuff going on at the time, it went out of my head.'

'It's all over with now, but I will admit that Rosie was pretty pissed off about it. But listen, that's before we knew your mum was ill. We were more upset that you didn't tell us about your problems. Don't keep it all in next time, eh?'

Finn nodded, accepting his friend's wise advice. 'Anyway, how's life with you and Rosie? It can't be long now till the baby's due?'

The evening flew by and soon Finn was making his way back to his flat above the restaurant, ready for a good night's sleep. In bed though, sleep wouldn't come. He kept going over all that had happened, trying to reassure himself he'd done the right thing. He was resentful about the agreement he'd made with Fuller and he kept worrying how it would all play out once the manager arrived. For all he knew, the new guy had no idea how to run a restaurant, either. And what if he was clueless about good food? It was a recipe for disaster. He couldn't face the embarrassment from the rest of the community if the restaurant failed a second time. He wasn't sure his career as a chef would ever recover from that level of failure. But there seemed to be no way out of what he'd agreed to, not if he wanted to clear his debt. He would have to get on with it and hope he could escape without too much further damage to his reputation. If he recovered his good name, he could leave and go and work some-where else. That thought only plunged him into a deeper state of misery. His heart was still in this restaurant and it would be hard when the time came to let it go for good.

After a restless night, he got up early and went downstairs to the bistro, planning to do some cooking to take his mind off everything. But when he reached the kitchen, he took one look at the fine layer of dust on the worktops and the cooker – which had stood unused for weeks after his mum's death – and decided he would have to give the place a thorough overhaul before any cooking could take place. It had been a while since he'd had the job of cleaning the kitchen, but right now he wanted to keep busy. The kitchen was the only place he'd ever enjoyed such work and he took real pleasure from seeing the end results. Even filling the bucket with warm, soapy water was therapeutic, and for a while the process did take his mind off his worries.

Finn was halfway through washing down the metal worktops and scouring the two cookers before he remembered he should probably wait for instructions from the new manager before he did anything. He paused and leaned on the mop, propped up precariously in the bucket, and considered his position once more. Despite enjoying being back in his beloved kitchen, there was no denying he'd been handed a poisoned chalice, and all before he'd even met the new manager. He had no idea what to expect from Fuller's employee, but he assumed the worst. That was wrong of him, but Fuller himself hadn't given him much confidence. He hoped he might never have to see that man again.

He sighed and pushed his floppy fringe out of his eyes with the back of his hand. He squeezed out the mop and rested it against the worktop by the industrial double sinks before heaving the bucket over to the back door. There was a drain outside that he preferred to use for this kind of dirty water. Intent on the job in hand, he leaned against the door with his back, swung the bucket round and, in a less than accurate fashion, threw the water towards the drain. A strangled squeal immediately followed. He looked up to see a young woman staring in horror at her now soaking wet feet.

'I'm so sorry,' he mumbled, as the immaculately dressed woman in her smart business suit stood stiffly on one leg to tip out the water from first one designer shoe and then the other, almost losing her balance. The gentleman in him wanted to help her, but instinct told him this particular woman wouldn't react well to being touched by a complete stranger. Trying not to laugh, he put his bucket down and folded his arms in anticipation of the battle he was sure would follow.

'I'm sure there's a better, more hygienic way to get rid of dirty water,' she complained, smoothing down her skirt in an effort to regain her composure.

The woman's clipped tone grated, and Finn wondered what on earth she was doing there.

'Maybe there is, but I've not found it in four years of running this restaurant.'

'You're Finn Anderson?' she demanded, her eyes wide.

'And who are you?'

'Olivia Fuller. I'm your new manager.'

———————

Olivia put her hand out towards the grumpy-looking man before her and his eyes locked onto hers for a moment. Then he wiped his hand down his apron before reaching out. For a moment, his large hand enveloped hers, but then he withdrew it so quickly she was sure he must have been reluctant to touch her. Her skin warmed and a slight blush crept up her cheeks before she regained her usual calm exterior.

'As the new manager, I would like to come in and have a look around, so if you don't mind...' She gestured towards the doorway he was blocking, and he moved back to let her in.

She swept through the kitchen, trying to ignore the way her feet were squelching in her brand new court shoes, glancing either side of her as she went, and on into the main dining area. The chef followed warily. Olivia sensed his eyes on her at all times, as if he was wondering what might happen next. She looked around the dining room at the peeling wallpaper, and the gingham tablecloths that had also seen better days. Together with the dark wooden panelling and furniture, they gave the bistro a rather claustrophobic feel. She was going to have her work cut out to transform this place into somewhere customers would want to come and eat. She brushed off the seat of a chair with her hand before sitting down gingerly on the edge, and pulled out her iPad from her satchel. She was poised to start tapping when she remembered the grimy state of the chair she'd just touched. She quickly delved into her bag for her hand sanitiser.

The chef, obviously unable to contain himself any longer, let out a roar of laughter.

'I'm glad you find the state of this place amusing, Mr Anderson. It needs a lot of work doing to it but not to worry, we'll have it ship-shape in no time.' She stared at him, daring him to contradict her.

'What do you think it needs doing to it to make it "shipshape" as you put it?' It was his turn to stare at her now, as if she was speaking a foreign language.

'Well, at first glance, I'd say the exterior and interior both need repainting and the furniture needs changing to something more modern. Then we need to bring everything else inside up-to-date. Gingham tablecloths and blackboards are cheesy in this day and age.' She wrinkled her nose. She wasn't sure if this bad-tempered chef was going to laugh again or be outraged.

He looked round the restaurant in the same way she had done a moment earlier. Perhaps he was looking at it properly for the first time in a long while. She waited for him to agree with her, but when his eyes met hers again, all she saw was a flicker of what looked like regret.

'You have done a good job in cleaning the kitchen, though,' she threw in, trying to soften the blow of the criticisms. All she received in return for her comment was a grunt. Then she remembered some-thing else. 'Oh, and the name of the place needs changing, too.'

'What's wrong with Le Bistro Français?' He folded his arms.

'Do you serve only French food here, Mr Anderson?'

'Mainly,' he conceded. 'But that's not all we do.'

'You've answered your own question, then.' She nodded to confirm she was in the right.

'But it's always been called Le Bistro Français.'

'All the more reason for a change.'

'And do you have a massive budget for all this from your boss?'

'My father has given me a good budget for redecoration, yes.'

'Oh, so your father is your boss, is he?' He nodded knowingly.

'My father owns La Riviera, the company that has bought your restaurant, yes. I'm going to be managing this project on behalf of the company.'

'The first thing you'll need to do, then, is to get some sensible clothes to wear while you "manage this project".' He drew some air quotes around her words, and then waved his muscled arm up and down her slight figure, indicating her expensive cream suit and now sodden court shoes. Her eyes flickered as his muscles tensed but then she looked back at him again.

'My clothes are perfectly sensible for the work I will be doing.' She thrust her chin out, certain her work suits would be as appropriate here as at the office.

'Not if you're working in a restaurant for months on end.'

'Oh no, Mr Anderson, I won't be here for months on end. I have only six months to turn this business round and I intend to meet that challenge. So I won't be needing any new clothes for such a short space of time.'

'Have you ever worked in a restaurant before?'

'Well, no... no, I haven't.' Finn's mouth dropped open so she hurried on. 'But I'm an experienced businesswoman and I assure you I can get up to speed quickly. Now, I'd also like to take a look at your accounts, please. Do you have them to hand?'

His bravado disappeared at the mere mention of paperwork, which didn't fill her with confidence. 'Er no, not to hand. I'll get them for the next time we meet. I didn't even know you were coming today.'

Olivia consulted her to-do list and frowned. 'The final and most important thing, of course, is your cooking.'

'My cooking?' he echoed.

'To put it simply, Mr Anderson, I want to know if you can cook, otherwise we're lost before we've even started. I'd like you to make me your signature dish, please.'

'My signature dish? What the hell do you mean by that?'

'Surely you're not telling me you don't know what a signature dish is? I don't think you can call yourself a chef if you don't know that term.' Her lips twitched as she teased him.

'I know full well what a signature dish is, and you know that's not what I meant.'

Olivia raised her eyebrows but said nothing.

Finn went on. 'I want to know why you're asking me to cook it. I don't need your approval, you know.'

'Not to put too fine a point on it, Mr Anderson, the only way I can find out if you can cook is if you make me something to eat. Then I'll know whether the reason the restaurant failed is because you can't cook, or whether it's down to something else.'

CHAPTER THREE

Finn set off early the next morning for his regular fish supplier in Barnstaple, just half an hour inland from Lynford. His old Volvo estate was on its last legs but still managed to get him everywhere he needed to go, and it had the space for him to carry most things he had to purchase. He had a few recipes in mind. He thought about the ingredients he would need for each one, depending on what fish was available at the supplier's. He was hoping to get some sea bass fillets to pan fry with wild mushrooms and prosciutto, or failing that, some halibut.

It was a beautiful spring day as he drove along the road away from Watersmeet Bridge and Lynford into town, and the bright sky lifted his spirits. The prospect of cooking again had also cheered him up and he wanted to make a good impression on Olivia. She'd got under his skin yesterday, in an annoying way on the one hand, but on the other hand, there was no denying her enthusiasm for the job in front of them. He shouldn't be trying so hard – he still resented the Fullers for swooping in and taking over his restaurant – but he couldn't help himself. Well, he would just make this one meal for her, so she would know without any shadow of a doubt that he was a good cook, and then he would get down to the business of working for her and her supercilious father.

He was in luck at the supplier's. They had plenty of sea bass in, so he bought four fillets, in case anything went wrong, and he also bought some samphire the supplier was keeping for regular customers that day. He picked up the other ingredients he needed at the delicatessen and at the greengrocer's in Barnstaple before popping into the independent wine merchant's and buying a couple of bottles of Sauvignon Blanc from the Loire Valley. He was on his way back to the restaurant a little after ten, happy at the prospect of cooking in his kitchen again. Even if he was their employee, it would always be his kitchen.

Once back at the restaurant, he did his prep of the shallots, garlic, prosciutto and wild mushrooms. He took a tub of his fish stock out of the freezer and left it on the side to defrost while he peeled and thinly sliced a couple of potatoes. Once everything was ready to cook, he took a short break to prepare a table for them to eat at when Olivia arrived at midday. He covered one of the tables with one of his few remaining tablecloths and put out napkins, glasses and cutlery. Satisfied, he then went back to the kitchen to cook, just as Olivia knocked on the back door.

He greeted her cheerfully. 'Morning.'

'Good morning, Mr Anderson.' She gave him a brittle smile, maintaining her formality of the previous day. Today she was dressed in a tailored, dark navy suit, looking every inch the businesswoman. She looked amazing. The suit fitted her in all the right places, but she didn't look like she belonged at the bistro.

'I'm just about to cook. The table's set, if you'd like to go through.'

A couple of minutes later, he brought the wine in and poured her a glass to drink while he saw to his cooking. She was busy studying something on her beloved iPad and barely even looked up. He shook his head as he made his way back to the kitchen, willing himself to get a grip and to focus on his dish.

Within twenty minutes, he was serving up sea bass fillets with sautéed wild mushrooms, sage and crispy prosciutto, accompanied by pan-fried potato slices and the samphire, which he had cooked at the last minute and then tossed in butter. He took the heated plates through to the dining room and served Olivia hers with a flourish, deciding not to tell her what was on it so he could see how knowledgeable she was.

He watched as she took her first mouthful, ignoring his own food as he waited for her reaction.

'Mmm. That is delicious,' she said, after finishing her first taste. 'I've never had sea bass with porcini before.'

He raised his eyebrows. She knew her food. He proceeded to demolish his meal, savouring every last mouthful. He didn't know when he might get to eat this well again. He was careful to taste the wine with the food, eager to know whether it was a good match or not. Olivia had hardly touched her wine.

Olivia patted her mouth gently with her napkin before placing it on the table next to her now empty plate. 'One thing's clear now – you are an excellent cook. That was a wonderful dish, made with all fresh ingredients, I'm sure?'

He nodded and his chest puffed out with pride. He was pleased to know he'd lost none of his cooking skills when everything else had gone to pot.

'I've eaten at some of the best restaurants in Bristol and I think you could easily give them a run for their money. Where did you train as a chef?'

'I learned all my skills from the man who used to own the restaurant before me. I worked my way up from washing the dishes when I started, to owning the restaurant when the previous owner retired.' Finn gave a small shrug, disappointed in himself once again for letting Bob and his wife, Jen, down. Deep in his heart, he knew they would have understood him wanting to be with his mum, but his guilt still overwhelmed him.

Olivia took a sip of her wine at last. 'Why do you think the restaurant failed?' She looked him in the eye, not unkindly, just openly.

He rubbed the palm of his hand against his stubble and wondered how much to tell her. 'Maybe it's because I'm not interested in the business side of things. All I want to do is cook.'

'Well, I like to think I'm good at the business side of things, so I hope we'll make a good team.'

Finn gave her a tight smile. Things were only going to get harder from here on in, as she became aware of the full extent of his lack of business skills.

Olivia left the restaurant shortly afterwards, having agreed to meet with the stubborn Mr Anderson the following day to discuss everything else she wanted to achieve before the restaurant reopened. There was definitely a lot to do, but she was up for the challenge, and knowing Mr Anderson could actually cook made things a whole lot easier. Still, there had to be another reason why the restaurant had failed when he was such a great chef, and she couldn't work out what it could be. He wasn't ready to tell her yet, that much was obvious.

She allowed herself a little chuckle as she walked down the cobbled street towards the river back to her hotel. Although Mr Anderson had been hard work so far, she was warming to him and to his business. She had been pretty sure he would prove to be a good cook because the kitchen had been spotless when she'd walked through it yesterday. A bad chef wouldn't have cared that much for his workspace. And she'd been proved right today, of course, when she'd tasted his *signature dish.* She laughed out loud then, to the consternation of some ducks that were floating along the river. She paused in the middle of the bridge to look at them, remembering how affronted the chef had been when she'd asked him to cook for her.

To her right was a plaque. *Watersmeet Bridge,* it announced, *where the east and west rivers meet.* Looking up Olivia saw that there were indeed two rivers flowing towards their meeting point under the bridge, and she was enchanted.

A soft breeze blew gently through her hair as she stood on the ancient stone bridge, and the spring sunshine warmed her face. For once, she hadn't tied her hair back that morning. She felt... she didn't know how to describe it. She'd never had this feeling before, but she supposed she felt free. She was already comfortable in this little seaside village after only one day. The restaurant had lots of potential and she'd never met a man like Mr Anderson... Finn, as he'd insisted she call him. He was very different from the men in the office back in Bristol – thoughtful and dedicated, and that gave her hope for their working relationship. Her mind was racing with all these thoughts, so she inhaled deeply, and blew the breath out slowly. She warned herself not to let down her guard. She had a job to do and she couldn't afford to let anything else get in the way of it.

She turned away from the gurgling rivers with a sigh and continued up the gentle hill towards her hotel, thinking about how much her life had changed in just a couple of days. Now that her father had shown he had faith in her, she had the chance to prove herself to him at last and, at the same time, to make him proud of her. After trying unsuccessfully to get hold of Damian Carter, the CEO of Café Express, the day before, she had sent him a quick email to let him know she couldn't accept his job offer after all, and now she couldn't wait to get started at the restaurant. With her business expertise and Finn's cooking skills, they might have a chance at turning the restaurant's fortunes round. And the sooner they got going, the quicker they could make a profit and she could get back to Bristol.

As she lay in the bath a short while later, indulging her body in the jasmine-scented bath oil provided by the hotel, she was still thinking about the restaurant, and particularly about the name. They needed to come up with something more modern, but she was stumped for ideas. It was more like a bistro than a restaurant but she didn't want the name to hint in any way that it only served French food. Olivia decided to leave that thought percolating at the back of her mind while she tried to solve other problems.

She turned her mind to the refurbishments. She planned to spend half her father's budget on the jobs that needed doing urgently and to keep the rest for contingencies. Painting the whole restaurant inside and out, in addition to getting the sign rewritten, was going to take up a good chunk of that sum, as would buying new furniture.

Once she'd got dried and wrapped herself in one of the hotel's luxurious white bath-robes, she decided to send a quick email to her father's PA. She needed to know when the budget money would be transferred to her, so she could get going with all the renovations. A minute later, her iPad pinged with a reply from Mrs Bell. She hadn't expected to hear back from her so soon.

'Miss Fuller,

Your father has asked me to advise you that he has had to withdraw the budget for your project for the moment, due to unforeseen circumstances with other businesses. He sends his apologies but he asked me to tell you he was sure you'd manage.

Yours,

Mrs Bell.'

Olivia gasped. How dare he? Now what was she going to do? She thought for a second, trying to keep calm and not let this setback get the better of her. Cash flow could be difficult for her father at times but her budget for the restaurant was such a small amount she couldn't imagine that was the real reason behind him withdrawing it. On an impulse, she dug her phone out of her bag and rang his private number. It rang for ages and then diverted to his voicemail. Deciding against leaving a message, she hung up.

Her mind was in a whirl once again. Was her father deliberately making things difficult for her? He'd held out for long enough on even allocating her a business to turn round. Why would he make it easy for her now? Well, he obviously didn't know his daughter as well as he thought. As she went downstairs for dinner later on, she was already planning how she would get out of the situation and turn things in her favour.

'I'm afraid I had some bad news last night,' Olivia began, as she sat with Finn in the restaurant the next day. She straightened her skirt out of habit and crossed her ankles under the table. 'My father has withdrawn the budget he was going to give me for refurbishments, so now we're going to have to get creative if we want to do everything on my list before our reopening.'

Finn didn't reply, which Olivia took to mean he was as concerned as she was about what they would do.

'It's okay,' she went on. 'I've already had some thoughts about how we can get round this, so there's no need for us to be despondent.'

'Well, I admire your determination, that's for sure. Go on then, tell me what's on your list.'

'As I said before, the exterior of the restaurant needs repainting and we need to agree on a new name, which will have to be painted by someone with expertise at signwriting. First of all, do you know anyone who could paint the outside for us as a favour? Someone who might be happy to be paid in meals for example.'

'I do know someone, actually. My friend, Ed, works as a painter and decorator and he might be up for it.'

'And I was thinking we could paint the dining area ourselves, to save some money.'

Finn pulled himself up to his full, seated height. 'Hang on, I do have some standards, you know, and I pride myself that I've reached the grand old age of thirty without ever painting a single room.'

'Neither have I, but I'd be willing to give it a try. It might stretch your friendship with this Ed to ask him to do all that for no pay as well.'

'Okay, I'll ask him and see what he says. What's next on the list?'

'The name of the restaurant.'

Finn groaned.

'Wait!' Olivia held up her hand. 'I've had an idea. I think you want something simpler, less French, and at the same time more in keeping with your community.' She paused for effect.

'Well, don't keep me waiting. Spit it out.'

'What about calling it the Bistro by Watersmeet Bridge?'

'I quite like that,' he mumbled.

She rolled her eyes. 'Sorry? Did you just admit I've had a good idea?' Now it was her turn to look proud of herself. 'Well, I wasn't expecting that to be so easy.'

'Hang on, shouldn't we check with your father before we make such an important decision?'

Olivia bristled. 'This has nothing to do with my father. I am the manager and you are the chef and if we're happy with it, then that's what we'll go with.' She paused to study Finn, disappointed.

'All right, then. I think that name could work, given our location, and it has a nice feel to it.' He smiled at her and she relaxed.

'Next item is furniture,' she said, getting straight back to business. 'I would have liked to buy all new chairs and tables, but we can't afford that now, obviously. I think we should try and sell what we have at auction, which would then give us the money to buy new stuff.'

'I don't mind a bit of repainting and changing the name of the place, but I don't want to lose everything. I like the furniture. It gives the place character and keeps Bob's legacy alive.'

'Bob?'

'The former owner.'

'Well, I understand your desire to honour Bob, but I do think we need to move with the times.'

'But we don't have the money to do that now, so why not make things easy on ourselves and keep things as they are?'

'Let's leave that for now. I'll come back to it once I've given it some more thought. Talking about money, that's the other thing we need to discuss. Budgeting.'

'Budgeting?' He swallowed nervously, wondering how honest he should be.

'Do you hire your linens or do your own laundry on site?'

'God, I hire them of course. There's no way I could be washing, drying and ironing, as well as cooking and running the restaurant. I'd never have the time.'

'I understand that, but how much does all that cost?'

'I honestly couldn't tell you without looking at one of the invoices.'

He looked Olivia straight in the eye but even so, she was pretty sure he was lying to her. She narrowed her eyes ever so slightly.

'I will need to sit down and go through all the expenses at some point soon. You know that, don't you?'

He nodded but didn't say anything.

'One of the things I'm particularly concerned about is the menu,' Olivia continued.

His hackles rose. 'The menu? Why?'

'Well, it's very long.'

'And? What's wrong with that?' His brow creased.

'If you have a long menu, that means you're either buying in stuff and then throwing it away when it doesn't get used, or you're using a lot of frozen food.'

'My food is all fresh.' He glared at her.

'That's what I thought. So you must have been throwing stuff away, and wasted food costs money. Is that what you were doing?'

'Well, yes, I used to end up throwing food away because I didn't know what people were going to order from the menu, but there's...' He fell silent, probably hoping he could get away without any further questions. But Olivia was dogged.

'Come on, Finn, I need the full story here.'

He covered his face with his hands for a moment before dragging them down his cheeks and resting them back in his lap. 'I used to overbuy food in case I got a dish wrong because I'm a bit of a perfectionist. I did it with wine, too, because I'm always looking for the perfect food and wine match.'

The blood drained from Olivia's face. 'I think I ought to look at the paperwork sooner rather than later, then.'

After showing Olivia into his office, Finn hotfooted it out and made his way down the street towards the river. She had gasped when he'd shown her the mess of paperwork on his desk, and he couldn't bear to wait around to hear what she might have to say. It had been mean to leave her to sort everything out, but she had all the right organisational skills, whereas he was useless with admin. In any case, it would do him some good to get out of there and feel some fresh air on his skin, after being indoors for most of the day. He missed being by the water if he stayed away from it for too long. He could hear the river tumbling over the rocks on its way to the sea as he walked.

He decided to go in search of Ed. He wanted to talk to him about the painting work they needed doing, but also to seek his opinion on all that had happened since Olivia's arrival. Ed had told him he was working over on the other side of the bridge, decorating the whole downstairs of someone's house. He'd said Finn could come round whenever it suited him. Finn thought about Olivia as he strolled alongside the river towards the bridge. Her passion for reviving the restaurant was infectious and she had some good business ideas, too. In some ways he almost regretted his plan to leave, but at the same time, she was so uptight he wasn't sure if they would ever see eye-to-eye on everything. The difficulty was that she seemed perfectly suited to turning the restaurant round and on top of that, she was determined, all of which would be great under normal circumstances. But this wasn't a normal situation. He resented her for swooping in along with her father to take over his restaurant, and now she wanted to bring in lots of changes too. He sighed. Maybe it was time for him to accept that some changes would have to be made if the restaurant was to have any chance of success. He stopped in his tracks at that thought and heard a harrumph behind him as a little old lady out walking her dog gently bumped into him.

'What are you doing stopping in the middle of the pavement like that?' she muttered, guiding her chubby terrier past him.

Whose side am I on? I shouldn't be thinking about the restaurant's future if I want to leave in six months. And if I ask Ed for help, he'll say 'yes', because he's too kind-hearted, like all my friends. But the fact is that Olivia and I both want the same thing – to restore the restaurant. It's just that if I help her, what do I get from it, apart from clearing my debt and regaining my reputation?

He started walking again, but his pace grew slower and slower under the weight of the realisation that he had to help Olivia restore the restaurant if he wanted to move on at the end of the six months. He reached the house, a lovely Victorian semi, a few minutes later, gave a quick knock and walked in. He proceeded down the long, tiled hallway towards the kitchen, where he could hear Ed singing along, in his own inimitable way, to a Bruce Springsteen classic on the radio. He found Ed up a ladder, painting the ceiling with a roller. His head was covered with specks of white paint, as if he'd been caught in a hail storm.

'Ah, Finn,' he called out. 'Time for a tea break. Awesome.'

He came down the ladder, gave Finn a fist bump, and turned to fill the kettle up at the sink before putting it on to boil.

'How's the job going?' Finn asked, trying to avoid answering any questions that Ed might have for him.

'It's fine, you know. It's painting, man.' Ed gave a tiny shrug of his broad shoulders and broke into one of his enormous smiles. Finn envied his friend's simple approach to life sometimes. 'What brings you out here to see me in the middle of the day, anyway? Something must be up, by my reckoning.'

'I came to talk to you about Olivia.'

'So you're already on first-name terms?' Ed joked with a wink. He stood up again to make two cups of strong tea. 'Come on then, tell me all about it.' He put the tea on the table and pulled out a packet of biscuits his customer had left for him.

And Finn filled him in on his latest news. 'I don't know what to do, Ed. Should I help her or should I carry on feeling bitter against her and her father for taking over my restaurant? I could tell her you'd said no to helping us with the painting, but I reckon she'd just come and find you and ask you yourself.'

'I must say, I like the sound of Olivia already. What have you got to gain from going against her? Her dad sounds like a slimeball but she hasn't given you any reason to dislike her, from what you say.'

'I feel I should be working against her on principle, I suppose, and it's also that she wants to repaint and modernise and change the name. And I don't want to lose the character of the bistro. I'm worried she wants to turn it into a soulless, identikit chain restaurant that would appeal to corporate types.'

'Well, a bit of painting won't hurt. It'll probably do the place some good to have a makeover.'

'But I already feel like I've let Bob down by losing the restaurant. I don't want to lose all my memories of working with him, too.' Finn was exhausted by the to and fro inside his mind.

'To be honest, I think you'd be honouring Bob by working with Olivia to modernise the place and get it up and running again.'

'Yeah, I suppose that's true. Are you sure you wouldn't mind doing all that painting for free? You know we can't afford to pay you in money at the moment.'

'Of course. I know you'd do the same for me.'

Finn stood up to get ready to go. He was glad they'd discussed the problem, but he was still not quite convinced they'd worked out a way through it. 'When shall I say you'll come by?'

Ed gathered the mugs and put them in the sink, popping another couple of biscuits in his mouth as he did so. 'I should be able to come in some time over the next few days. Don't be specific with a start date, though. I have no idea when I could actually begin.'

Finn gave Ed a quick man hug before setting off to make his way back to the bistro, still pondering what to do for the best.

CHAPTER FOUR

There was so much paper in Finn's office, Olivia was almost buried in it. She'd spent the past hour trying to sort it into similar piles but had made very little headway. There was paper everywhere, leaving her nowhere to put a document down safely before it was somehow drawn back into the general mess. Finally, she left the room in search of a large box to put it all in. She found two good-sized boxes in the kitchen back room and decided to fetch them both; she could use one for invoices and another for everything else. She paused a moment, and then headed back to the office to start the sorting process all over again. When she was finished, she'd at least be able to talk to Finn more clearly about the state of the accounts.

'Hello! Anyone here?'

'Yes, I'm in the office,' Olivia replied at the sound of Finn's voice a short while later.

'Oh, my God, I can see the desk and the carpet.' Finn gazed at his office as if he'd never seen it before. 'You've obviously been hard at it while I've been gone. Would you like a cup of tea?' He had the grace to look guilty at having left her to sort out the chaos.

'That would be wonderful, thank you.' She groaned as she uncurled her back from the position she'd been stuck in for the last half an hour, and then she stumbled out, blinking, into the bright lights of the kitchen. She was glad she'd chosen to wear trousers for the work she'd been doing, but when she went to smooth them, they were covered with dust.

'You've done a brilliant job, you know, and in extra quick time, too.' As Finn turned to smile at her, she blushed bright red. 'What did I say?' He laughed awkwardly, trying to make light of things.

She waved her hand in front of her face, as if that might make her embarrassment magically disappear. 'It's just that I'm not used to getting praise and you caught me off guard.'

Finn reached out to touch her lightly on the arm. She was mesmerised by the gesture, and her skin tingled as goosebumps formed.

'Well, I'm glad if I caught you off guard with such a simple thing as a compliment. But I'm sorry if I embarrassed you.' He turned back to make the tea and she took advantage of the time to compose herself, berating herself for allowing him to see her at her most vulnerable. There was something about him that made her want to talk to him, to let her barriers down without fear of mockery. She drew in a deep breath and let it out slowly.

'Anyway,' she began, in a slightly shaky voice, 'how did you get on with Ed? Any joy?'

'Yes, he said he'd do it.' Finn took a long slurp of tea. She noticed he didn't make eye contact. Great, she thought. She'd embarrassed him with her show of weakness. She wouldn't be doing that again in a hurry.

'Oh, that's brilliant news. Well done to you, too. You must have been convincing.' She beamed at him this time and was pleased to see him smile back at her excited expression. 'When can he start, did he say?'

'He couldn't say a specific date but he said he'd come in some time in the next few days if he can, to talk to you about it in more detail.'

Her smile fell a little, but not much. 'Well, that will have to do, I suppose. I thought while I carry on sorting out your office, maybe you could research auction places where we could try to sell the furniture. Unless you know of somewhere already?'

'I thought we'd agreed not to sell the furniture. If we just do a repaint, the furniture will be fine.'

'Okay. How about a compromise? Let's wait and see what difference the repainting makes. If we think it looks good enough afterwards, we'll keep the furniture, but if not, we'll sell it. Agreed?'

Finn nodded but didn't say anything.

Olivia didn't know what to make of that response so she stood up and went to the sink to wash out her cup before making her way back to the office. She sensed Finn following behind her, and it made her nervous for some reason. She'd just entered the room when her foot caught on some old box files stacked by the door, and she tripped. She put her hands out in front of her, trying to break her inevitable fall, and was surprised when Finn's large hands slipped easily round her slim waist, saving her at the last minute. Her body fit snugly against his as he pulled her towards him.

'Oh!' Her soft gasp hung in the air in the brief silence that followed. The touch of Finn's warm hands against her hips made her feel safe and protected from the harsh reality of the outside world. She was also acutely aware of each part of his body where it met hers.

Her chest rose and fell as Finn breathed in, and then pushed her gently away. The fleeting moment passed, but she was taken aback by the frisson of attraction she had experienced at his touch. He was still behind her, not saying anything or even moving. Perhaps he was unsure what to say because she felt the same way herself. She heard him pick something up before leaving the room, taking all the tension away with him. A few moments later, the front door of the bistro slammed shut.

Now she would have to wait again to talk to him about the accounts. She sighed and turned to survey the office. It looked much better and she was even able to put her laptop on the desk. She sat down, turning her attention to the drawers next. She pulled out the top one. Sitting on top of yet another pile of invoices was a photo. When she looked at it more closely, she could see it was Finn when he was a bit younger, with an older woman who must be his mum. The resemblance between them was striking. She smiled as she stared at it. They looked happy together. She turned the photo over. 'I thought you might like this one, from Dad.' Olivia frowned as she considered the words.

Finn couldn't believe what had just happened between himself and Olivia. Her body had fitted so perfectly against his and he had only just about been able to keep himself steady. The intoxicating smell of her hair and the soft swell of her hips in her tight jeans had captivated him so much, he almost couldn't bring himself to let her go. It was only the gentle press of her hands on his that had brought him to his senses. Up till then, he'd been struggling to have a single coherent thought.

As the harbour came into view, he drew up next to the railings, setting his laptop bag down between his feet. The thought that he might be attracted to Olivia, and that she might feel the same way about him, had taken him completely by surprise. He hadn't had a relationship for so long; what with running the business and then spending time with his mum, he'd almost forgotten what an attraction between two people was like. He was still giddy with the adrenaline rush he'd experienced, but reality was slowly beginning to seep back in. He couldn't afford to have these feelings for Olivia if he was to work alongside her in the restaurant, day in, day out. Yet there was definitely something about her, a vulnerability that he was drawn to, and a large part of him wanted to know her better. But he had to keep focused on his end goal: to work out his six months and then leave to start another restaurant of his own some-where else.

Finn raked his hands through his hair, staring at the water as it lapped against the boats below. What was he going to do? There was no way out of his predicament. He and Olivia would be forced to work side by side if he wanted to regain his reputation and to clear his debt. Fuller had left him in no doubt that if he went back on his promise to stay for the full six months, he would find himself in debt all over again. He would have to avoid any kind of relationship other than a professional one with Olivia, or otherwise there was a serious risk both of them would get hurt, and he didn't want that to happen for either of them.

He picked up his bag with a renewed sense of determination, and retraced his steps along the harbour wall at the river's edge. He was captivated as always by the boats and dinghies bobbing up and down in the water, their reds, blues and yellows mingling together in a bright, colourful mass. They were just what he needed to take his mind off things.

'Hey, Finn!'

He looked up at the sound of his name being called to see Zoe, his former waitress, running towards him, her long black hair flying out behind her.

'Hi, Zoe, how's it going?' he asked as she fell into step beside him, struggling to catch her breath.

'Pretty good, thanks. I heard you're going to reopen the bistro. Is that right?' Her eyes sparkled with excitement and he felt bad again for having to let her go.

'Yeah, the bank found me a buyer at the last minute, and they want me to stay on as chef at the restaurant.'

'Well, that's great news. I'm pleased for you.' Her soft Irish lilt was balm to Finn's ears. He'd missed Zoe's calming influence, and her friendship, since she'd left the restaurant.

'I hear you've got a new job. How are you getting on?'

Her pretty face fell. 'Jeez, I hate it, Finn. Sitting in an office all day doesn't suit me. It's a job, I suppose, but I'd much rather be back at the restaurant.'

Finn's eyebrows shot up. 'Zoe, I'm not in a position to offer you your old job back. There's a new manager now and I don't know if we'll be hiring anyone until we get back on our feet. I'm sorry.'

'No, I know, it's okay. Just to say, that if you ever do want someone again, you will ask me first, won't you? I'd love to come back.' She grinned and he was grateful for her understanding.

'I will, you can be sure of that.'

'What's the new manager like, then?' Her eyes twinkled.

'You've been talking to Ed, haven't you? The swine.' He chuckled at the thought of Ed and Zoe gossiping about him.

'Well, go on then. What's she like?'

'She's... er, she's nice. She's keen to get the bistro up and running again and she knows about business, which, as you know, was never my forte. I'm hopeful we can get back to our better days with her help.'

'That all sounds great. I'll have to pop in once you reopen and you can introduce me to her. What's her name?'

'Olivia.'

'Well, it was lovely to see you, Finn. Good luck with everything.'

They said their goodbyes at the bridge, promising to meet up again soon at the pub. Finn felt even worse than he had before, knowing that Zoe hated her new job. It was his fault she wasn't working at the bistro any more. In fact, it felt like everything was his fault. He wasn't sure he would ever be able to make it up to her, either. He picked up his bag and returned to the restaurant to face the music.

Olivia tucked the photo away, feeling guilty for snooping into Finn's personal papers. She continued sorting the paperwork in his cramped office for about half an hour, but found she couldn't focus on it. Her mind kept returning to what had happened between them and how good it had made her feel. There was an attraction between them, that she couldn't deny, but they also had a job to do and that would only be made harder if the two of them became involved with each other. She'd been down that road before and knew precisely how that turned out.

When she heard a knock at the back door and the handle being turned, she was glad of the distraction from both her thoughts and the boring paperwork sorting she had been mired in. It couldn't be Finn coming back this soon, and she was curious to find out who it was.

She reached the door just as an enormous man came into what now seemed like the tiny kitchen.

'Er... hello, can I help you?' she ventured with a surprised smile, gazing up at the man's huge frame.

'Ah, I was looking for Finn actually,' he began, scratching his shaved head. He paused, seemed to collect himself and said, 'You must be Olivia.' He extended his hand.

She took the bear-like paw he was offering and stared at him. 'I am. And you are?'

'I'm Finn's friend, Ed.' When she still looked puzzled, he added, 'The painter and decorator guy.'

'Oh, hi. Finn said you might be calling in, but I wasn't expecting you so soon, sorry. Come on in, anyway. Would you like a drink?'

'No, I'm fine, thanks. I drink far too much tea and coffee in my job as it is.' He gave her a devilish grin and she wondered whether there might be something in the water down this way. Two gorgeous men in a matter of days.

'Finn's not here right now, but I can talk to you about what we're trying to do. The first thing I need to make sure of is that Finn told you we don't have any budget to pay you with. We can pay you in meals when we get up and running again. Is that going to be okay?' Olivia gave him a tentative smile. When Ed didn't reply, she rushed on. 'How about I help you with your accounts, too? Would that be useful?' It was a gamble, but knowing how small business owners often hated doing their paperwork, she hoped it was one that would pay off.

'Now you're talking.' Ed looked delighted at that suggestion.

Olivia nodded, pleased to have found his Achilles heel, and turned to lead the way through the dining area and out of the front door. They stood side by side in front of the building as Olivia explained their plans.

'So, first of all, I want to have the exterior repainted. This burgundy colour is nice, but it's too dark. I'd prefer a pale blue to remind everyone of the sea. And then we're going to rename the place, too, so we need to have the sign redone.'

'What are you going to call it?'

'The Bistro by Watersmeet Bridge,' she said proudly.

'That's a great idea. I like that a lot. Well, I can definitely do the repainting, but I wouldn't be much good at painting the sign. I know a few people I could talk to about that, so I'll find out and let you know.'

'The important thing is that they understand we can't pay them for the time being. I feel awful when I know it's your livelihood, too.'

Ed gave her a small smile which she didn't know how to interpret, but instinctively she understood he was on her side.

'Don't worry about it, I'll handle it. Now, Finn mentioned you were thinking about repainting the inside yourselves. But why don't I do that as well, while I'm here?'

Olivia could have thrown her arms around Ed at that point, but didn't want to scare him off. 'That would be wonderful. Thank you.'

He opened the door and stood aside to let Olivia go first. They chatted inside about colour choices for the dining and service area, following the same idea of the colours of the sea. Just as they were finishing up, the kitchen door slammed shut and a moment later, Finn appeared.

'Hey, Ed, I thought you said you couldn't make it here today,' he said pointedly, giving Olivia a quick glance.

'I had a few minutes at the end of my job and thought I'd take the chance to pop in. Olivia and I have talked about the work you need doing.'

'Yes,' she said. 'The only question now is when can you start work? I'd like to get the restaurant open again within a fortnight.'

Ed and Finn both turned to her with open mouths. Finn regained his composure first. 'A fortnight? That's optimistic.'

'I don't see why. If Ed gets on with all the painting now, that will allow us to sort out the furniture. We'll then have plenty of time left to talk about the menu and anything else we need to do before opening day.' She smiled confidently and turned her attention to Ed.

'Well, I am very busy,' he stalled momentarily, 'but I don't think your job would take long. I could make a start in a couple of days, which would give me time to get the paint and any other materials I need. I can't promise when, though.' He swallowed nervously and Olivia wondered if she'd pushed him too far.

'That's perfect, thank you.' She looked at Finn in time to see him give Ed another piercing look. 'Well, thanks for coming in, Ed. It was great to meet you and I'll see you later in the week, hopefully.'

Olivia went back to the office to grab the invoices box and her bag. Then she set off back to her hotel, eager to escape any more close encounters with her new chef.

Finn waited until he was sure Olivia was gone before turning sharply.

'What's going on, Ed? When we talked about it earlier, you said you didn't know when you could start. And now you've potentially agreed to get started within the next few days. It would have been good to have a heads up you were coming.'

'I know, I'm sorry. I came round to see you but found Olivia instead, and she got straight down to business. When I told you earlier I had no idea when I could start, I hadn't met Olivia, had I? You didn't tell me what a lovely person she is, and I couldn't say no when she asked me. And neither of us knew she wanted to reopen so quickly. She's clearly a determined lady.'

'I know, right?' Finn groaned. 'I'm finding it impossible to say no to her, too. Still, I suppose it won't hurt for you to get started on the painting, and to be fair, it's in everyone's interest for us to reopen as soon as we can.'

'That's right. You need to think positively. It's a second chance for you. As long as you complete the six months, you'll have cleared your debt, and you still get to work in the restaurant, even if it's not yours any more.' Ed rushed on at Finn's grimace. 'You've got a good opportunity here.'

'You're right. But there's still so much to do and I don't think she realises how big this project is that she's taken on.'

Ed scratched his shaved head as if that might give him an answer to Finn's troubles. 'Have you got time for a pint?' he asked instead, happy to bury his head in the sand.

'Now, that's the best suggestion you've had all day.'

They walked out onto the street and made their way slowly up the hill, away from the river this time, and on to the village pub. They got their pints and sat down at a table in the window, both of them taking a long drink of their beer before speaking again. Finn gazed out at the harbour in the distance, where the wind had picked up to make the water a lot choppier.

'I saw Zoe when I was down at the harbour today. She asked me if there was any chance of her getting her job back.'

Ed's eyes lit up at the mention of Zoe's name. 'What did you say?'

'I had to be honest and tell her we won't be able to hire anyone else until we get back on our feet again.'

'How did she take it?'

'She was fine, but I could tell she was disappointed. I feel bad about putting her out of a job she loved, and I've missed her company as well.'

'The thing is, you're going to need a waitress and Zoe's the best there is. Do you think Olivia is up to taking on Zoe's job, as well as managing the money and everything else she'll have to do?'

'I honestly don't know. She doesn't strike me as someone who could do waitressing but then what do I know? She knows her food, but I'm not sure she's strong enough to deal with demanding customers every lunch-time and evening, like Zoe is.'

'And sorry to keep on, but how are you going to manage in the kitchen on your own without a sous-chef or a washer-upper?'

'Christ! Can you give me a break, man? I'm already broken as it is.'

Ed was right, though. Finn would have to bring these things up with Olivia when he next saw her. He was not looking forward to that conversation at all because there was no chance of any spare money to pay staff with.

'And was that a box full of invoices she took away earlier?' Ed chuckled as Finn took a swipe at him.

'She's already talked about the expenses with me, and I did confess to overspending on my food and wine purchases.'

'Yeah, she's in for a shock when she sees all the invoices.'

'I think it's time you bought the next round, after making me so damn miserable, and when you come back, I've got a bone to pick with you about gossiping about me with Zoe.'

Ed looked suitably abashed and hurried off to the bar to avoid any further recriminations.

Finn watched his friend lumber up to the almost empty bar and pondered all they'd discussed. Just for a moment, he let his imagination run wild about the future. Olivia had already made some good suggestions, and as Ed had said, this could be a great second chance for him to make a go of it. She could teach him about the business side of things, so he could maybe even take back control of the restaurant on his own again after she left.

Then he stopped himself. He couldn't daydream like this, not when the reality was so brutal. If he was going to get the restaurant back, he would have to buy it back, and right now, he didn't have a penny to his name.

Still, even if he didn't get to stay at the bistro, maybe some day, he could think of owning his own restaurant again, when he was a bit older and wiser. He'd be damned if he'd do anything more to let Bob and Jen down.

CHAPTER FIVE

The following morning, after a restless night worrying about her relationship from here on with Finn, Olivia went down early for breakfast at her hotel. She wanted to leave herself plenty of time before Finn was due to pick her up for their trip to Barnstaple. Despite her bad night, she was ready for a full English breakfast today. She picked up a copy of the *South Western Daily* on her way into the dining room and took a seat near the window overlooking the river below. While she waited for her breakfast to arrive, she skimmed through the first half of the paper, only interested in getting to the financial section. As she turned the final page of the leisure section, her eyes landed on the headline on the front page of the business news.

'*SW restaurant chain, La Riviera, rumoured to be in financial trouble.*' Olivia gasped despite herself. Why was she only finding this out from the paper and not straight from her father?

The article carried on. '*George Fuller, owner of the chain, has long been known for his love of expansion, relentlessly buying up failing restaurants, turning them round and adding them to his chain, or selling them on if they don't fit his brand. Now, insiders are saying that the money for this constant expansion has run out, and the board's patience along with it. How long will Fuller last at the company he founded and has run for the last 25 years?'*

Olivia counted to ten and tried not to let her imagination run wild, but deep down, she was worried. Her father had always wanted to expand, that much was true, and there was a time when that was right for the company. But her reports on the independent restaurants they'd bought up over the last few years had become steadily more gloomy as he failed to turn them round more and more often. They had been forced to sell most of them on again but increasingly at a loss. This was why she was so determined to make a success of the bistro. Her father needed to recoup his money and make a profit, and her knowledge of why the businesses that had gone before had failed should prove invaluable in helping her reach her goal. Still, it was going to be an uphill struggle in this economic climate. In her heart, she wasn't surprised that the board had called time on her father's reckless squandering of money on restaurants that would be better left alone.

On impulse, she decided to try calling her father again to see what he had to say for himself. She found his name under her contacts and listened as the call connected. This time he answered straight away.

'Olivia, darling. How are things going?'

'They were going pretty well until I saw an article in the *South Western Daily* saying that La Riviera's rumoured to be in financial trouble...'

Her dad coughed. 'That old rag. Surely you know by now not to trust what you read in the papers. They make it up as they go along, you know.'

'Well, it has the ring of truth about it. Don't forget, I've been writing reports about our acquisitions for the last three years, so I know exactly how many restaurants we've failed to turn round and been forced to sell on again.'

Her dad sucked in air through his teeth, a sure sign he was

annoyed at her for challenging him. 'As I have said, Olivia, we are not having *financial problems* or any other kind, for that matter. Perhaps you've got too much time on your hands down there if you're spending it reading pointless articles like that.'

Her father's defensive stance only served to confirm Olivia's suspicions. She went on the attack, rather than backing down as she normally did. 'Then why did you withdraw my budget for refurbishments, if money isn't an issue for you at the moment? It was a small amount to you but would make the world of difference to me in trying to get the bistro back up and running.'

'That's merely a cash flow problem, my dear, which you'd understand more about if you'd had any experience of running a business. Now, let's move on to other things and leave this to one side. How are things actually going? Rupert was asking me the other day and I need to give him a report.'

Olivia was seething. 'Things at the restaurant are going well and we've got round the issue of your cash flow problem perfectly well on our own. If I lack experience, that's because you've taken this long to let me manage a restaurant. And as for Rupert, he's supposed to be on sick leave, so why is he even asking for a report? It sounds like he's meddling for the sake of it to me.'

'Perhaps it would be better if you gave him the report yourself. He is still my operations manager and, as such, responsible for the performance of all the restaurants we own, so you do answer to him and he has my full support. If he thinks you're not up to the job, he'll tell you so and he'll pull you out of there quicker than you can say "failing restaurant". So if I were you, I'd make sure you have a proper report ready when you do call to speak to him. Now, if there's nothing else, I have got rather a lot to do today. Goodbye, Olivia.'

Olivia stared at the now silent phone in her hand. Her goal of managing a restaurant on her own was fading before her very eyes, and what's more, she was now forced to deal with her ex, and that was about the worst thing to happen to her for quite a long time.

Finn had been awake since four in the morning. He tossed and turned, trying to go back to sleep, but his thoughts overwhelmed him and sleep finally became impossible. He got out of bed at half past five and went through to the lounge. His mind was so busy that he decided against coffee and went for a cup of camomile tea instead. After stirring in a spoonful of locally made honey, he sat down in the armchair, trying to calm his mind.

Olivia had been in his thoughts, despite all his efforts to stop thinking about her. He closed his eyes and tried once more to banish her at least to the back of his mind. He'd also spent a lot of time thinking about his mum during the night. He still missed her terribly, but he found it so hard to talk about his feelings of loss. He'd hardly spoken to his dad since she'd passed away, let alone, Declan, his brother. They were probably finding it as difficult to deal with their grief as he was. Maybe he should call his dad to see how he was coping. They still had their differences, but now that his mum was gone, perhaps it was time to let the past go, and move on. He sipped his cooling tea and debated whether to call his dad. He glanced at the clock to find that it was only half past six, too early to call yet, so he decided to take a shower first.

His dad picked up on the first ring when he called him a little while later, almost as if he was waiting for Finn's call.

'Hey, Dad, how are you?'

'Not too bad, son, how about you?' His dad sounded weary, and Finn felt guilty for not having called sooner.

'Yeah, about the same. Sorry for not calling before now. I had to, erm... put the bistro up for sale after Mum... you know, and I've been dealing with all that since then.'

'Oh no, I'm so sorry, Finn. Ah, what a mess this has been for all of us.'

'Well, it's not all bad. We did find a buyer and he's asked me to stay on at the restaurant for the next six months while we get it back on its feet.'

'That sounds a bit better, I suppose, but it must be hard working there but not being in charge any more.'

His dad was more perceptive than Finn had given him credit for. "How about you, Dad? How have you been getting on?'

'I miss your mum, of course, and to tell the truth, I wish we'd never moved so far away from Lynford. Now I'm on my own, it feels so lonely.'

'Yeah, I can imagine. Listen, I do want to visit Mum's grave. It's just taken me a while to build up to it. Maybe I could come and see you then?'

'That would be grand, Finn. Let me know when you're coming.'

Finn said goodbye to his dad, feeling much better.

He left the flat a few minutes later, deciding on a whim to get his breakfast from the bakery and to test the waters with Rosie. She and Ewan had been such good friends to him, and he regretted the way he'd them let down when he'd dropped everything to go to his mum.

The air was bracing as he walked up the high street, but it was good to be out and about. When he reached the bakery, the queue was snaking out of the door. He was pleased to see how well Rosie and Ewan were doing, but maybe now wouldn't be the best time to apologise to Rosie for the problems he'd caused. That was if she would even talk to him after all that had happened. He was just thinking about coming back another time, when Rosie saw him. He couldn't turn away now, so he joined the queue.

'Finn, what can I get you?' She looked wary, but her eye contact didn't waver.

'Two croissants please, Rosie. Great to see you're so busy,' he said as she turned round to get his pastries.

'Yes, it's taken a while to get there, but we've done it.'

'I'm so sorry for all the problems I caused you earlier in the year.'

'I know you are, and I was cross about it at the time, but when I found out about your mum, I felt terrible. I wish you'd told us about it. We would have been there for you, you know. We go back a long way.' She gave him a tentative smile then.

'I am sorry, but thank you. I'd better let you go, but I'll see you soon.'

'Definitely. Don't be a stranger.'

He left the shop feeling like a great weight had been lifted from his shoulders. He hoped his other past suppliers would be as gracious as Rosie and Ewan had been. He was dreading seeing some of them again when he went into town with Olivia later that morning. It would be embarrassing enough seeing them again after all that had happened, without Olivia being witness to it.

He was about to cross the road when he came face to face with Jamie's dad.

'I want a word with you, Anderson. I hope you know how much you let my boy down. I never wanted him to work at your restaurant anyway, and I've been proved right, haven't I? He should be concentrating on his A levels, not wasting his time doing your dirty work. I've heard that you're going to reopen the place now, but you listen to me.' He jabbed Finn in the chest. 'You leave Jamie alone to concentrate on his studies. He'll be much better off without you.'

He stalked off without letting Finn say a word in his own defence. Hanging his head, Finn walked back to get his car before going to meet Olivia, feeling more like a failure than ever.

Olivia escaped the dining room and went to wait for Finn outside. It was a beautiful early spring day and the sun was warm enough to heat her face, even at nine o'clock in the morning. As she took in the view from the clifftop down to the harbour, where seagulls were circling in the almost cloudless sky, she found the sea a calming influence after the phone call with her father. She needed to talk to him face to face to find out what was going on. Maybe she could return to the city for a few days once the restaurant reopened and got going again. She would give Finn all the tools he needed and then she could go home for a break and to see her friends. Most importantly, she wanted to find out from her father what was going on with the business.

She turned at the sound of a car's horn giving a gentle toot and saw Finn pulling into the hotel's sweeping gravelled car park. She walked briskly back across the grass to meet him, but as she drew nearer and caught sight of his battered old Volvo, she began to slow down. When she drew up next to him at last, he wound down his window, with some effort.

'Morning.' He smiled. 'All set?'

'Well, I was until I saw the state of your car. You don't seriously expect me to sit in this worn out old car all the way to Barnstaple, do you?' She gestured at her business suit and pulled a face.

'I hope you're not insulting Bessie. She's seen me through a lot of tricky moments.' He stepped out, causing Olivia to move back, and went round to the passenger side to open her door for her. 'Your carriage awaits, princess.'

He was in an unusually cheery mood, Olivia thought, but she had the feeling it was only for show. She wondered briefly whether something had happened.

She followed him round the back of the car, tutting at the dirty, rusted paintwork and stopped in front of the passenger seat. She leaned over and peered in.

'The seat and the footwell are at least clear of any rubbish. I suppose it might be okay.'

'I know it's not the luxury you're used to, but I think you'll survive.' Finn rolled his eyes.

Olivia got in, and he closed the door firmly behind her as she did up her seat belt. She sat stiffly as Finn climbed in next to her and started the car. A few minutes later, they were on their way. Olivia had wondered if things might be awkward after what had happened between them the other day, but Finn seemed to be back to his usual self, so she didn't bring the subject up. Instead, she tried to relax by looking out the window, enthralled by the scenery. They crossed over first one river and then another, before taking the winding moorland road out of the village and heading for the main road that would take them all the way to Barnstaple.

'I tried repainting one of the bistro chairs last night, but it looked awful. So I've got a couple of tables and chairs in the back of the car to show them at the carpenter's today. They said this would be enough to give them an idea of what they'd need to do to refurbish the whole lot,' Finn told her as they progressed through another picturesque village on their journey.

'That's good. I think it's a good compromise to refurbish the old furniture and spruce it up a bit.' Finn smiled. She was glad they'd managed to agree on a new way to solve this problem.

They sat in silence for a few miles and Olivia enjoyed the lush Devon landscape visible from the car window.

'I like the colour you chose for the outside of the restaurant,' Finn said a few minutes later, glancing quickly at her before returning his eyes to the road.

'Thank you. I'm glad you like it. I can't wait to see it once Ed gets going, and it will brighten the inside of the bistro.'

'Have you had a look at the invoices now?' Finn asked, not looking at her this time.

She studied him for a moment. His face had taken on a worried look. 'Yes, and the income too.'

'Did you come back for the accounts books yesterday?'

'Yes. Obviously you weren't there or we might have talked then about the financial situation.'

Finn sucked in a breath. 'How bad is it?'

'As bad as you think it is, from the look on your face. But I have ideas about how we can cut our costs to maximise our income, and cutting back is the only way we can make a go of this.'

'I think your idea to cut the menu is a good one. What else have you got in mind?'

'I think there's more to the food side than just the menu. I don't think you were charging enough for the food, or the drinks, and perhaps your food portions were too generous, I don't know. But judging by what you served me the other day, portion size could be an issue.' Olivia glanced over at Finn in time to see him swallow nervously before she continued. 'The other big costs are for laundering linen, and of course you used to pay two members of staff, which is an expense we don't have to worry about straight away.'

'It would be pretty difficult to run the restaurant with just the two of us, though.'

'I hope you don't mean me. I don't know the first thing about being a waitress or working in a kitchen, come to that.'

'Well, you'd better get used to paying for employees again, then.'

Olivia pursed her lips and folded her arms. 'Where on earth do you think we're going to find money for staff, as well as everything else?'

Finn shrugged. Olivia chewed her lip as she considered the situation. 'I'm happy to help out front of house, and perhaps with other things over time.' She did want to help. It was just that she'd had so little practical experience.

'That's a start then, but there's a lot more to running a restaurant than that.'

After a successful day in Barnstaple, sorting out the refurbishment of the tables and chairs, Finn was not looking forward to the following day at all. Olivia had asked him to meet her in the coffee shop in the village to discuss the restaurant's finances. She wanted to meet somewhere neutral, she'd said, so they could both talk freely. He didn't like the sound of that one little bit. Obviously they would need to talk everything through, but their discussion would only highlight how everything had gone wrong. The business had taken a dive after Dan, his finance manager, had left, and he had taken the decision to go to his mum's bedside in the hospice. Their conversation would only serve to remind him of why he was in the awful position of being an employee and no longer the owner of his own restaurant.

Finn arrived at the café first and after getting himself a coffee, he took a seat at a table in the window so Olivia would spot him when she came in. A few minutes later, he saw her walking along the street towards him, her long, auburn hair blowing out behind her rather than tied back, as it had been when she first arrived. Dressed in jeans again, and a pale green sweater, rather than one of her formal business suits, she looked amazing. The casual look suited her and she seemed a bit more relaxed, although he was sure she would always find it hard to let herself go completely.

'Would you like a coffee?' he asked as she came in and approached his table.

'Yes, thank you.'

Her rosy cheeks made her look even more beautiful and he found it hard to take his eyes off her. He stood, breaking the spell, and made his way to the counter. He returned a couple of minutes later with another coffee, which he set down on the table next to her. The coffee shop enveloped them with its warmth and the enticing smell of roasting coffee beans and freshly made cakes, and Finn began to relax.

'Let's start with the menu,' she said, after a quick sip of her coffee. 'If we're going to open at lunch-time, I think we should have a fixed lunch menu only, at a set price for two or three courses, and we should limit the choice to a maximum of three starters, three mains and three desserts.'

'I agree with all of that. It sounds very sensible. What about the evening menu?'

'We increase the list of choices to five items in each section of the menu and still offer the set price menu. That way there should only be two extra courses to prepare for the evening. You could choose one dish as the special, perhaps?'

Finn nodded, relieved she'd started with a topic that it was easy for them both to agree on. 'This means that I'd be buying more of each item, but it would be a much shorter list. We'd have to print a new menu every day, wouldn't we? Could we get ourselves set up for that?'

'Yes, that's not difficult as long as we have a decent colour printer and some premium paper.'

'Okay, what else?'

'You do also need to discuss your food costs and related pricing with me, as well as the portion sizes.'

'Yes, agreed. I'll need some help with that.'

'Linen is the next item. Your bill is astronomical and we can't afford to keep paying it. Once we have our refurbished tables with their newly sanded finish, I think we should ditch the tablecloths altogether and just have thicker, paper serviettes. That will save us a ton of money.'

'Fair enough. I do like the linen, but I understand it's a real drain on our finances.'

'The other high cost is from purchasing wine and spirits. It looks like you do all that yourself, is that right?'

'Yes, and I know it's been expensive.'

'Well, here I do think we should outsource. Is there a good local independent wine merchant you use?'

'Yes, in Barnstaple, near the fish supplier. What did you have in mind?'

'We could ask them to supply all our wines and offer to credit them on the menus, but ask for a deal in exchange. We'd also want sale or return.'

'How good are you at negotiating?' Finn closed his eyes momentarily at the thought. Negotiating wasn't one of his strengths, that was for sure.

'That's fine. I can sort all that out.' He released a sigh of relief and she stared at him for a minute before eventually looking back at her list. 'Next, as you mentioned yesterday, we need to talk about staff. You had two members of staff before, yes?'

'That's right, Zoe and Jamie.'

'This is a bit radical but is there any chance that they might work for free or for reduced pay while we get started again?'

'Absolutely not. We can't ask them to work without pay. I won't do it, Olivia.' He sat back in his chair and folded his arms.

Olivia put down her pen and looked him clearly in the eye. 'Well, we can't afford to pay two more people as well as you. So you need to think laterally.'

He would have loved to offer to go without pay but he simply couldn't afford it. He needed to build up some savings of his own for the future. 'There's another issue,' he said. 'Zoe would be delighted to come back, but I bumped into Jamie's dad yesterday and he told me to stay right away from him because he needs to concentrate on his studies. I don't want to cause family problems for Jamie by asking.'

'Okay, so we have two major problems: no money to pay for the two extra staff we need, and only one member of staff available anyway, even if we manage to sort out the finances.'

Olivia pulled a frustrated face and in that moment, Finn would have liked to kiss her. Instead, he responded with a grimace of his own. 'One thing that might work is to pay them on a shift by shift basis when we actually have some money coming in. I think they'd accept that. How about you?' Even as he made the suggestion, Finn frowned, wondering how they might respond to this idea.

'Yes, that could work,' Olivia replied. 'We might have to take it one step at a time and see how busy the restaurant is, day by day, week by week, until we build up the reputation again. Okay, so if you talk to Zoe and ask her if she'll work as waitress again on our opening night on that basis, and how about I go to see Jamie and talk things through with his parents, to see if I can persuade them to let him come back as our washer-upper and prep cook whenever he's not at school?'

'I think that will work with Zoe but I'm not sure whether you'll persuade Jamie's dad. He was furious when I saw him yesterday. If you could swing it, it would leave me to do all the main cooking and you to oversee front of house, which would be all we'd need.'

'Well, I've had no experience of working in a restaurant before but if I stay front of house, I'll probably be fine. Just don't ask me to do any waitressing.'

'Zoe loves waitressing, so between the two of you, I think it will all be great. We just have to keep our fingers crossed you can persuade Jamie's parents.' He made to stand up but Olivia waved him back down again.

'Let's not get too carried away yet. I have a few other items on my list.'

CHAPTER SIX

Olivia headed back up the main street side by side with Finn towards the restaurant. She was pleased with how their meeting had gone, although she still had concerns. She would need to keep a tight hold on the reins to stop Finn's perfectionist tendency and with it, his need to overspend on every last thing. She glanced at him from underneath her eyelashes, hoping he wouldn't see her studying him. His hunched shoulders, so evident when she'd first arrived, were becoming a thing of the past and his stubborn, grouchy demeanour was also softening and only appearing when she challenged him. Suddenly, Finn stopped and turned to her. He must have seen her staring at him, she thought with embarrassment. Olivia's mouth went dry, as she wondered what he was about to say.

'Look!' He pointed ahead of them and she followed his instruction.

'Oh, it's beautiful.' She ran up the street until she drew level with the restaurant and could see the newly painted first coat for herself. Finn joined her a few seconds later and they stared in wonder at the pale blue colour that transformed the building.

'It really does look like the sea. That was an inspired idea you had there.'

Olivia broke into a big grin; she couldn't help herself. 'Do you like it, Finn?' she asked, turning to face him.

'I love it, Olivia.'

Finn looked deep into her eyes, and for a moment, Olivia forgot where she was. It was just the two of them standing on the pavement, and nothing else. Finn reached out and took her hands in his, drawing her gently towards him as if he was about to kiss her, but before things could go any further, she pulled away and withdrew behind her invisible barrier. Getting intimate with a man she was supposed to work with was a very bad idea. It was her golden rule, and it was the only way of ensuring her sanity, as she had been constantly reminding herself. Now she found herself worried about hurting Finn's feelings if she said the wrong thing.

'Finn, I...' she began, her eyes wide as she studied his face. 'We can't let personal feelings get in the way of the job we have to do here.'

'Is that really what you think?'

'I just know from experience,' she said quietly.

'Well, I'm sorry to hear that, Olivia.' And with that, he turned on his heel and disappeared round the corner towards the back of the restaurant.

Olivia heaved a sigh. She did like Finn. More than that, she was attracted to him, and the last thing she wanted to do was to hurt him, but this was for the best. She was sure he understood that deep down. She carried on up the street towards her hotel, leaving the restaurant behind her and trying not to dwell on what had almost happened between her and Finn. She could think of nothing else though, no matter how hard she tried. Why did these moments keep happening between them? She was fooling herself by pretending not to know the answer to that question.

Once safely back in her room, she took refuge in her work. She fired up her laptop, planning to send an email to Rupert updating him on how things were going. They'd already achieved so much and she was proud of the fact that she'd managed to complete some of the tasks on her list without any budget. She was confident they could open within another week, and then once some money came in, some of the pressure would be off. There was still a lot to do before then, though, including promoting the reopening. She was hopeful that by sending this report she could get Rupert off her back and keep control. She sent a brief update, and copied her father in, for good measure.

As she thought about all the things she was going to do next, she couldn't ignore the little niggle at the back of her mind telling her she was only keeping busy to stop herself from thinking about what might have happened had she not pulled away from Finn.

Desperate to focus, Olivia moved on to planning a website for the restaurant and setting up some essential social media accounts. She couldn't believe this hadn't already been done; they would be vital marketing tools in the months to come. She also wanted to explore the local community to see whether they could get some free promotion by working with other businesses. The high street was a busy one and she was sure there were opportunities to investigate there. It was only as she was making a checklist for herself that she understood how hard it must have been for Finn to be both chef and business owner all on his own once Dan had left. The previous owner had at least been able to share the workload with his wife. Just as she was reflecting on all these thoughts, her mobile rang. She stared at the screen in horror as Rupert's name flashed up.

'Hello?'

'Olivia, I just got your update about the restaurant.'

No preamble, just straight to the point, despite them having had no contact in months.

'Good, so you can see how well things are going now.'

'I wouldn't go that far. You're making a big mistake by planning to reopen so quickly. You need to give more thought to what went wrong last time before you reopen again. You don't want to get it wrong a second time.'

'I'm confident we can reopen on schedule. You shouldn't get involved like this when you're supposed to be off sick.'

'I hardly need remind you that I'm the Operations Manager of the company, and as such, I've had a lot more experience than you. Although I'm still on sick leave, it's only my leg that's broken. My brain is fine. I don't want to have to come all the way down to Devon to make sure you're doing what I want you to do, Olivia, but I will if necessary. I want you to give me your word that you'll take a couple more weeks before reopening to make certain you get everything right.'

Olivia didn't reply. She didn't want to give him her word. She was already invested in this project, and she wanted to push ahead so she could prove herself capable to her father, particularly since she only had six months to do it.

'Olivia?'

Rupert sounded annoyed at the other end of the phone. The last thing she wanted was him coming down here and lording it over her.

'Yes, of course,' she said at last. As she hung up, she blew out a long breath. She was about to go past the point of no return. For the first time in her life, she had lied about her intentions to her boss. Now she was under even more pressure to get everything right.

Finn came in through the back door into the kitchen, slamming it shut behind him. He braced himself on one of the kitchen work surfaces and counted slowly to ten, trying to get his frustration under control. Why was Olivia shying away from him? What she said made sense, but he was convinced she was hiding her true feelings.

'Hey, Finn, is everything okay?' Ed appeared in the kitchen wearing his paint overalls.

'I'll be fine,' he managed to grind out.

'I saw you and Olivia outside. It looked like you were arguing about something.'

'That's not all we were doing,' he muttered. He rubbed the back of his neck, immediately regretting saying quite so much even to his best friend.

'You didn't kiss her?'

Finn shook his head. 'I wanted to, but she rejected me, which is no more than I deserve, I suppose.'

'I don't blame you for wanting to. I guess she's just trying to be professional, and you know you shouldn't get involved with her.'

A flash of jealousy went through Finn at Ed's words. 'Why not? I like her and I know she feels something for me too.'

'You can't carry on like this. If you're going to be working together, you need to back away from any kind of intimate relationship and focus on the restaurant.'

Finn stayed silent as Ed drifted back into the dining area to clear up his things. He was surrounded by sensible advice but he didn't want it. All he wanted was to spend time with Olivia and to get to know her better.

'Will I see you down the pub later?' Ed asked before he left.

'Only if I can cheer myself up before then.' Finn had no intention of going down the pub. He would only get blind drunk and he didn't want to behave like that with Olivia around to see the consequences the next day.

Once Ed had gone, Finn decided he would have to get on with something else to distract himself. Ed was right. He should focus on the restaurant instead and not waste any more time dreaming about what might have been with Olivia. He wandered through to the kitchen and took out his notebook. Then he jotted down his recipe ideas and made a list of his favourites to see if he could create a six-week programme of meals to make life easier. If he worked on seasonal items, he should be able to come up with a simple plan of menus with dishes he could swap around if something wasn't available on a particular day. It took no time at all to write down his top thirty favourite dishes, which were a good mix of starters and mains. He'd have to do a separate list of desserts, of course, but he wasn't as concerned about that. Being open five days a week and offering only five choices a day was quite limiting; he would have to repeat some dishes during the week, but the menu would be changing and it would be flexible. He was already more fired up about it than he had been for a long while.

He reached for his laptop to do some research into seasonal ingredients, and while it was booting up, he made himself a cup of tea. He was pouring the water into his cup when he heard his email ping. He hardly ever got any messages these days and he frowned. Probably just some junk mail. Still, he went over to have a look, blowing on his freshly made tea on the way.

He set the cup down and clicked on his email. Damn! The message was from Mr Fuller and the title was 'A gentle reminder'. Finn swallowed nervously.

'I have just received a message from my daughter telling me how well her preparations are going in the lead-up to the reopening of the restaurant. She tells me you have been very helpful and she thinks you have a good working relationship. She goes on to say she believes you will make a real success of the business this time. In fact, she seems too confident of your abilities after such a short space of time spent working together. This has led me to wonder whether you might be forgetting your place.

I obviously need to make it clear to you, Mr Anderson, that you're my employee now and as such I expect you to do what you're told. And I'm telling you to stay well away from my daughter, unless you want to find yourself out of a job, with nothing further to do with your beloved restaurant, and what's more, still in debt. This is the last glowing email I expect to receive from my daughter about your abilities.

I hope I have made myself clear on this matter.'

Finn groaned. The email only served to confirm how precarious his position now was. How could this man be related to Olivia? At least she was nothing like him, thank God. He was delighted to read her thoughts about him and about his ability to make a go of the restaurant this time, though. Her confidence in him was reassuring and it only made him like her more. But now he'd have to be extra careful not to get too close to her and arouse her father's suspicions even further.

By the time Monday morning rolled around, Olivia was dreading seeing Finn again. They had so much to do and she needed him on her side if they were to make any progress. She could only hope he'd got over her rejection the other day and he wouldn't let it interfere with their working relationship.

After resisting the draw of the hotel's breakfast buffet, feeling she wouldn't be able to eat much anyway, she made her way across the bridge towards the restaurant. A light drizzle was falling and her hair immediately regained the curls she spent so long trying to tame every morning. She was sure this was a sign of the sort of day it was going to be.

As she drew closer to the restaurant, the light blue façade cheered her up at once. Somehow Ed had managed to swirl hints of white into the final coat of blue paint, giving it the appearance of water lapping gently on the shore. She hoped customers would want to go in as much as she did now. As she stood across the road, staring at Ed's handiwork, she saw Finn through the window. He was just coming into the dining area, carrying some of the refurbished chairs. She couldn't wait to see them in place and hurried round to the kitchen door to see what was happening, her earlier reluctance to see him again all but forgotten.

Finn was helping the delivery man carry in the final items as Olivia reached the back door. She waited for them to finish before trying to go inside.

'Morning, Finn,' she said hesitantly as the van drove away. She bit her lip, wondering if he was still going to be upset with her.

'Morning, Olivia. Come on in and see the furniture. I think you'll be pleased.'

She couldn't have been more surprised by his change of mood. It was as if he'd never tried to kiss her, as if she had never rejected him. On the one hand, she was pleased – she didn't want there to be any tension between them – but on the other, she was sad he had moved on so quickly, even though that's what she'd told him to do and what she'd tried to do herself. She sighed, trying not to let the situation get to her, and followed him through the kitchen.

The chairs and tables were all neatly laid out in their places around the dining area, their lightly sanded finish adding to the brighter ambiance in the room. She could imagine all the tables laid out with crockery and cutlery ready for their first service and the thought of how close they were to opening thrilled her.

'Oh, Finn, they do look lovely. Well done for putting them all in place already.'

'It didn't take long and it was a real pleasure to see them transform the place. It feels so light and airy now in here, especially with the new exterior. Ed texted me to say his bit is all done now and that he's found someone to do the signwriting – my old waitress, Zoe. She'll be along later today.' He gave her a big smile, but it didn't quite reach his eyes.

'That's all great news. Zoe sounds like she's worth her weight in gold.'

'She is, and when she comes, I'll talk to her about working on a shift by shift basis. I don't think that's exactly what she had in mind when she said she'd love to come back and work here if the opportunity arose, but we can only ask.'

'Well, she may get the chance to come back sooner than she was hoping.' She paused. 'I spent yesterday working on the website and updating our social media accounts with the date of our reopening.' She took a deep breath, and blocked out all thoughts of what Rupert would have to say. 'I think we should reopen on Saturday evening.'

'Saturday this week?' Finn's eyes widened.

'Yes, I know it seems soon, but I honestly believe we're nearly there now. You'll just need to do some work on the menus and we'll need to sort out some staff, but if we work hard, I think we can do it, especially if we can get Zoe on board.'

Finn blew out a long breath and thought about what she'd said. 'I did some work on the menus yesterday, so that's not too hard now. If I speak to Zoe later when she comes to do the sign and you go round to see Jamie, we can hopefully persuade them to start back at least for Saturday. Jamie will have to convince his dad about it, too, but if he does, we could possibly open on time.' He didn't look convinced.

'I'll pop round to see Jamie and his dad today. We'll have to start promoting our Saturday night menu everywhere, but I can take care of that, and then afterwards we'll have a couple of days when the restaurant is closed to assess how everything went.'

'It would probably be a good idea for me to go and see my fish supplier again today to alert him to our plans. You could go and see the wine merchant while I do that, if you like?'

'That sounds like a good plan.'

'Perhaps you could look over my menus with me before we go back to Barnstaple to see what you think we could offer on Saturday?' A hint of vulnerability passed across Finn's face and her stomach fluttered with a feeling she couldn't identify.

'I'd love to do that with you.' She sat down at one of the tables, delighted he'd asked for her opinion and more certain than ever of her growing affection for him, despite all her efforts to resist him.

By the Saturday morning, the day of their reopening, Finn was ready, as well as eager to run the restaurant again. He and Olivia had decided to go for a soft launch first to make sure everything was in hand. Olivia had done a great job of advertising on Facebook and Twitter, as well as on their brand new website, and she had distributed flyers around the village. As the new season hadn't started yet, it was only local people who had made reservations for tonight, and Finn was hopeful they would all be on his side, willing him to make a success of things second time round.

Every table was now booked and he had a solid menu planned that would appeal to his customers. Olivia had overseen their wine delivery the day before, and they had spoken to both Zoe and Jamie about taking back their old jobs, at least for one night. Zoe had been delighted, even after he'd told her about the lack of money to pay her with until after the first shift. Jamie was still unsure. Still, Olivia had persuaded him to work for the opening and after that, they would have to see. Jamie had promised to tell his dad and get his agreement, as Olivia hadn't managed to catch him when she went round. Finn hoped to God he had kept that promise.

After a quick coffee and a couple of slices of toast for breakfast, he made his way downstairs to wait for the fish delivery. The driver always came to him early, and today he was even more grateful for that.

'Hey, Finn.' Jamie ambled in looking like he was still half asleep, in the way of most teenagers first thing in the morning.

'Thanks for getting up so early. I know it must have been hard,' Finn joked as he walked past him to go and greet the delivery driver, who was just pulling in. By the time Finn had taken out the first box of fish, Jamie was in place to take it from him and put it in the large kitchen fridge. They made a good team and the delivery was all safely put away in no time. There was no let-up, though, as the fruit and veg man turned up a few minutes later, along with Olivia and Zoe who were going to set up the dining area.

'Morning, Finn, Jamie,' Zoe said as she walked past. 'Good to see you earning your keep.'

Finn laughed at her banter, aware of how much he'd missed it. He glanced at Olivia as well, but didn't say anything. This past week, he'd devoted all his energy to the business and to getting the restaurant back open, steering well clear of anything like an emotional attachment to his new manager. He was professional in his relationship with her, of course, but when he was on his own, with too much time to think, he regretted not being able to get to know her better. For now, it was best to keep things as they were.

He spent all morning prepping food for the evening with Jamie's help, while Olivia and Zoe set up the dining area. By the time they stopped for lunch, he had the final menu planned out precisely in his head. His sea bass fillets recipe, so carefully prepared that first day for Olivia, was one of his main dishes, along with a seafood and pasta ragout. The fridge was full of all sorts of delicious ingredients, including his fish stock, freshly made that morning with Jamie's help.

'Can you type out the menu after lunch for me please, Olivia?'

'Yes, that won't take me long. Are you all set?' At Finn's nod, she went on. 'The dining room is pretty much finished now. All we need to do is get the front window of the restaurant ready this afternoon and prepare some cocktails, I think. Is there anything else you can think of?'

'No, but I must come through and see what you've done with the dining area. That might spark some thoughts, but otherwise I think we're nearly there.' He heaved a sigh of relief and Olivia smiled at him, obviously feeling the same. He looked at her for a second longer than was necessary as they shared the pleasure of a job well done, before reluctantly looking away.

When Finn walked into the main restaurant, he could hardly believe the transformation. The tables now all had cutlery, crockery, glasses and serviettes in place and they'd all been decorated with a small vase, ready for some fresh flowers. Zoe had made some bunting in pastel shades to match the exterior of the bistro, which they'd hung around the walls, along with some watercolour paintings of local sea views. He recognised the artist from paintings he'd seen around the village. There was nowhere else for artists to show their work since the local community centre shut down and he was glad they'd been able to help.

'Those paintings look fabulous, Zoe, and so does the bunting. Well done. I love it. And where did all these knick-knacks come from?' He pointed at a wooden lighthouse and some painted wooden seashells dotted on window ledges and shelves around the restaurant.

'Olivia found those in the craft shop down the road. They gave us a discount for displaying some of their cards as well.'

Finn turned in a circle, trying to take in all the changes. He found he couldn't stop smiling.

'I think the tourists will love this when the season proper starts, don't you?' Zoe asked.

'I do.' He silently thanked goodness for Olivia's brilliant organisational skills. Not only had she done all these practical things, but she'd also reminded him about utilities, licenses and insurance renewals. He couldn't have done it without her. Now everything depended on his cooking skills to make the night ahead a success. He pushed the kitchen door open, planning to do one final check over the menu with Jamie, only to find Jamie's dad glaring at him.

CHAPTER SEVEN

'Mr Murphy, Jamie. What's going on?'

Finn glanced from father to son, trying to stall for time before the inevitable explosion happened.

'You know damn well what's going on.' Mr Murphy was red in the face and was clenching and unclenching his fists, putting Finn on edge. 'I told you to stay away from my son, and you did exactly the opposite. You've lured him back here, away from his studies, and you've done it all behind my back.'

Finn studied Jamie's body language. He was scowling for all he was worth, with his arms tightly folded across his chest. Olivia had asked Jamie to check with his dad before agreeing to work, but obviously that hadn't happened. Finn didn't want to get Jamie into more trouble but he did want to reassure his father.

'I admit we did ask Jamie whether he could work tonight, but we also asked him to discuss it with you before making a decision. The last thing I want to do is to come between Jamie and his studies. I know how important they are. At the same time though, Jamie is really good at this job, Mr Murphy, and there's no-one else I trust to work by my side as much as I do your son.' Mr Murphy harrumphed a little but didn't say anything. The redness in his face was fading and his shoulders had dropped a little.

'Why didn't you discuss it with me, lad?' He turned to his son at last.

Jamie shrugged. 'Because I knew this was how you'd react. You never listen to me. You just jump to conclusions.' Jamie sneaked a look at Finn, his young face reddening in embarrassment. Finn gave him a reassuring smile.

'And you enjoy this job, do you? Are you as good as he says you are?' Mr Murphy jerked his thumb in Finn's direction without taking his eyes off Jamie.

'I really like this job, Dad. Finn knows what he's talking about and if he thinks I'm good at it, then I trust his word.'

Finn swallowed, proud of Jamie for being brave enough to speak freely.

'And you've allowed time to catch up with your studies if you work tonight, have you?'

Jamie rolled his eyes. 'Of course.' Finn heard the 'I'm not stupid, you know,' even though Jamie didn't say it.

'And it's only for tonight, is it?' Mr Murphy brought his attention back to Finn.

'Well, we want the restaurant to continue. If it goes well tonight, I'd like to speak to Jamie about how we can manage his time while he studies and does his exams. With your permission, of course.'

Jamie grinned at him from behind his dad.

'I suppose that will be all right. But mind you let me know whatever you plan after this, both of you.'

'Okay, Dad, thanks.'

'I'll see you later, son.' He nodded at Finn without another word and left the kitchen.

Jamie and Finn stared at each other for a good few minutes without speaking. Then Jamie went to get his apron.

'What shall I get started on now?' he asked, as if nothing had happened.

Finn consulted his plan for the evening. 'Right, then. You can make a start on the marinade for the chilli prawns and I'll start removing the crab meat.' He put the recipe on the magnetic bar in front of Jamie and left him to get on with it, trusting him to ask if he was unsure. When he returned from the fridge a few minutes later with the crabs, Jamie was hard at work.

'Did you mean what you said to my dad about me being good at this job?'

'Of course. We make a good team, and I know I can rely on you to do your bit.'

Jamie didn't ask anything else, but Finn was glad he'd had the chance to tell him how much he appreciated his work. They fell into companionable silence for a few minutes until Zoe poked her head through the hatch.

'Hey, Finn, how's it going?'

'All good at this end. What about out there?'

'Yes, we're getting there. I just wondered when you wanted to go through the menu with me?'

'I can do that any time. I should probably include Olivia, so she knows what's being served in case anyone asks her. Will you be all right on your own for a bit, Jamie?'

At Jamie's nod, Finn made his way through to the dining room. He cast his eye around the place once again, taking in the simple elegance of the room now it had been set up properly. The refurbished tables and chairs looked like new and the minimal tableware set them off perfectly. The whole room seemed so much bigger after repainting. He had to give it to Olivia, she'd been right about everything.

'Well done, both of you,' he said. 'It looks amazing out here. I still can't quite get over it.'

'How are you getting on?' Olivia asked. 'We thought we might have heard voices out there.' She frowned in concern.

'Nothing to worry about. Jamie's dad was a bit upset about us taking him away from his studies, but it's all sorted now. Shall we go through the menu so you know how to answer any questions?'

'Let me just finish replying to this email.'

Finn turned to speak to Zoe but before he could speak, Olivia interrupted them.

'Oh, damn.'

'What is it?'

'Another email has just come in from my father's Operations Manager. He's probably trying to interfere as always.' She closed her laptop and ushered them away. 'I'll look at it later. It's probably nothing important and we have enough to deal with right now.'

Just before half past six that evening, Olivia turned the 'closed' sign on the front door to 'open' and took the fresh orange and yellow gerberas out of the buckets they'd been standing in all afternoon. She began to put the flowers in the glass vases on the tables, glad she still had something to occupy her mind for the last half hour before people started arriving. Everything was ready, but she was still nervous. Although she wouldn't be serving, thank goodness, she would have a lot to do, getting drinks orders ready and preparing bills. She was worried about managing her time so that she could pull her weight in the restaurant team. When she'd finished the flowers, she turned towards the bar to find Zoe waiting, a look of determination on her face.

'All set?' Olivia asked.

'Yes, the flowers were the last thing. I just want the customers to come now so we can get started.'

And within minutes, they were turning up at the door. Olivia and Zoe shared greeting responsibility and showed people to their tables, following that up with a free welcome drink to celebrate the reopening. Zoe seemed to know a lot of people personally, and Olivia understood then what an asset she was to the restaurant. The sign she had painted had already received lots of compliments, as well.

While Zoe took orders, Olivia got as many drinks ready as she could so Zoe could take the food orders straight to the kitchen. The short menu was going down well with the customers, who seemed to prefer not having too much choice. Olivia had emphasised the freshness of their local ingredients by naming the local suppliers on the menu, and this was obviously winning people over. Soon Zoe was delivering delicious-looking starters of chilli prawns, calamari or crab cakes to all the different tables.

'One customer just told me those were the best crab cakes they've ever had in the area.' Zoe grinned at Olivia as she headed to the kitchen again, this time with an order from a recently arrived table of four. She came out carrying plates of the sea bass Finn had cooked for Olivia that first time. She was confident that dish would go down well with their customers.

What with preparing drinks and greeting people at the door, Olivia didn't have a second to think for the first hour of service. She had never worked so hard before, and she had a new respect for all restaurant staff. As people moved on to their main courses and some decided against having dessert, she switched to preparing bills. She had created a feedback card and she was delighted to see most tables filled them in and left them with their payments. She didn't have any time to look at them, but she had a feeling the feedback was going to be good.

Around nine o'clock, Finn popped his head round the kitchen door to survey the dining area, which was now only about half full. Olivia took in his red face and dishevelled hair, both signs he must have worked flat out to make the evening a success. She was pleased by the way they had all worked so well together. Finn disappeared again after a second, because there were still dessert orders to fulfil, and she returned to her bill preparation.

'Table six would like their bill now, please,' Zoe said on her next visit to the bar area.

'Here it is,' Olivia replied. 'I've just got it ready, as they're drinking their coffees.'

'They told me they're so glad to see us open again. They used to come here a lot before and they've missed having that chance. They loved the sea bass fillets.'

'Oh, that's excellent news. Finn will be so pleased.'

Olivia took them the bill and thanked them for their feedback.

'It's good to know you enjoyed your visit and how much you enjoyed the sea bass fillets. That's one of my personal favourites. You will fill out the feedback card, won't you?' She had a quick wander round to see how the other tables were getting on. She didn't speak to anyone else, but she overheard some very positive comments and she made a mental note to pass the feedback on to the others.

By ten o'clock the restaurant was empty. Finn and Jamie emerged blinking from the kitchen to join Olivia and Zoe in the main dining area. They all stood together feeling shell-shocked for a few moments, but with tired smiles on their faces.

'Wow! What a first night,' Finn exclaimed finally, lifting his apron to wipe his brow. 'Thank goodness we only went for the one sitting and a shorter menu. I'd forgotten how full on it is working non-stop like that. Jamie's done a great job supporting me through the evening and the kitchen is almost clear. Thanks, kid.' He tousled Jamie's hair, much to his consternation, but Jamie looked happy, too.

'And Zoe's done a brilliant job front of house. We've had nothing but good comments all evening. I've kept all the feedback cards to look over later, but I have a good feeling about it all.'

'Are you sure you've never done this sort of work before, Olivia? You were great tonight. You were always one step ahead of me what-ever I needed. Thank you.' Zoe gave Olivia a big grin and Olivia returned it.

Once Zoe and Jamie had made their way off into the night, Olivia turned her attention to the email she'd received from Rupert. It had been worrying away at the back of her mind all evening. She skimmed through it, ignoring his repeated warnings to take her time before reopening. She'd already proved him wrong on that front, she thought to herself with great satisfaction. It was only when she reached the last two lines that her breath caught.

'I will be down to see you some time this week to discuss my plans for the future of the restaurant and how we're going to put them in place, including a sensible date for reopening.'

Finn was so pumped up he'd found it hard to get to sleep after the great success of the reopening. He'd been delighted with how well they'd all pulled together and Olivia had been vital to their transformation. It would seem like a lifetime until Tuesday lunch-time when they were going to be properly open again. Despite not falling asleep until around two in the morning, he was still up at eight, ready for his meeting with Olivia. He appreciated the chance to talk things over with her and to know what she thought about all the different elements of their situation.

When Olivia knocked on the kitchen door at nine o'clock, as agreed, he opened it with a big grin on his face, only to be met with the sight of her with her suitcase in hand. His face fell.

'What's going on? Why have you got a suitcase with you?' He couldn't bear for her to leave now, when everything was going so well.

'It's all right, don't worry,' she reassured him. 'I'm just going back to Bristol for a couple of days while we're shut to catch up on a few things and to get some new clothes. I'll be back on Tuesday.'

'But will you be back in time for Tuesday lunch-time's service?' He shouldn't complain, but she was his good luck charm. He didn't know if he could maintain the success without her.

'I should be back by then. But even if I wasn't here, I think you'd manage without me, like you did before with just Zoe working front of house.'

Finn wasn't so sure about that. He followed Olivia as she walked through to the dining room, set down her suitcase and took a seat at one of the tables for four. She took off her padded jacket and hung it on the back of her chair before pulling her laptop out of her backpack. When Finn didn't say anything, she glanced up to find him staring at her with a marked frown on his face.

'What's the matter?' she asked.

'Zoe can't work this Tuesday lunch-time, she has to go to her day job. I was counting on you to manage the lunch-time sessions until she feels confident enough to leave her office job and just work with us again.'

'What?' she asked sharply. 'Why didn't you tell me that before?'

'I didn't think I needed to. I thought you'd be here. I didn't know we might need a contingency plan.' He forced himself to remain calm and not be petty, despite his concerns.

Olivia picked up her phone and searched for Zoe's number.

'Hi, Zoe. Yes, I'm fine, how are you?'

Finn studied Olivia's face as she reacted to whatever Zoe was saying: her clear blue eyes and the light sprinkling of freckles on her upturned nose. As he looked at her, all his concerns melted away. It was only a matter of time before he would be drawn by her charms once more, if she let him. He wanted to taste her lips... He shifted uncomfortably, thinking of fluffy kittens to try and take his mind off what was happening elsewhere in his body. He willed himself to return to the conversation between Olivia and Zoe so he could find out what was happening. To his disappointment, Olivia was just saying goodbye.

'Well?'

'Zoe will cover the lunch-time session this Tuesday just in case I'm not back. She says she's owed some time in lieu. Okay?'

'I still wished you'd picked a less awkward time to go back to Bristol, and that you'd discussed it with me first.' Finn hated himself for being petulant, but he needed Olivia and she seemed oblivious to that fact.

'Look, can we focus on our review of last night, please? I have a train to catch.'

'Well, in my opinion, last night was perfect. There's nothing to review.' Finn crossed his arms.

Instead of rising to his bait, Olivia smiled at him. 'One of the things that occurred to me was that we had a lot of empty tables by nine o'clock, which is great in terms of workload, but in the summer we'll want to encourage more people to come in around that time. I think we should give some thought to how we can best manage two sittings. Maybe we could ask people to specify whether they want their table for the whole evening when they book? If they do, fine. If not, we can rebook it at nine for another table and maximise our profit while not annoying those people who want to stay for a bit longer. They'll spend more money if they stay for longer, I'd hope anyway, and that should absolutely be our objective, don't you think?'

Finn didn't reply straight away, still irritated with Olivia for deciding to go home at such a critical time. Then he caved. He was as desperate as she was to plan the restaurant's future. 'I agree. It could put pressure on staffing if we do go to two sittings, but that's something we can look at further down the line.'

'I had a quick look at the feedback cards and the comments were mostly good. The few negative ones were minor issues, so nothing to worry about in general. I'd like to carry on giving out the cards, though, if that's all right with you. They'll be a good source of information for us as we continue from here. Was there anything else you wanted to mention?'

Finn shook his head, not wanting to go on about her leaving. He was pleased with how things had gone for their first night. Now all they had to do was to keep on doing the same – and he would feel a lot more confident about that if Olivia was by his side.

Once on the train back to Barnstaple, Olivia let out a long breath. It had been a difficult morning. The look on Finn's face when he had seen her suitcase had made her feel so guilty, although she didn't admit that to him. Last night had been such a great success and now she felt she was letting him down. She tried to make herself feel better by thinking about seeing her father and catching up with friends, but in her heart, she was sad to be leaving. The thought threw her off balance. She had never expected to enjoy being in Devon quite so much, and she was surprised at how attached she'd become to the place in such a short period of time. She had become so much less formal and more relaxed, too, and that was good for her.

By the time she reached home, she was worn out and even more fed up. Her father had replied to the email she had sent him. He wouldn't be able to make it home in time for dinner but hoped to see her tomorrow morning at breakfast. That was quite unlike her father. He was usually so protective of her, relishing every opportunity to spend time with her and to find out what she was doing. She'd also been planning to persuade him to tell Rupert to back off and not come down to Devon, but now she would have to contact Rupert herself.

Dreading the prospect of spending a lonely evening at home, she texted round a few of her friends, only to find they were all too busy to see her, too. As she thought about it, she realised none of them had been in touch with her in the couple of weeks since she'd been away, as if they hadn't missed her at all. So much for a triumphant home-coming. In all fairness, she hadn't bothered to contact any of them either, so maybe those friendships didn't mean as much as she'd thought.

She let herself in, expecting Mrs Thomas to berate her for not letting her do her job.

'Hello? Anybody here?' she called out, but only silence filled the hallway. It was unusual for Mrs Thomas not to be around. Perhaps something terrible had happened. After dropping her bags on the tiled floor, Olivia made her way through to the lounge. She was surprised to see her father's paperwork scattered across the low coffee table in front of the sofa. He was scrupulous about keeping his work in the office. Perhaps he no longer needed to be quite so tidy now she was away. Still, Mrs Thomas would usually tidy up after him if he didn't do it himself. Seeds of doubt sowed themselves in her mind. She went to the table and began to gather the papers together, but as she did so, one of them slipped onto the carpet. She stooped to pick it up and the letterhead caught her eye. It was from her father's company accountants. She scanned the contents quickly, feeling guilty even as she did so. The accountants were advising against the company's suitability for floating on the stock market. She checked the date and confirmed it had been sent only last week. As far as she was aware, her father had always been adamant that they would never list the company on the Stock Exchange, and the board had always been right behind her father in that aim. Why was this being discussed again now?

Olivia couldn't articulate why straight away but the letter left her feeling distinctly uneasy. Her father was up to something. But what? She put the letter back in the middle of the mass of papers, trying to conceal that she had been snooping. She would just have to keep her question to herself for now and bide her time until she could find out more.

She checked all the rooms downstairs to see if Mrs Thomas was busy working somewhere and when she didn't find her, she made her way upstairs. After finding no sign of her there either, she went to unpack her things in her bedroom before going out to eat for the evening. Olivia tried to make sense of her thoughts as she walked around the crescent, past the other Georgian houses, towards Clifton Village. She managed to get the last table at her favourite pizza restaurant, where she sat in the window, sipping a glass of rosé and considered the situation.

As far as the housekeeper was concerned, it must simply be her day off. With regards to the business, there was no point asking her father for any information. Experience told her he would clam up. The main reason for a privately owned company to float on the Stock Exchange was to raise capital from the sale of shares, but going public also brought with it new costs and new dangers in the form of liabilities. Her father had always used these reasons not to float the company, so why had he changed his mind? She could probably wheedle more details out of the three vultures at the office, but that would mean having to go and talk to them. She hoped her father wasn't involved in something that would have terrible repercussions for the business, or for himself.

Having got nowhere with her first problem, she turned her mind to Rupert. She bet he knew more than she did about what was going on with the business. Sometimes her father treated him more like his son than his employee, and she resented Rupert for that as well as the awful way he had treated her during their brief relationship. Her father still didn't know they had been together, and she had no desire to tell him. He would be furious. She would just have to email Rupert and tell him there was no need for him to come to Lynford, and that she had everything under control.

CHAPTER EIGHT

In the old days, Finn's first instinct after Olivia's departure would have been to spend all his time down the pub while she was away, drowning his sorrows and wallowing in self-pity. The new Finn didn't want to do what the old Finn would have done. Olivia had helped him turn over a new leaf, and while there was still a long way for him to go, he was already starting to feel better about things. He spent the rest of Sunday cleaning the kitchen and giving some thought to new menus. The day flew by as he kept himself busy, giving him hardly any time to miss Olivia.

As he ate his breakfast on Monday though, he realised there was little left for him to do, and he was dreading a long, slow day with no sense of purpose. By the time he'd had his shower, it was still only just coming up to ten o'clock, so he made a spur of the moment decision to visit his mum's grave as he'd been meaning to do for a while.

He was soon in the car and driving out of the village on his way to Taunton. His parents had moved there when they'd retired, not long after Finn had taken over the restaurant from Bob and Jen. They'd never been back to Lynford since and he hadn't been to visit them either. He'd only seen his mum at the hospice when she was near the end of her life. By then it was too late for them to be reconciled, because her dementia was so advanced, but he'd been glad to see her before the end.

The church where his mum was buried was in a little village on the outskirts of the main town. He pulled into the empty car park and turned off his engine, steeling himself for the task ahead. It had been so hard to deal with her burial, but it was even harder to come back now. He let out a long breath and stepped out of his car. He remembered exactly where her grave was and made his way steadily towards where it lay, in the far corner of the graveyard, underneath a cherry tree.

'Here lies Mary Anderson, beloved wife of Brendan, and mother to Declan and Finn. Taken too soon.'

His heart hurt once more as he read the inscription and tried yet again to make sense of it all. She'd been so young, only in her late fifties, but, as Finn had learned, dementia could often claim people early.

'Oh, Mum, I'm so sorry. I miss you so much and I wish we'd had more time together.' If only his dad had told him earlier about her illness, at least he would have been able to make things up with her before her death. But that was only part of it. They should never have let their differences over his chosen career keep them apart for so long. He sighed at the pointlessness of it all. He crouched down to look at the tidy flower arrangement next to the gravestone, fingering the delicate snowdrops, narcissi and tulips all huddled together in a neat wicker basket. His dad must visit often to keep the grave looking so well-cared for. He stood up, stretching his legs, and after one last look at his mum's grave, he turned to go. That's when he saw his dad standing there watching him.

'How long have you been there?' Finn asked.

'A while, son. It's good to see you.' His dad came forward and put out his hand.

Finn shook it, despite his lingering resentment over their past disagreements. Seeing his dad face-to-face was harder than speaking to him on the phone. He inhaled deeply and forced himself to speak.

'How often do you come here? The grave looks well-tended.'

'I try and come every week. It makes me feel like she's still here, you know.'

Finn nodded. His dad had loved his mum more than anything, that much he did know. 'How have you been getting on since I spoke to you, Dad?'

'It's still as hard. As I mentioned on the phone, it's lonely living here without any close friends or family nearby. At least I can visit your mum's grave, though.' He gave Finn a brief smile and in that moment, Finn wanted all the past resentments to be over with. His mother's death had shown him how fleeting life can be, and he didn't want to miss out on any more time with his dad.

'You should come and visit me at the restaurant. You could explore the village like you used to.'

'How is everything at the bistro now? I know how difficult it was for you when your mum was ill.'

'It's a long story, but at least I'm still there. My debt will be cleared as long as I stay for six months and then I'll have a fresh start somewhere new.'

Finn's dad's face fell. 'Ah, Finn, I'm sorry to hear all that. I know how much it meant to you to own the place.'

Finn thought back to when his dad had refused to lend him the money to buy the place when he needed it. He was glad, at least, to know his dad now understood how important the bistro was to him. 'So would you like to come over and visit some time?'

His dad nodded and gave him a proper smile this time. 'That would be grand, Finn.'

'Have you heard from Declan recently?' Finn hadn't been in touch with his brother since their mum's funeral, either, and he wished he'd made more of an effort to speak to him.

'Not since your mum... no.'

They walked out of the graveyard together and shared an

awkward hug as they said goodbye back in the car park, promising to see each other again soon.

On the drive back to Lynford, Finn was in a better mood than he'd been in ages. Seeing his dad had lifted his spirits, and although it would take some time to rebuild their relationship, he was hopeful for the future. He still needed to make contact with Declan, but that would have to be another day. It had been even longer since he'd spoken to his brother after their falling out. He'd accused Declan of being the favourite son when his dad had refused to lend him the money for the restaurant, lashing out at his brother in his frustration. He'd always regretted the things he'd said to Declan that day, and he wasn't sure it would be as easy for them to put the past aside and move forward.

On his way home, Finn decided he could afford to pop into the pub for a quick drink with Ed and anyone else who might be there. It was a few minutes after one when he arrived and Ed was already at the bar.

'Hey, Finn, how are you?'

'I'm good, thanks. I went over to see my mum's grave this morning, and I bumped into my dad.'

'Crikey, how did that all go?' Ed plonked a pint of local bitter in front of him, and took a sip of his own.

'It was fine, much better than I was expecting, and I'm glad I went. I even asked him to visit.'

Ed clapped him on the back. 'That sounds good. You've both had a tough time of it, and it will be good for you both to lean on each other.'

Finn took a small sip of his beer. He hoped Ed was right.

'Hi there, Finn, how's things?'

Finn looked round to see Zoe standing at the bar. Ed had

wandered off as she approached, which seemed odd, but Finn didn't linger on it.

'Yeah, not too bad, thanks.' He smiled warmly. 'How are you?'

'I feel great since working at the restaurant the other day. I can't wait to get back to it tomorrow.'

'Yeah, thanks for stepping in to cover lunch.'

'When does Olivia get back from Bristol?'

'Tomorrow morning. She should be there for the lunch-time service.'

'Oh, that's good. It would be difficult without her at lunch-time if we get busy. I can't even remember how I managed without her before.'

'Well, she said she should be back, so we'll be fine.'

'Is Jamie coming in too?'

'Yes, he'll be there. Apparently, he only has lessons till ten tomorrow.'

'Okay, I'll get there for about eleven then, if we're opening at twelve.'

'See you then.'

As Zoe walked away to join a group of friends, Ed exchanged a look with her, and Finn wondered if there was anything between them. Then Ed was standing in front of him and the thought disappeared from his mind.

'Do you fancy another?' Ed asked as he finished his pint.

'No, thanks,' he replied, standing up. 'Olivia's back tomorrow. I've got to finish planning menus for the coming week and get some preliminary cooking done before we open again this week. And I need to be up bright and early to go and get some ingredients in Barnstaple.'

'Well, good for you. I won't keep you then.'

Finn sauntered back to the restaurant, his mind full of new recipe ideas. As he went to go round the back, he saw a black car with tinted windows coming down the high street. The executive look of the car made it stand out on the cobbled street, and Finn wondered who could be inside. Probably tourists making their way to the grand hotel across the bridge where Olivia was also staying. He carried on towards the kitchen entrance, stopping to fish his keys out of his pocket. When the black car pulled into the courtyard behind him, he gave it his full attention, an ominous feeling settling in the pit of his stomach.

The car came to a stop a few feet away from him. The driver got out but didn't say a word to Finn, despite catching his eye. Instead, he went straight to the passenger door behind him, opening it wide.

'Give me a hand, for God's sake. How do you think I'm going to get out of this thing otherwise?'

Finn's eyes widened. Who was this irritable man and why was he here? A straight leg, covered in plaster from the thigh down, appeared from the back seat first, followed by the other leg, which eventually found its way to the ground. The driver was having to pull the passenger out bit by bit, while being criticised the whole time.

'Get me my sticks then, will you? How do you expect me to stand without them?'

Finn repressed a chuckle, knowing instinctively that this man wouldn't appreciate him laughing at this critical moment. Finally, the driver got the passenger to standing point and the bad-tempered man moved towards him.

'Where's Olivia? I want to see her now.'

Finn was indignant at the stranger's pompous manner. 'And you are?'

'Not that it's any of your business, but I'm Rupert Parker. I'm Olivia's boss. Now where is she?'

'Olivia's not here. She's gone home to Bristol to see her father, who I thought was her boss. She's never mentioned you.'

'And who the hell are you to question me?'

'I'm Finn Anderson, the chef here.'

'Well, in that case, I'm your boss too. Now, stop asking me all these infernal questions and show me somewhere where I can sit down.'

Entitled idiot, Finn thought as he turned away to open the back door, trying to calm himself. He held the door open, allowing the man access to his restaurant against all his better instincts. The driver shared his look of relief that they'd both managed things so well this far and then climbed back into the front seat of the car, looking pleased that he didn't have to come in and join them.

Finn followed Rupert inside. What on earth was going to happen now? And why hadn't Olivia told him about her boss or that he was going to visit while she was away?

Olivia couldn't wait to get back to Lynford. After a disastrous visit home, she'd had to admit to herself that she was happier down in Devon, which was why she'd decided to come back early. The only thing she'd had going on in her life before she'd come to manage the restaurant was her work, but her trip home had only emphasised how lonely her life had become. She'd not been able to see any friends – she was actually wondering if she even had any – and her father had also been away. Now, as she arrived at the station on the Monday morning, she realised she hardly missed her comfortable but empty life in Bristol at all.

She picked up a copy of the free city newspaper for the train journey and set off to find the platform for the train that would take her back to Barnstaple. Once settled in her seat, she began absently flicking through the pages, glancing at the headlines but not taking them in as she worked her way towards the business section. She was unprepared for the headline that caught her eye on the next page:

'La Riviera to sell off unprofitable restaurants in bid to resolve cash flow problems'.

Olivia skimmed the first paragraph to check whether the headline was true, her heart pounding at the thought her dad's company might be in real trouble. As she progressed through the paragraphs, she could see that the journalist could only quote 'sources', and no-one specific. However, the sources did confirm that the board had thrown out a suggestion to float the company on the Stock Exchange, which backed up the letter she'd seen at home among her dad's paperwork. It must have been her dad who put the idea to the board, but why would he have gone against his principles? He'd *never* wanted to float the company before. But his obsession with expansion demanded a regular supply of cash. Clearly, the company no longer had that spare cash, and the board had finally put its foot down. So where did that leave the bistro? It could hardly be said to be failing when it hadn't even had a chance to get going yet. They had to give it a chance to prove itself. All this might be rubbish anyway, she reassured herself. Anonymous sources weren't reliable. But her father's refusal to discuss it with her last time she asked made her more doubtful this time round that he'd been telling the truth.

Not long after she'd finished reading the article, the train pulled in to Barnstaple and she managed to get a taxi straight away to take her on to Lynford. She worried about the situation with La Riviera for the whole of the car journey, but as soon as she stepped out of the car at her hotel, she was distracted by her surroundings. Spring was on its way and there were already golden yellow daffodils and vibrant crocuses in the hotel's borders showing off their colours for all to see. After quickly dropping her bag in her room, she set off for the bistro, keen to get back and to see how Finn had got on in her absence. As she made her way along the cobbled streets, saying hello to the people she knew, she acknowledged she'd already established a sense of belonging. She was happy here, and she wanted to make a real go of things but so much of that depended on her relationship with Finn. As long as they could work together and keep their relationship professional, everything would be all right. She was sure then they could prove to the board that their restaurant was worth keeping should it come to that.

As she approached the restaurant, she stopped on the other side of the road to admire the stunning blue exterior once more. She was pleased at how far they'd come in such a short space of time. She could imagine Finn in the kitchen hard at work on the food prep for the coming week, and her pride threatened to overwhelm her. She took a deep breath and stepped out to cross the street.

She went round to the back to catch up with Finn, admitting to herself that she was looking forward to seeing him after only a couple of days apart. When she entered the courtyard, she was surprised to see an executive car parked there. The driver was reading a newspaper in the front seat. He looked vaguely familiar, but she couldn't think how she knew him.

She entered the kitchen to find Jamie busily prepping ingredients for Finn's fish stock.

'Hi, Jamie. Why are you here on a Monday?' she asked.

'I asked Finn if I could come in and give him a hand.'

'Where's Finn, then?'

'He's in his office with the visitor.' Jamie pulled a face, leaving her in no doubt of his feelings towards the visitor, and she couldn't help but grin.

'Who is it, do you know?'

'Some stuck-up bloke called Rupert or something similar.'

Olivia's heart sank and she turned abruptly towards the office, wondering what she would find when she got there. She couldn't imagine Rupert and Finn having anything in common. As she approached, she heard Rupert's braying voice.

'I still can't believe you've gone ahead and opened despite all my warnings.'

'That was my decision, nothing to do with Finn,' Olivia replied as she arrived at the entrance to the poky room. In Rupert's moment of surprise, she took in the squash in the room – caused by his broken leg taking up most of the space – and the weary, hunted look on Finn's face. His look quickly changed to one of relief when he saw her.

'And where the hell have you been?'

'I'm sure Finn has explained where I've been,' Olivia said. 'And I don't answer to you so don't talk to me like that, please. Finn, I know you need to get on. You can leave this to me now. I'm sorry you've had to deal with this unexpected intrusion.' She gave him an apologetic smile, but he didn't look pacified. She waited for him to make his escape before turning her attention to Rupert.

'Whatever you want, you'd better make it quick, because I have work to do and I'd much rather be getting on with it than wasting time in here with you.'

It was clear Rupert wasn't going to get the ball rolling, so Olivia went on. 'Didn't you get my email telling you there was no need for you to come?'

'It was precisely because I did get your email that I decided to come. I told you not to open yet, but I could sense from your message you hadn't taken any notice. So I decided to come and see for myself.' He paused. 'Besides, I wanted to see you again after all this time.'

Olivia's mouth dropped open. When she'd recovered, she carried on. 'And here I was, hoping I would *never* have to see you again. Our relationship was a sham, so don't pretend to have any feelings for me. And don't expect to charm your way back into my affections either.' She took a deep breath and tried to calm herself and lower her voice, aware they could probably hear her in the kitchen. 'I want to know what's going on with the business. I've seen a couple of reports in local papers saying La Riviera is in financial trouble, and my father is being very secretive about the whole thing. Now today, the latest report said that some of the less profitable restaurants are going to be sold.'

'And that's precisely why I told you not to be in such a hurry to reopen in case this one is going to be sold off.' Rupert moved in his seat, trying to get comfortable, and by the look on his face, failing miserably.

'But how could that be? We need a chance to prove ourselves

before any decisions are made about the future, and going on our first night, I think this bistro has a lot of potential.'

'Really?' Rupert sneered. 'This place is a backwater. I can't see you ever making enough money at it to give us a decent profit. No, my first instinct is to add this one to the list your father's been compiling. That is, if he hasn't already done so himself.'

Olivia was stunned. Her father had been making plans all along, and not only that, but keeping them from her as well. She needed to proceed cautiously with Rupert if she wanted to find out more from him and not give away her own plans.

She softened her tone a little. 'I think closing this place would be a big mistake, Rupert. Trust me, there is potential here and I think we can make a profit pretty soon, which would help the business, wouldn't it?'

'Well, as you've already opened, I suppose it wouldn't hurt to give it a go, but I wouldn't hold out your hopes as far as the business is concerned. Things are getting tough and the board are doubling down on only the essential activities for the time being.'

Rupert struggled to push himself up from the chair and get to standing. Olivia wanted to help him, but she didn't want to give him any reason to think she was changing her mind as far as their relationship was concerned, so she opened the office door instead.

'I mean what I say though, Olivia. You do report to me, so I don't expect you to disobey me again. I'm getting better every day now. I should be able to come back again soon and check on how things are progressing. Please keep in touch with me in the meantime.'

Olivia saw him out of the back door and watched as his driver helped him into the car before driving off. She shut the door and leaned against it, closing her eyes, and blew out a huge sigh. She hoped Rupert never managed to find his way down to Devon again.

'Is everything all right, Olivia?' Finn's worried voice penetrated through her relief, and she opened her eyes.

'Sort of. I got rid of him, at least. I'm so sorry, Finn, that I had no chance to warn you. I had no idea he was coming.'

'You should have told me about him. There's no telling what he might have done if you hadn't turned up when you did.'

'He's all mouth really, but I know him of old, so I know how to handle him. Anyway, aren't you glad to see me back early?'

Finn nodded but he looked grumpy and anxious at the same time. 'So what else did he want?'

'Nothing, just to moan at me for going ahead and opening up against his advice.'

Finn raised his eyebrows. 'I think you're hiding something from me.'

She stared at him, trying to decide how much to say. She couldn't bring herself to tell him about her former relationship with Rupert, because it was all too humiliating, and she was still trying to keep things professional between her and Finn. But she needed his help if she was going to make a success of the restaurant. 'Come with me,' she said after a long moment, leading the way back to the office. 'I think you'd better sit down,' she said.

If she could play even a small part in delaying the problems her father was dealing with, she would have proved herself as capable. The problem now was that she didn't know how much time she had to make her plan work. Six months had seemed like plenty of time. Now she might have only a few weeks to prove the bistro could turn a profit. And more than all that, she owed it to Finn, Zoe and Jamie not to let everything come crashing down all over again. The community couldn't withstand any more upset, and she wasn't sure that Finn would ever recover.

CHAPTER NINE

Since the opening night, the restaurant had been pretty full at lunch and dinner every day. Finn was desperately hoping this would be enough to stop them being troubled by that oily shark, Rupert, ever again. He'd been stunned when Olivia had told him about the company's problems, and had agreed with her about pressing on with their plans. The main problem they had in the foreseeable future was being too busy, particularly when Zoe and Jamie were still occupied elsewhere. Olivia had planned a staff meeting to talk about how their first week had gone, and he had been tasked with the job of going to the local bakery and getting breakfast in for everyone.

It was a crisp but sunny morning, his favourite kind, and he breathed deeply as he strolled along the street, taking in the salty sea air. It never ceased to amaze him how wonderful a place he had chosen to settle in. As a young child, he had lived just outside Lynford, but as soon as he started working at the restaurant, he'd been sure he'd always want to live near the water.

'Morning, Rosie. How are you? It can't be long to go now, can it?'

Rosie smiled at him with the air of a woman who has had quite enough of being asked that question. 'No, just six weeks,' she replied, stroking her nicely rounded stomach.

Finn marvelled at the way Rosie seemed to have her life so sorted out. When they'd been at secondary school together, they'd talked about their respective dreams – hers was to open a bakery and his to take over the restaurant from Bob and Jen when they retired. They'd both achieved that, of course, but Rosie's business was thriving. Not only that but she'd got married to Ewan and was about to have her second child.

'Could I have four croissants and four cinnamon pastries, please?' he asked, forcing himself to focus on the present rather than dwelling on the past.

'I'm glad to see the restaurant open again, Finn. It looks like everything's going well for you this time.' She glanced at him as she pulled a bag open and started placing croissants inside it using a pair of tongs.

'Yes, it's much better this time round, thanks in large part to Olivia, my new manager.'

'Ooh, yes, I've heard lots of good things about Olivia.'

'You should try and come along one evening. It'd be great to see you and Ewan again.'

'I'll mention it to him tonight and see if we can make a booking soon. No time to waste.' She laughed and Finn joined her.

As he sauntered back out into the sunshine, he was grateful for the support the local community was giving him, especially after things had gone so wrong for him. He just hoped the success of their first week would continue and he'd be able to show them their support was justified.

By the time he got back to the restaurant, everyone else had arrived and Olivia was making coffee. He noticed she was making instant coffee rather than using the machine, and he made a mental note to show her how to use it later. It would be useful for her to be able to prepare the coffees in the restaurant.

'Thanks for coming,' she said, once everyone had sat down and helped themselves to a pastry. She opened her folder and gave a list to each of them. 'I've prepared a short list of items for discussion today, starting with staffing. We've had a good first week and it's been really busy. Even with the four of us though, we've struggled to keep on top of things.'

'If we can rely on being this busy, I might give up my day job now,' Zoe confirmed.

'Well, it would be great if you could always be here, Zoe, but whether this level of business is going to continue, we simply don't know. I wouldn't want you to put all your eggs in one basket.'

'I know what you mean, but I'm tired working both jobs. I want to work here again, not in some stuffy old office.'

'We're not even into the real tourist season yet, so we should expect even more customers then. But I doubt we'll be able to sustain that number of customers once all the tourists go home,' Finn said.

'Can we come back to that one?' asked Olivia. 'For now, we can't pressure you, Zoe, but you know we'd love to have you here guaranteed all the time. And then, Jamie, in your case, we don't want you here all the time, for the best possible reasons. We want you to pass your exams.'

Finn admired the tactful way Olivia handled everyone in the meeting. She was thoughtful and understanding and he could see from the look on Jamie's face that he adored her. He wasn't the only one. Then he immediately scolded himself for letting his thoughts run away again.

'We need you to tell us when your latest date for working here is so we can make contingency plans.'

'My first exam is mid-May, so I ought to start studying properly within the next week or two. I have a friend, Harry, who might be able to take over for me. Would you like me to talk to him? He's in the year below me. He does have to go to school more often than me, though, so we'd have to share it between us.'

'That's great, Jamie, thank you. You know he'd only be covering for you, don't you? This job is yours for as long as you want it. Isn't that right, Finn?'

Finn nodded and smiled as she blushed. Even though she was the manager and didn't have to ask his opinion, she had no idea how much it meant to him that she did. He owed her so much already and he was determined to concentrate on paying her back properly. The restaurant was going to be a resounding success this time round. He only hoped her father would keep believing in them and not decide to sell up.

Olivia finished the last mouthful of her full English breakfast in the hotel dining room, enjoying the fact that she didn't have to be anywhere today. It was Sunday again and now she'd been here a while, she was feeling more at home, both in the village and in the restaurant. The local community had welcomed her into their fold and she was more and more surprised by how comfortable she was here. Still, there was a long way to go yet. It was already nearly a month since she'd arrived. She only had five months left at most to make a success of the business before her father would be on the case and selling the restaurant again. They'd got off to a flying start, though, and she had every confidence they could sustain this level of success through the summer.

'Miss Fuller!' She turned at the sound of her name being called as she left the dining room a short while later. One of the reception staff was waving a piece of paper at her.

'Thank you,' she said, taking the message from her. She realised she'd left her phone in her room.

'Be ready at 11 o'clock. We're going out for the day. See you later, Finn.'

She smiled to herself. Where could he be taking her? That old familiar anxiety rose up at once, telling her she shouldn't be spending time with him outside work. But another, slightly stronger voice said it might be fun to let her hair down for once. It would be great to have a day out, away from all the stresses and strains of running the restaurant.

She was back down in the lobby a short while later, looking around to see if Finn had arrived yet. When she didn't see him, she went outside to the car park. His car stuck out like a sore thumb, but she'd grown used to that. He was standing next to it, looking out for her. He was carrying a small rucksack on his back and he was wearing sensible walking shoes. What had he got planned?

'Morning, Finn. This is a surprise. What are we going to do today?' She grinned at him, excited despite herself.

'I thought we'd go for a walk along the coastal path and have a picnic on the way. What do you think?'

'That sounds lovely, thank you. I'm touched you planned that for me.'

Finn cleared his throat, possibly out of embarrassment at her gratitude. 'Have you got any better shoes? Those ones look a bit flimsy for the coastal path.'

She looked down at her expensive loafers and burst out laughing. 'Wait right there, I'll be back in two ticks.'

She dashed inside, climbing the stairs two at a time to her room on the second floor. She ran cheerfully down the corridor, grinning from ear to ear. Once in her room, she dug out her old trainers, unable to remember why she'd brought them with her but glad she had. When she finally returned to Finn she was a little out of breath but raring to go. They set off, leaving Lynford behind them. It took about fifteen minutes of walking through and out of the village to reach the official path. They climbed higher and higher, so eventually they were looking down on the sea from quite a height. They saw a stone-built lookout post along the way and Olivia was impressed by Finn's knowledge of local history as he told her all about its maritime history.

'Have you always lived here, Finn?' she asked, as they left the lookout post behind and made their way towards an ancient-looking stone church.

'Born and bred in the area, yes. I've only lived here in the village since I started working full-time in the restaurant, but I've explored almost every part of the area over those ten years.'

'And what about your family? Are they still here?'

Finn took a deep breath. 'My dad still lives nearby, but I haven't seen much of him since my mum passed away. My brother lives abroad, so I don't see much of him, either.'

'I'm so sorry to hear about your mum, Finn.' Olivia fell silent as she remembered the terrible sense of loss when her own mother had died. She waited to hear if he would say any more about his family, but he didn't volunteer anything further and she didn't want to push him. She found it as hard to talk about her family, and she couldn't judge him when she kept her own struggles to get on with her father very private most of the time as well.

'Families can be trying,' she said at last. 'I still live with my dad in Bristol, but he's become more and more distant in the years since my mum died. Sometimes I feel like he cares more for his work and the likes of Rupert than he does for me.' Tears welled in her eyes, catching her by surprise. It had been a long time since she'd thought of how much she missed her mum. Most of the time, she buried her feelings at the back of her mind and didn't share them with anyone, but there was something about Finn that encouraged her to let them out.

***

Finn studied Olivia's face, taking in the depth of her obvious sorrow.

'I'm sorry to hear about your mum, too. When did she die?'

'Oh, it was a long time ago now, when I was nine, but I do still miss her.'

'That must have been hard on you. Do you have any siblings?'

'Nope. Only child.' She laughed, trying to shrug off the cloak of sadness that had descended over them. 'Anyway, tell me about this church.'

Finn stared at her for a long moment, understanding her need to change the subject, but torn by his need to comfort her. He sensed it would upset Olivia more if he tried to make her feel better, so he let it go. At least he had a better idea now why her father was so protective of her, but he still had no idea why he was so hard on her. He felt bad for ever resenting her arrival.

'Okay, well, apparently what you can see now is a rebuilding of an earlier church. This one dates from the 18th and 19th centuries. There's been a settlement here since the Domesday Book, though, and a manor house too.'

They carried on walking past the Iron Age hill fort, where Olivia marvelled at the massive ramparts, and Finn made her laugh as he recounted the stories of possible battles in the area between Saxons and Vikings with silly names.

'They are silly, but they're original compared to the names we have now,' Olivia said after she'd managed to stop laughing. 'I could just see myself with a son called Odda one day.'

'Would you like to settle down and have children in the future? I thought you might be more of a career girl.'

Olivia blushed. 'Well, I do like my work, but I also want to marry and start a family one day.' She looked at him and smiled. 'And how about you? Do you want to marry and settle down one day?'

She was prying, but he had asked her so it was only fair that she ask him.

'I would, but I haven't had much luck with relationships so far. It's hard to find someone who's as interested in the restaurant as I am. It's all-consuming and that can be hard on a relationship.' He glanced at Olivia, who was listening to every word, and she looked up at him when she sensed him watching. They shared a lingering look but neither of them said anything.

They carried on down the path towards the woods and followed it along the river for about another mile before Finn stopped.

'This is a good spot for lunch. Let's head off down one of these little side paths and find somewhere to sit.'

'This is such a beautiful setting.' The boughs of the trees hung overhead and the sun dotted in and out of the leaves, warming their faces every now and then.

They soon found somewhere free of stones and laid out the picnic blanket Finn had brought with him. Olivia waited eagerly to see what he had packed for them to eat. She hadn't been aware how hungry she was until he had mentioned food. As if on cue, her stomach rumbled, and Finn laughed. He passed her a bag and when she looked inside, she let out a sigh of pleasure.

'Mmm, Cornish pasties. It's a long time since I had one of those.'

'Shhh, you're in Devon now.'

Olivia chuckled as she laid them out on the two picnic plates Finn had brought with him. He brought out cherry tomatoes and a tub of chopped, dressed salad, too. He handed her some cutlery, as well as a cup of locally made apple juice.

'This may be the nicest picnic I've ever had,' Olivia said. 'Thank you so much for going to all this trouble.'

'It's my pleasure, and the least I owe you for helping me to get the restaurant back on its feet.'

'Can you tell me more about what happened before, if it's not a sore subject?'

'Well, as you've gathered, I'm not so good at the business side of things. And that was fine until Dan, my business manager, left. My forte is cooking and socialising with the customers, but even though we were busy, the money wasn't stretching far enough. Then my mum fell ill and everything went from bad to worse. I couldn't be in two places at once, so eventually I didn't have enough coming in to keep paying my loan.'

'And that's when we stepped in. At least you're clear of the loan, though, which must be a relief?'

Finn swallowed, realising she didn't know about the clause forcing him to stay for six months. 'Yes, it feels good not to have to worry about the loan or the lease. It hurts that it's no longer my restaurant, but I'm glad to be cooking in it again.'

'I'm sorry about that, truly I am. I hope my dad told you you'll always be chef for as long as you want to be?' She looked pointedly at him, but he couldn't bring himself to tell her what her dad had forced him to agree to.

'We haven't discussed that, no.' He released a sigh as Olivia looked away, relieved she didn't have any more questions for him.

'Well, I'm going to bring that up with him next time we discuss things.'

'How much discussion have you already had with him?'

'Hardly any, to tell the truth. It's difficult to get to speak to him directly. It's almost as if he's avoiding talking to me at times.'

Her forehead creased in a frown and Finn had to stop himself reaching out to smooth it away. He was finding it so hard to remember she was his boss. For a moment he'd felt she was keeping something else from him, and he desperately wanted to know what it was. Now was not the time to ask her though.

'Let's not talk about business any more,' he said, jumping up and brushing off his jeans. He started packing away and Olivia helped before standing up to continue their walk.

After the picnic, they carried on steadily along the riverbank until they found themselves in a steep-sided valley. They finally came to a dramatic summit with spectacular views between two cliffs, looking out across the trees and the river into the distance. They stood side by side, savouring the sight of the bay far below them and the water lapping at the edges of the sand. Once they'd caught their breath, they continued up a steep hill, passing a hotel beautifully located at the top with views across the bay, and soon found themselves back where they'd started.

Olivia stopped next to Finn's battered car and watched as he stowed the picnic bag back in the boot. 'Thanks for making this such a great day,' she said as he turned back to face her.

'It was my pleasure. Thank you for your company.' He paused and seemed to consider saying something else so she waited. She didn't want this to be the end of their time together when she'd enjoyed his company so much. 'Listen, a group of us sometimes meet up in the King's Head on a Sunday evening and I wondered if you'd like to join us. Ed and Zoe should be there tonight and it would be good for you to meet some of the other locals.'

His eyes were bright with enthusiasm, and Olivia didn't want to seem churlish by saying no. She gave it some thought, trying to decide as always, whether it was a good idea to get more involved with both Finn and the local community. She finally decided there was no good reason for her not to go. 'I'd like that. What time shall I meet you there?'

Finn beamed. 'See you there at seven.' He leaned forward to kiss her cheek and her face warmed from his contact. She was disappointed when he pulled away. If he had persisted, she would have given in easily. There was something about the connection between them that made it hard to keep resisting him. Maybe it was a good thing he had pulled away after all.

Once she'd said goodbye to Finn and watched him drive away, she went back into the hotel and up to her room for a rest before the evening. She flopped down on the bed and kicked her trainers off, groaning as her aching feet were set free. She nestled against the recently fluffed up pillows, her eyes heavy and within no time, she had dozed off. She awoke with a start half an hour later at the sound of her mobile ringing. When she picked it up, she gasped to see her father was calling her.

'Hello, Dad. How are you?'

'I'm fine, Olivia. I wanted to apologise for missing you the other weekend. I've been busy lately but I would have liked to have seen you.'

Olivia sensed there was more to his explanation, but that he wouldn't tell her any more details over the phone. Perhaps it had something to do with that letter from the accountants. She couldn't mention that, though, because then he'd know she'd been snooping.

On hearing his apology, her resentment towards him softened. 'That's okay, Dad, I know you're busy. I hope you're not working too hard.'

'I don't have anything else to occupy my mind. It does me good to keep busy. Now, how are you getting on at the restaurant?'

As always, her dad didn't linger on the niceties. 'It's going well, thanks, Dad. As I told you in my email, I'm getting on well with Finn and the rest of the team, and we're making it work together. We've been open again for a couple of weeks now and we've had a regular flow of business the whole time. I'm confident we can make this work. I did want to ask you about the restaurant's future actually.'

'That's if the restaurant has a future.'

Olivia counted to ten in her head, trying not to let her father provoke her, as he always seemed to want to do. 'We're working hard to make sure it does, and surely that's what you want, too, to make good on your investment? Especially since you have problems with the business overall.'

'What are you talking about? I've already told you the business is fine.'

'Well, Rupert told me otherwise when he came to visit me. He says you're thinking of selling off some restaurants, and I don't want the bistro to be one of them. I'm determined to make a success of it, and with Finn's help, I know we can.'

'I will be having words with Rupert, in that case. If I do decide to let your project continue, I'm sure it will do well during your time there, but I'm not convinced it will survive once you leave. That good-for-nothing chef has probably never succeeded at anything in his whole life.'

'Dad! How can you say that? You don't even know him. He's a great chef and a hard worker. He needed some help with the business side of things, that's all, and that's what I'm good at.'

'It sounds to me like you've grown fond of this man in a very short space of time. I hope you're not letting your emotions cloud your judgement.'

Olivia started to pace the floor of her hotel room, forcing herself to ignore the sexist comment from her father. 'My experience in life is that a happy work environment leads to a successful business, and I have nothing to gain by not getting on with the people I'm working with. I'm teaching Finn what I know so he can carry on running the restaurant when I leave. I hope you'll support me in that plan.'

'It's early days, Olivia. I think I'll need more evidence from you and that restaurant to prove it has a long-term future. And as for whether I want that chef involved long term, that remains to be seen.'

She seriously wondered why her father had even bothered to call. All he seemed to want to do was wind her up. By the time he said goodbye, Olivia was feeling just as resentful as she had before he'd called.

CHAPTER TEN

Finn knew it was only a matter of time before Mr Fuller would be breathing down his neck once more about staying away from his daughter. Olivia was certain to keep her word about trying to persuade him to keep Finn on as chef, but ironically, that would only alert her dad to the fact they were getting on well together, and worse, spending time with each other outside work. Who knew what her father was capable of?

Finn busied himself in the kitchen, trying to take his mind off the business side of things. There was no better way to spend his day off than prepping his fish stock for the restaurant, and soon his thoughts became more positive. He had Zoe and Olivia front of house and they made a dream team, and in the kitchen, he either had Jamie or one of his friends to help him prep and keep on top of the clearing up. Even more than that, he and Olivia were developing a real friendship, and if it weren't for the power her dad had over the business, he'd say to hell with it and go all out and romance her. He smiled as he thought about the day they'd spent together, and how comfortably she'd fitted in with the crowd at the pub. Not for the first time, he wondered what it would be like if she decided to stay at the restaurant. If she made up her mind to stay, then he would too. They were a great team, and she gave him the confidence he had lacked for so long. He could also see the qualities she had as a businesswoman, which her dad seemed oblivious to. He released a long sigh. It was all a dream, and he knew it deep down. Olivia had a comfortable, easy life in Bristol and he fully expected her to go back to it when the six months were up. And for his part, he would have to move on to pastures new. He couldn't imagine Mr Fuller letting him stay on once Olivia left.

He put all the fish shells, skin and bones in the deep pan and then cut up some carrots and celery to add to them. This was what he loved doing, and he didn't want to give it up now he'd been given a second chance.

He'd just picked up a fennel bulb and started slicing it thinly when his mobile rang. He groaned, dreading who might be at the other end of the line. He wiped his hands on his apron and swiped across the screen. A local number, thank goodness, and not Mr Fuller.

'Hello, Mr Anderson, it's Mr Stephens.'

It might not be Mr Fuller, but Finn wasn't sure if a call from the bank was that much better. 'Hello, what can I do for you?'

'I've just had a call from Mr Fuller's office. I have bad news, I'm afraid.'

'Do I need to sit down?' Finn asked, his heart pounding.

'You may need to, yes. I've been told Mr Fuller's company, La Riviera, is in some financial trouble. Despite all their efforts to release some cash by selling off less profitable restaurants, it's now become clear they will have to sell the company.'

'What? Oh, God. Where will that leave me and the bistro?'

'At best, I think it leaves the bistro being sold on to whoever buys La Riviera, as part of the deal. At worst, it could mean the bistro is sold off, which might well leave you without a job.'

'What about my debt to the bank? Has that all been paid off?'

'Not quite, but La Riviera is committed in writing to doing so, and that will have to happen before the company is sold. To be honest, Mr Anderson, I think Mr Fuller's decision to buy your restaurant and to pay off your loan might have been the final straw. How is the business doing now?'

'Well, the restaurant is on top form – better than ever before, thanks to Olivia.'

'Olivia is Mr Fuller's daughter?'

'Yes, and she's a whizz at all the stuff I'm no good at. If I'd had her on my side before, Mr Stephens, I'm sure I'd have been paying off the loan in no time. Olivia did tell me that her father's company was having problems, but I thought she'd secured a stay for us. I assume she knows about this turn of events, but I'm surprised she hasn't mentioned it if she does. If Olivia were to stay here, I know we could maintain a successful business, but this new development could mean a complete change in her plans. I imagine she'll go back to Bristol if the restaurant is to be sold.' The reality of the situation hit Finn hard and he plonked himself on a bar stool, not trusting his legs to support him any longer.

'Hmm, that is a real problem. However,' Mr Stephens continued after a brief pause, 'if you had accounts to show how well the restaurant has been doing, and a commitment from Miss Fuller to stay for the longer term, then you would be in a good position to buy the restaurant back yourself, should the opportunity arise.'

That wasn't what Finn had been expecting Mr Stephens to say. All at once, he went way up in Finn's estimation. His mind began to buzz with wild thoughts and he stood up to pace the kitchen. 'I need to speak to Olivia, don't I? And sooner rather than later, from the sounds of it.'

'Good luck, Mr Anderson. I'll be in touch again soon to see how you're getting on.'

Finn rang off and stared at the phone in his hand. What on earth were they going to do? He'd speak to Olivia and find out what she was thinking. Maybe, if he was lucky, he could persuade her to stay, and they could fight for the restaurant together. He dropped the phone on the worktop and ran to the back door.

Olivia opened the kitchen door only to find Finn rushing towards her.

'Olivia, I was just coming to find you.'

She was still catching her breath, having run all the way from her hotel. 'Finn... I have news... bad news... I'm sorry.'

Finn patted her arm. 'Don't worry, I've heard. I've not long got off the phone to Mr Stephens at the bank.'

He turned and led her into the kitchen. Once she was sitting down, he went to get her a glass of water. By the time he returned, she was able to speak normally.

'I can't believe it, Finn. I've been hearing rumours about my dad's company for a week or so, but every time I asked him about it, he was so evasive, and Rupert didn't tell me much, either. But I had no idea things were so bad the company would end up being sold. It wasn't even my dad who called. It was Rupert.' Olivia pulled a face.

'So now we know, when will you be leaving?'

'What do you mean? I have no plans to leave. That's what I was coming to tell you. I want to stay here and fight. I've already invested so much in this place and I want it to succeed. I don't want it to be sold on again now. If La Riviera does get bought out, I want the bistro to stand out as the one successful independent that my father's company bought.'

Before she could say another word, Finn took her face in his hands and kissed her full on the lips. He pulled back at once, much to her disappointment, and for a long moment the kitchen was silent.

'I'm sorry, Olivia, I shouldn't have done that. I'm just so pleased you're going to stay and help me make a go of things.'

She touched her lips gently, still feeling the impression of Finn's lips on hers, and the impact of the kiss right down to her toes. 'Can you do that again, please?' she whispered.

'Wha–?' he began before he understood. This time, he took a slow step towards her and pulled her gently to her feet. Then his lips were on hers, and he was kissing her so softly. Her lips parted and the kiss between them deepened, as Finn stroked her back gently. Olivia slipped her arms round his neck without even thinking about it, enjoying the sensation of his curly hair caressing her skin. She heard his groan of satisfaction as it rumbled through his chest, and the sound filled her with deep pleasure. She turned her head slightly, brushing her hair against his stubbly cheek. The sensation was so arousing, she pulled back, worried things might get out of hand if they didn't stop.

'Finn.' It was as if she was really seeing him for the first time. He wanted her to stay and fight! They could unite and be on the same side, rather than circling each other as they'd been doing ever since she arrived. 'You want me to stay?'

'Of course I do. We make a great team, and I know we can make a success of the restaurant together. But you do have to promise me one thing.'

'What's that?' she asked with bated breath, taking a step away from him, wondering whether the kiss they'd shared had meant anything to him on a deeper level.

'Not to keep any more secrets. We're either in this together or not at all.'

'Okay, that's fair. I have a question for you, too.'

'Go on.'

'What do you want to get out of all this, apart from seeing the restaurant succeed?'

'Well, success is a pretty good reward in itself. But I also want to clear my name so I can rebuild my reputation.'

'And?' She wanted to hear him say it.

'And... In an ideal world, I would buy the restaurant back.'

Olivia clapped her hands together. 'Excellent! That's what I want too. I want you to want this for yourself more than anything. And I know we can do it, Finn.'

Finn grinned at her enthusiasm. Then his face fell. 'There's something else I've been meaning to ask you about.'

'Oh?'

'Did anything ever happen between you and Rupert?'

Her cheeks heated. Now there was no escape from telling him about her past relationship. 'Yes. And it's the biggest regret of my life.'

Finn's eyebrows rose. 'You don't have to talk about it if you don't want to. I just wanted to know. I'm sorry he left you feeling like that, though.'

She shrugged. 'I've moved on now. I'll tell you about it another time if that's okay.' It was still raw, but she had learned a harsh lesson from the experience. Even as that thought went through her head, she worried about the kisses she and Finn had shared. She had good reason for not getting involved with someone she worked with, even though her instinct told her Finn was almost the polar opposite of Rupert in temperament and personality. She was even starting to believe Finn wanted to be with her because he liked her, and not because he could curry favour with her father.

Finn moved closer and took her hands. 'I understand if you want to tell me about it some other time. Just know that I am nothing like him,' he said, as if reading her thoughts. 'I won't ever push you to do something you're not ready for, I promise.'

She nodded, grateful he'd been honest, but also thinking about the work ahead of them if they were committed to getting the restaurant back. They'd have their work cut out with both Rupert and her father, and they would have to use every trick in their arsenal to get past them both.

Olivia and Zoe were just clearing up the dining area after a busy lunch-time service the next day when the bell above the door tinkled.

Thinking that one of the customers must have forgotten something, Olivia came out from behind the bar. She stiffened involuntarily, pulling her shoulders up straight and standing to attention.

'Dad! What are you doing here?' They kissed each other on the cheek and Olivia flushed at the awkwardness between them. She wished she'd called him back, after all the messages he'd left yesterday. She might have been able to persuade him not to come.

'As you haven't been answering my calls, I thought it was about time I paid you a visit to see how things were going with my investment,' he replied smoothly. He removed his coat and gloves and handed them to her, as though it was understood she would look after them for him. She took them without hesitation, even though by doing so she was reinforcing his hold over her, but as she turned round, her unhappiness at having her father in the bistro was clear for all to see. She put her head down and avoided Zoe's gaze.

As she went to hang up her father's coat, she noticed Finn had come back out into the dining area. He paled at the sight of her dad standing at the entrance. Their first meeting obviously hadn't left him with a good impression of her father. And Finn probably thought even less of him now he knew the company was being sold.

Olivia wanted to take Finn's hand to give them both courage, but she couldn't do that in front of her father. Nor did she know how Finn would react to such a public display of affection in front of their work colleagues, when they'd only shared a couple of kisses. Jamie had also joined them in the dining area and was watching the scene unfolding in front of him with great curiosity.

Finn walked forward and held out his hand. Her dad looked at him for what seemed like ages until she thought he wasn't going to shake it. Then at long last he did, after Olivia moved to his side and gave him a nudge. She frowned at him, wondering why he was being so rude, and ignoring her instinctive desire to seek her father's approval.

'Ah, yes, the man who let this restaurant fail the first time round.'

'Dad, for goodness' sake,' Olivia hissed at him.

'It's all right, Olivia,' Finn said. 'Your father's only speaking the truth.'

At least Finn had some manners, unlike her father. She admired his honesty. He could have retorted, but he remained patient and didn't rise to her father's bait.

'Well, we're working as a team now and it's not going to fail this time,' Olivia replied, sticking out her chin. She willed her father not to embarrass them in front of Zoe and Jamie by revealing that the company was being sold, and possibly the restaurant with it.

'As I've already told you, my dear, that remains to be seen. Now enough of this chit-chat. I'd like to see the accounts and to talk to you somewhere in private.' Her father drew himself up to his full height and proceeded to ignore Finn and the others.

'All the paperwork is at my hotel. Why don't we go there and let Finn get on with his prep for tonight?' She touched Finn lightly on the arm and went to get her father's coat again, eager to get him away from the restaurant and her friends. She threw a desperate look at Zoe and Jamie, wishing they would go out to the kitchen, but they remained rooted to the spot.

The two men stared at each other, neither one of them wanting to be the first to look away. Olivia saved the day by coming back with the coat, but she looked nervously between Finn and her father, trying to defuse the tension.

'Get your things, Olivia. I'd like to get started and ensure I have time to eat here this evening.'

'You want to dine here this evening?' Finn said, flabbergasted.

'That's what I said, yes. As I've invested in this place, I want to make sure the food is at least half-decent, before I–'

Finn and Olivia gasped at the same time, and her father fell silent. Olivia dashed off to get her things before he could put his foot in it again, shooing Zoe and Jamie out of the dining room on her way. As she returned, she caught the tail end of what her father was saying to Finn.

'...the sooner I get rid of this place, the better.'

War might break out at any time, either between the two men or between Olivia and her father, so she rushed forward, giving Finn no time to reply. Finn moved to look at the bookings screen on the computer and gave a small smile.

'I'm sorry, Mr Fuller, but we're fully booked tonight, and indeed for the next few nights, so we won't be able to fit you in.' He shrugged nonchalantly. 'But do give us a call if you're expecting to be in the area again soon, won't you?'

Olivia had to stifle a giggle. Her father gave her a damning look before turning abruptly on his heel and leaving the bistro to wait for her outside.

'I'm sorry, Finn. I should have expected he'd come here and start throwing his weight around.'

'Don't worry, I've got a thick skin. Good luck with your meeting and I'll see you later.' He smiled at her affectionately, and she followed in her father's footsteps to try and find out more about what he was up to.

Olivia tried to keep up with her father as he marched towards her hotel. She had no idea why he was in such a desperate hurry to get there, but she didn't even have the breath to call out to him and ask him to slow down. Then suddenly he stopped, as they reached the middle of the bridge. She caught up and stood next to him, watching his face as he gazed at the water cascading over the rocks below.

'Olivia, this is beautiful. I had no idea what a lovely place this is.' He stared at the meeting point of the two rivers, as entranced as she had been the first time she'd seen it.

'I know. It's taken me by surprise how much I enjoy living here, too.' She turned to face the river and smiled as she looked at the gurgling waters down below. There was something about water that was so calming and it seemed to be having that effect on her father.

'We need to talk, Olivia,' he said, still looking at the river.

'About the restaurant? Yes, I know.' She frowned as she tried to reconcile the nervous look on her father's face with the confident one she was used to seeing, and the arrogant display he had put on at the restaurant.

'Partly, yes, but I need to talk with you about some other things as well.' He turned to face her at last and she noticed the slight bags under his eyes. 'Let's go to your hotel now.' He offered his arm and she took it for the remainder of the journey. His pace seemed to get slower and slower, as if he didn't actually want to get there and tell her what he had to say at all. The butterflies in her stomach fluttered more violently with every step she took. They finally arrived at the hotel and, after collecting her key from reception, Olivia led the way up the stairs to her room.

Her father refused her offer of a drink and took a seat in the armchair, and she sat opposite him on the small sofa. She smoothed her skirt out of habit and looked over at him, wondering what this was all about.

'Since your mother passed away,' her father began, clearing his throat, 'all I've ever wanted to do was to protect you because I... I love you. I hope you know that in doing that, I never meant to dictate to you how you should live your life, but I'm ashamed to say that that's what I've done.'

Olivia's eyes had widened from the minute her father started speaking, but she couldn't find any words. She couldn't remember the last time he'd told her he loved her. She waited for her father to continue, desperate to hear his words of affection after all this time, but also hoping she would soon have the opportunity to tell him her ambitious plans for the restaurant.

'When I understood you were about to leave the company to take up another job offer,' he held up his hand when Olivia tried to interrupt, 'I had to act at once to stop you from moving away. I couldn't bear that. So when the team found this restaurant for me, and then Rupert had his skiing accident, it seemed as if everything was falling into place. That's why I sent you here.'

'How did you know I'd been offered another job?'

'Rupert has his ear close to the ground.'

'So it was him who told you? And that was what led you to give me a restaurant, not because you believed in my ability to succeed?' Olivia was finding it hard to catch her breath. No wonder everyone thought she was so pampered. All she'd ever wanted was to make her father proud of her, and to do it on her own terms.

Her father nodded, suitably embarrassed by his manoeuvring. 'I chose this restaurant because it had already failed and the chef was desperate to sell the place. He was bound to take a low offer, because all he wanted to do was pay off his loan.'

He looked up at Olivia to find her mouth open in shock.

'Okay, let me get this straight,' she said, finding her voice at last. 'You only let me come and manage this restaurant to stop me from taking a job somewhere else and because, in the absence of dear Rupert, there was no-one else who could do the job. On top of that, you chose a restaurant that had failed before. Why?'

'Because I thought it would be harder, or maybe impossible, for you to turn round a restaurant like that, since...' He couldn't bring himself to finish.

'Since what?' Olivia's voice rose a notch in pitch, despite her efforts to keep calm.

The silence in the room was deafening.

'Hang on, did you expect it to fail because I hadn't had a lot of experience either, so between us it was bound to be a disaster?'

A few moments passed and all that could be heard was the sound of a clock ticking on the desk beside the hotel stationery.

'Why did you want me to fail, Dad?' Olivia asked, breaking the near silence.

'I didn't want you to fail, Olivia. I wanted to keep you with me, and the only way I could achieve that was to put you in a position where you were more likely to fail, so you would come back home again.'

Olivia took a minute to digest that information and to find her voice again. 'Except I haven't failed, have I, Dad? In fact, you under-estimated me. Those years I spent poring over reports served me well, and as I've told you, Finn and I are working well as a team. I think we can turn the restaurant's fortunes round. When you sell the company, I want this restaurant to be the flagship indie the new company can be proud of.'

'I am proud of what you've done, Olivia. But I have more to tell you, and what I have to say will explain why I've confessed all this.'

CHAPTER ELEVEN

As he prepped for the evening service, Finn could think of nothing else except what Olivia and her dad could have been talking about all afternoon. He'd had to work so hard not to tell Olivia about her father warning him off, and now he had no idea what Mr Fuller might be saying to her. Things couldn't carry on like this, not if he wanted to have any kind of relationship with her. He'd have to come clean, but he didn't relish that conversation one bit. On top of that, he wanted to know whether her father would accept their plan to carry on running the restaurant, or if he would want to recoup his losses straight away.

He was just washing up at the end of the afternoon when his phone rang.

'Hello Mr Anderson, it's Mr Stephens here. I'm calling to confirm I can make the meeting with you and Olivia tomorrow afternoon at four o'clock here at the bank. Is that still a good time for both of you?'

'I don't know anything about a meeting. I presume Olivia arranged this. Did she say why?'

'I understand Miss Fuller wants to open a business bank account with you, and of course both of you would be needed to do that.'

'I see. I'm still none the wiser, but I guess she'll get round to explaining it all to me before tomorrow. We'll see you then.'

Finn rang off, his mind full of concern. What was going on? He couldn't begin to imagine the kind of conversation Olivia was having with her father that would lead to her wanting to open a joint bank account. He groaned softly as he fired off a quick text to her, letting her know about the meeting. Then he tried to remain patient until she returned.

'Man, it sounds like something even worse has happened since I was here at lunch-time.'

Finn looked up to see Jamie ambling in to the kitchen for the evening shift.

He straightened up and tried to look like everything was fine. 'It's nothing. I've just had a phone call from the bank asking me to attend a meeting there tomorrow, and you know what banks are like. It's never good news, is it?'

Jamie nodded wisely, although Finn wasn't sure he understood what he meant at all, at his young age.

'What do you need me to get on with?' Jamie moved straight on to the job in hand and Finn set him to skinning some fish fillets, releasing a sigh of relief at his efficiency. He then busied himself with his final prep, trying to take his mind off wondering what Olivia was up to. He cast a sideways glance as he worked to see how Jamie was getting on.

'You've done a great job with those fillets. All the practice you've had here is paying off.'

Jamie cleared his throat and Finn was surprised to see him flush at his compliment.

'I wanted to talk to you, actually,' Jamie mumbled a few moments later.

'What about?' Finn asked, opening the large fridge to take out some langoustines he'd bought at the market that morning. He was making his take on bouillabaisse, but a much lighter version than the traditional provençale stew most people expected. He'd already been gently simmering the onions, leeks, tomatoes and garlic for a while. Now it was time to add in the herbs, and the fish bones and trimmings before the long simmer for the final soup. He stopped at the counter and looked at Jamie, hoping to make him more confident by giving him his full attention.

'The thing is, when I've done my exams I'd like to train properly as a chef, like you. And I sort of... like, I wondered, you know, if you might take me on as an apprentice.'

Finn beamed at him and slapped him on the back. 'If you're sure that's what you want to do, I would love to have you as my apprentice. I know Olivia will agree as well. Have you talked it over with your mum and dad?'

Jamie swallowed again. 'Not really. They want me to go to university.'

Finn's face fell. He walked over to the sink to wash his hands and to try and compose himself for what he needed to say next. He turned back to find Jamie looking forlorn.

'I won't go back on what I've said, Jamie. I would love to have you working by my side, but I know only too well how things might turn out if you don't discuss it with your parents. In case you need reminding, I didn't see my family for a long time, and that's partly because I went off and did what I wanted without talking to them about it.' He didn't tell Jamie how his dad had thrown him out of the house when he'd said he wanted to buy the bistro and be a full-time chef. 'My advice to you – and it's up to you whether you take it – is to tell them your plans. Try not to get angry when they disagree. Just keep calm and tell them again. You can tell them you have my support for this but also that I told you to discuss it with them. Deal?'

'Okay, I'll do it for you, but I know my dad won't listen.'

'You might be pleasantly surprised if you show him how passionate and serious you are.' Finn wasn't entirely sure about that, having seen Jamie's dad's previous reaction to his son working in the bistro, but he wanted to encourage him. 'What do your parents think you should study?'

'Maths.'

'And you don't like maths as much as that, is that it?' Finn cut the heads off his langoustines and removed the skins while he talked, popping them into the pot of soup as he worked. He passed the whole hake to Jamie for filleting.

'I do. It's just that I don't want to study it for another three years. I like to apply it and there would be plenty of application in this job, I reckon.'

Finn laughed. 'Excellent reasoning, my friend. Good luck and remember they're only trying to look out for you.' Finn hoped and prayed that Jamie would listen to his advice. He only wished he'd listened to Bob when he'd given him the same talk all those years ago.

———

'Unfortunately, as you know, things have come to a head and the board have made the decision to sell the company.' Olivia's dad looked bereft as he explained the events of the previous weeks.

'Well, yes, I do know. It was a shame I had to hear it from Rupert. How on earth has this happened in such a short time?' Olivia felt as if the ground was about to give way beneath her feet as she considered the impact this was having on her father and his company.

'I've made one too many mistakes, my dear, in my blind quest to keep expanding. Now the money has run out and the board have caught up with me. This means I will no longer be making decisions about the restaurant you're running. It's likely the company will want to sell it on again, and soon.'

Olivia brought her hands to her cheeks trying to cool them down. Before she could ask her father more questions, he started speaking again.

'Not only that, but I invested my own money in La Riviera, and I'm going to have to sell the house. There will be little money left once the mortgages are paid off.' He fell silent.

Olivia hoped to God there were no more revelations to come. She stood up and started pacing.

'Dad, I don't even know where to start. You're leaving the company you've built up, and not only that, but you're selling the house I've lived in since I was born. I can't even begin to process all this. Are you still working?'

'Yes, but not for much longer. Do you remember Damian Carter?'

Olivia nodded, and blushed.

'I can see you dislike him as much as I do.'

Olivia didn't have the heart to correct him as he jumped to conclusions. Rupert obviously hadn't found out that it was Damian who'd offered her a job.

'Well, it's his company that's buying La Riviera. They brought him into the board meeting the other day to advise them on the way forward. He was adamant he only wants to keep the restaurants in the chain, not the independent restaurants.'

Olivia nibbled her lip. Her hopes for the restaurant seemed to be disappearing before her eyes. How would she tell Finn?'

'Had you and the chef harboured plans of keeping the restaurant going, in spite of the forthcoming sale of La Riviera?'

'His name's Finn, Dad,' Olivia said. 'And yes, we do want to keep the restaurant going. And while we're talking about Finn, why were you so unpleasant to him?'

He had the decency to look shamefaced under his daughter's scrutiny. 'I'm sorry, I was feeling provocative, and I suppose it was a last stab at wielding some power. I was also trying to look out for you, but I can see now I overstepped the mark. I apologise.'

'It's Finn you need to apologise to, not me.' She placed her hands on her hips and gave him a stern look.

'Valerie told me to tell you the truth, but look where it's got me,' he moaned, looking aghast at the thought of having to apologise to anyone.

'Who's Valerie? Do you mean Mrs Bell?' Olivia narrowed her eyes. 'Is there something else you haven't told me?'

'Yes, Mrs Bell. We've become... close over the years. For my part, she's become more than a friend, but I've yet to find out if she feels the same way.'

'I see. Well, I hope it all works out for you, if that's what you both want.' Olivia's natural desire for her dad's happiness kicked in, even in the midst of the disaster unfolding all around her.

'And I sense you've become close to this Finn, despite all my–'

Olivia frowned. 'What do you mean, despite all my–? That sounds like you've been up to something.'

Her dad released a faint groan. 'Olivia, I–' He raised his hands in a futile gesture, trying to get out of the trap he'd led himself into.

'Dad, just tell me the truth.'

'Very well. I warned Mr Anderson off. I told him he wasn't good enough for you, and he needed to leave you alone or he would have me to answer to.'

And suddenly, all Olivia's restraint vanished. 'How dare you interfere in my life in that way? That's shameful. If you loved me as much as you say, you'd be happy for me and you'd let me live my own life. This is the 21st century, you know and I'm not a child! I make my own decisions and my own mistakes. Do you know how much grief I've had to put up with in the office because I'm the boss's daughter? Your stupid rules about not acknowledging that fact have made me vulnerable to the misogynistic attentions of all those sexist pigs I work with in my team. And how would I know whether to trust anyone who made an effort to get to know me? Not that it matters – no-one dared to for fear of getting in your bad books, which has made it hell working there for the past three years.' No-one apart from Rupert, Olivia wanted to say, but still couldn't bring herself to do so.

She turned her back on him, furious and tearful at the same time. She folded her arms around her body, trying to protect herself from any more hurt, and understanding at last why she found it so hard to let herself go. She heard her father leave the room a few minutes later and decided that was maybe the best decision he had made in a long time. She threw herself onto the bed and sobbed, drained from all the standing up she had done to her father over the past hour.

———

It was gone six o'clock and still there was no sign of Olivia. Finn was frantic with worry. Just after half past six, the kitchen door opened and Olivia appeared at last. Finn and Jamie both turned towards her, but as soon as Finn saw her tear-stained face, he gestured to Jamie to leave them alone.

'Olivia, what the hell happened? I've been so worried about you.' He folded her into his arms as she sagged under the weight of her worries.

Finn stood numb as she filled him in on all the details – how her father had hoped she'd fail, how he'd been forced out of the company and would have to sell their home, and how the bistro would now be sold off. She pulled back to see his reaction. 'Oh and not quite content with all that drama, he admitted he'd warned you off having a relationship with me.'

'Oh, Olivia, Christ, what an afternoon you've had.' Finn pulled her close again and stroked her hair, trying to soothe everything away for her. 'I wish I could have been there for you. I'm sorry you had to deal with all those revelations on your own.'

She shrugged as she took a step back. She took a few deep breaths but didn't look any calmer for doing so.

'Can we talk after service?' she asked, her eyes wide and still brimming with tears.

'Of course we can. But listen, before you go, I want you to know something. Your dad did warn me off having a relationship with you just after you'd rejected me yourself, but I couldn't do it. I've loved every minute we've spent together and I hope we're going to spend much more time getting to know each other in the months to come.

Forget about what your dad did. All that matters now is what we want, okay?'

She nodded and tried to blink away her tears. Finn gave her a soft kiss on the cheek and she went off to the dining room to get started.

As always, it was a busy service, and they barely had time to speak to each other again. At the end of the evening, they caught up again in the kitchen, after all the customers and staff had gone. Finn took Olivia's hand silently and led the way upstairs. He poured them both a glass of white wine and they sat down, face-to-face, on two of Finn's threadbare pieces of furniture, ready to pick over the details of everything that had happened earlier in the day.

'Ever since I met your dad that first day at the bank, I've had the feeling he had an ulterior motive for buying my restaurant. Buying failing restaurants and turning them round is what he does, right? So why did he insist on the chef who made the business fail in the first place doing the cooking, with no investigation as to whether I was any good or not? And why pair me with you, when this is your first experience of running a restaurant?'

'Why didn't you say something before?'

'I wanted to, but I didn't think you'd believe me on the basis of a hunch. The important thing is we've succeeded, despite your dad's efforts to stop us. We work well together, Olivia, and we know we can make a go of this. The real question is, do we want to continue? We'll have to fight the corporate execs at your dad's old company, and maybe at the new one, and it could get ugly.'

'I want to stay and finish what we've started, and I'm not going to let those boring corporate execs stop me. The sale's bound to take a few months. What I'd love then is to buy the place back for you. I'm sure we can raise at least half the money in the months before the sale comes up.'

'If you really believe that, all we'd have to do is persuade the bank to lend us the rest when the time comes, and then work our guts out to pay the loan off.'

'That's why I called the bank and set up that meeting for us tomorrow afternoon. We can't waste a single minute.'

Finn nodded. 'And what will you do when the time's up, if you have no home and no job to go back to?' he asked softly. He was desperate to ask her to stay but didn't want to push her into making the decision too soon.

'I... I don't know. God, I hadn't even thought that far ahead, but you're right. There won't be anything for me in Bristol any more. I couldn't care less about the job or the money, but I won't even have a home of my own when I leave here.'

Finn reached out to her and she stood up to come and sit next to him. She let her head rest on Finn's chest and her tears fell once more. In that moment, Finn knew he had fallen in love and he never wanted to let Olivia go. He had no idea how he was going to tell her that, but he was determined to find a way. He would do everything he could to make the restaurant work this time round, with her help. He only hoped it would be enough and that he wouldn't end up in debt, with a second failure to his name.

Olivia woke early the next morning and immediately wondered where she was. She glanced around the unfamiliar room until her eyes adjusted to the gloom. Spotting Finn's watch on the bedside table, she sat up. This must be Finn's bedroom, and therefore Finn's bed. He was nowhere to be seen. She looked down at herself. She was wearing one of Finn's t-shirts but she had no memory of putting it on or how she ended up here.

She went to the door and peeked into the living area. Finn was scrunched up on the sofa and still fast asleep. It had been late when they'd finished talking, she remembered that much. Her mind stumbled as she worked out the rest. She didn't want to wake Finn when he could hardly have had any sleep, so she went into the bathroom.

She was just finishing getting dressed when she heard a knock at the door downstairs.

'Coming!' She heard Finn call.

She took a final look in Finn's tiny bedroom mirror at her unruly hair before going out to see who had been at the door. She was taken aback to find her father in the living room standing next to Finn, both of them waiting for her. Her father was shifting his weight from one foot to the other, and fidgeting with his hands.

'What are you doing here, Dad?' She was weary of it all now and couldn't face talking any more.

Her father cleared his throat. 'Well, first of all, I'm here to apologise to Finn for being rude the other day and for interfering in his relationship with you.' He looked directly at Finn, who, after a moment's hesitation, gave a brief nod of acceptance. The tension in the room dissipated at once.

'Thank you, Dad. That was the least you owed him, and me.'

'On that note, I wondered if you've made any decisions about the restaurant?'

'Well, as I told you, we're going to do everything we can to persuade your company to keep us on so we can prove ourselves to the new one. If they sell the bistro now, it will undo everything we've achieved so far.' Olivia didn't elaborate. She still wasn't sure whether to trust her father with everything they were planning to do.

'Then I have a piece of good news which might benefit you in your negotiations with the company. It's about the lease on the restaurant. I was going to take it over, but I haven't signed the contract yet. Technically, the lease still belongs to you, Finn.'

Olivia smiled at Finn's stunned expression and at her dad's use of Finn's name. She almost forgave her father for his misdemeanours. But not quite.

'That's excellent news, Mr Fuller, thank you for that. We could certainly use that as a bargaining chip.'

'That's what I thought, Finn. It makes sense to be prepared.'

Olivia sat down on the sofa and Finn joined her, waving her

father towards the armchair. She glanced at Finn, seeking his agreement to tell her dad their full plan. He nodded.

'Look, Dad, there's something else we haven't told you.'

Her dad's eyes flickered in surprise.

'We don't want to be sold off by La Riviera or be sold on to Café Express. We want to buy the restaurant back, and we've made an appointment at the bank to discuss a loan. We can only hope they'll go for it and support us.'

For once, Olivia wasn't waiting for her father's approval – they were going to do this anyway – but she was interested to know what he thought of their plan.

'Would you like me to come to the bank with you to give you some moral support?'

'As long as Finn doesn't mind, that sounds like a good idea to me.' Olivia looked to Finn to find him nodding but still frowning. She understood it would take him some time to forge a relationship with her father.

'How long do you think you'll be staying here, Mr Fuller?' Finn asked.

'I'll make my way home after the meeting. I can't delay putting all my affairs in order now.'

'What will you do?' Olivia understood suddenly what an awful impact this was going to have on him. His work had been his life for so long.

'I don't know yet, but I have a few ideas and it's time for a new phase in my life to begin.'

As Olivia and her father fell silent, Finn spoke again. 'We've had a cancellation this lunch-time. I wondered if you'd like to take that table so you can taste our food for yourself, Mr Fuller?'

Her father beamed and so did Olivia. 'That would be wonderful.' He stood and put his hand out to Finn. 'Thank you for being so forgiving. I didn't deserve it after the way I'd treated you. I wish you and Olivia all the best for the future.' He turned to leave, but Olivia caught his arm.

'Thanks for coming this morning, Dad, and for telling us about the lease.' She leaned towards him and kissed him gently on both cheeks. He gathered her into his arms and gave her the first proper hug she could remember for many years. When he pulled back, they both had tears in their eyes.

'I'm returning to the hotel to pack my things and check out, and I'll see you back here later to sample a delicious meal.' He gave them both a wobbly smile and made his way downstairs. Olivia followed him slowly, almost unable to believe the rollercoaster of emotions they'd all experienced in the last twenty-four hours. She found Finn waiting for her in the kitchen when she returned and she walked into his embrace.

'What a morning it's been and it's not even ten o'clock yet.' Olivia sighed as Finn hugged her a little bit tighter.

'Well, Miss Fuller, there's no rest for the wicked. I need to get dressed. We have a lot of work to do for the lunch-time service, especially as we now have a special guest coming.'

Finn's whisper in her ear sent shivers down Olivia's spine.

'Do we have to?' she groaned.

'Yes, we do.' He gave her a quick kiss and went into the bathroom, emerging fresh and raring to go.

Once downstairs in the restaurant kitchen, they surveyed Finn's meal plan and the jobs to do, which were all neatly displayed on the whiteboard above his work surface.

'You are a hard taskmaster, Mr Anderson,' she grumbled. She tied an apron round her waist and fetched a knife from the rack hanging on the wall.

'I'll make it up to you later, I promise.' He gave her a final wink and focused his attention on his cooking.

Olivia turned her attention to the vegetables laid out in front of her, awaiting Finn's instructions. She was glad to have something to take her mind off the meeting with the bank. She hoped having her dad with them would be a benefit rather than a hindrance, and that the bank would agree to their request.

CHAPTER TWELVE

Mr Stephens shook hands with them as they entered his office. Olivia was pleased to meet the man at last and, despite his slightly fuddy-duddy appearance, she was confident his brain was sharp. She wasn't going to underestimate him.

'Thanks very much for seeing us,' she began as she sat down opposite his desk, her father and Finn on either side of her. It was clear she was going to take the lead in the meeting and Mr Stephens gave her his full attention.

'How can I help, Miss Fuller?'

'My father is about to part ways with his old company, which is to be sold. Our position is now a bit uncertain and so Finn and I would like to talk to you about the bistro's future. In fact, we'd like to make the bank a new proposition.'

Mr Stephens blinked several times.

'I see.' He cleared his throat. 'What kind of proposition did you have in mind?'

'Well, the bistro has now been trading again for a little over a month. In those first few weeks, out of season, we made profits of £5,000.' Olivia paused to let Mr Stephens take in the information.

His crinkly old face lit up, and she was thrilled he was on their side.

'That's good news, Miss Fuller, and I hear the success is due in no small part, to your excellent business sense. May I ask again what your proposition is?'

Olivia released the breath she'd been holding. She hoped the risk she was about to take was worth it. 'What we want is to buy the bistro back from the company for the same price they paid for it. We would like the bank to lend us the money to do that.'

Mr Stephens' eyes widened this time but he said nothing, waiting for Olivia to continue.

'We'll put aside as much money as we can for the remaining five months that I'm here and, at the end of that time, I'm confident we'll be able to pay you back. I have a business plan and cash flow forecasts with me to support our request for the loan.'

'I have every confidence in your ability to do whatever you set your mind to, Miss Fuller, but may I ask why you think the bank should accept this plan after what happened to the restaurant before?' Mr Stephens rested his elbows on his desk and steepled his fingers.

'My projections show that in five months' time, the restaurant will be thriving, allowing us to pay the loan back before I leave. Finn will have his business back and he'll be able to carry on our success. It's surely in the bank's interest to keep local companies going, with a view to investing in them in the future.'

'Well, you've given this a lot of thought and done your preparation, and I admire you for that. I have to say though, that I think the bank would look even more favourably on your proposal if you were committed to staying at the restaurant.' He smiled kindly at her.

'I can't commit to the longer term at the moment,' she replied with a quick glance at Finn. She took in the disappointment etched on his face and wished she didn't have to hurt him, especially in front of other people.

'I can't make this decision on my own,' Mr Stephens said. 'I would have to consult with my colleagues. But there's no harm in you opening a new joint account at the bank and keeping all your profits there for the time being. There would be other expenses to take into consideration in the future, so it would be wise to put more aside than just the money for the loan. I'm sure your business plan has covered this.'

Olivia reached into her bag and withdrew the documents she had prepared. She passed them over to Mr Stephens.

'This meeting has been most instructive, Miss Fuller, Mr Anderson, Mr Fuller.' Mr Stephens stood up and nodded at each of them in turn. 'I'll put your request for a loan to my colleagues and come back to you as soon as I can.'

'Thank you.' Olivia stood and extended her hand.

'It has been an absolute pleasure to meet you, Miss Fuller, and to see what a great difference you've made to the restaurant's fortunes,' he said, shaking hands vigorously with them all.

Olivia left the bank manager's office certain he was on their side but not at all sure he would be able to persuade his colleagues. Without their agreement, her plan was already dead in the water.

After saying goodbye to her father at the station, Olivia was quiet in the car on the return to the bistro. She'd had so much to deal with in the last couple of days, and she needed some time to think.

'Are you all right, Olivia?' Finn asked.

'What? Oh, yes, I'm fine. Just thinking.'

'It's been a tough couple of days for you.'

She sighed. 'Now we've talked to the bank, all I can think about is what my dad has done. I can't get past how he set me up to fail like that. I've always known he was protective of me, but this is more than that. It hurts so much to know he would go to those lengths to keep me living at home.'

'Now I know your dad better, I don't think he meant to hurt you.

It's just that his protective nature got out of hand. He loves you so much, he's frightened you'll be successful and break away from him. The thought of being on his own when you leave home is what frightens him, I think, because it's been the two of you since your mum died.'

'That makes sense, I suppose, and it also explains him warning you off getting involved with me. It still makes me really angry, though, and I told him so.'

Olivia closed her eyes and let her head fall back against the head-rest. Her forehead was wrinkled with frowns for the rest of the journey. Every now and then she sighed, as though wrestling with a major issue with no solution in sight.

Finn pulled into the tiny car park behind the restaurant and turned off the engine. He touched Olivia lightly on the arm and she opened her eyes. She was still troubled and they sat in silence for a few minutes.

'I don't know what I'm going to do after this, Finn. I can't believe Dad's going to have to sell the house. Hell, he might even have sold it by now. And the thought of clearing out all my things, as well as my mum's, fills me with dread.'

'What's your house like?' Finn asked softly.

Her face lit up. 'Oh, it's so beautiful. It's a great big Georgian house in Clifton, overlooking the park. It's all I've ever known. It's luxurious, I suppose, but it's not that I'll miss. It's all the memories.'

They climbed out of the car and stood facing each other across the roof.

'Maybe you should go home and visit one last time before it's sold, so you can appreciate the memories properly before you have to start packing up.'

'That's an excellent idea. I might do that next weekend.' Olivia paused. 'I don't suppose you'd like to come with me?'

'I'd like that,' he said simply.

She gave him a beautiful smile. 'We need to call Zoe and Jamie together, and maybe get word to Ed and Harry, and as soon as possible.'

'We do? Why?'

'If we're going to gain back the bistro, we're going to need an action plan, and we need as many people contributing to that plan as possible, to give us ammunition.'

After another busy service, Olivia called everyone together in the dining room. It was getting on for half past eleven and everyone looked like they could sleep for a week.

'I won't keep you long, guys. It's been a long week for all of us and we still have tomorrow to go.' They all winced at the thought of it. 'I just wanted to let you know there have been some developments in the ownership of the bistro.'

They sat up and leaned forward a little as Olivia outlined everything that had been going on to a shocked Zoe and Jamie.

Jamie let out a little whoop at the plan to buy back the bistro using the lease as the bargaining chip, and was rewarded with a big grin from Olivia.

'So we're going to have to make sure we raise that money in the time I'm here. Then we can buy the bistro back, and you can all carry on without me when I leave.'

A hush descended as Olivia finished speaking. She looked round at them all.

'You can't mean you're going to leave us after all you've done, and after everything you plan to do in the next few months to turn everything round? We won't be able to carry on without you, Olivia.' Zoe's eyes filled with tears, which set Olivia off. Soon, Finn and Jamie were coughing in an effort to cover their emotion.

'I... I don't know what the future holds for me – it's all a bit complicated now – but I hope to be here for the next few months, and I'm going to do everything I can to raise that money.' She cleared her throat. 'Now, before it gets too late, I want you all to go home and have a think about things we can do to raise the profile of the restaurant outside the normal job of cooking and serving food here twice a day. Think laterally. All ideas welcome. Please ask your friends for their ideas as well.'

She stood up and turned to busy herself with something at the counter, trying not to let them see how touched she was that they cared enough to want her to stay. It was no longer about proving herself to her dad. All she wanted to do was to make a go of the restaurant for herself, for Finn, and for her new friends.

Olivia was thrilled to know the restaurant was fully booked for lunch that day. They were now into their fifth week and things were going well – so well, she was confident that if they could keep up this level of business throughout the summer, they would have no trouble in raising the money to pay the bank back.

She and Zoe had already established a good routine for getting the restaurant ready in the mornings, and they could usually get everything set up within an hour. As she was finishing putting the coffee machine on, Zoe and Jamie arrived together at the kitchen door.

'Ooh, give me coffee,' Zoe cried as soon as she closed the door behind them. 'I'm still surprised by how chilly it is first thing in the morning.'

Olivia passed them both a cup. 'Do either of you know where Finn is? I haven't seen him yet.'

'He told me he was going to the fish market this morning to get something for lunch-time service,' Jamie replied. 'He's left me a list of jobs to get on with until he comes, and he made his stock yesterday.'

'Excellent. Let's crack on then.'

She busied herself wiping down the tables and laying out new cutlery and napkins, while Zoe put out glasses, condiments and the lunch-time menu Olivia had printed out earlier. Olivia filled all the vases with water and Zoe popped in fresh flowers from the bunches she'd collected on her way to work. By the time they'd finished, it was half past eleven. Olivia went out to the kitchen. There was still no sign of Finn and anxiety began to gnaw at her about whether he would arrive in time. She pulled out her phone to check it, for the tenth time since she'd arrived that morning, but there were no messages.

Just as she was putting it away, Finn flung open the outer door with a flourish, grinning round at everyone.

'Thank God,' Olivia cried. 'I was starting to get worried. Are you going to be able to get ready in time?'

'That all depends on how well our Jamie here has got on.' He cast his eye over the work surface. 'And it would seem you've done a great job. Well done. We can do this. Now, Olivia, if you don't mind, we must get on.' He shooed her out of the kitchen and she went back to the dining room, happy to leave them to it.

She checked the menu, trying to see what he was up to, but there was no sign of anything unusual. She guessed it must be a special he'd been planning. The doorbell tinkled, announcing the arrival of their first guests, and she went to give Zoe a hand with greeting and seating them. As soon as Zoe had the first drinks order, Olivia got going, sorting out the various types of water – still, sparkling and tap – to suit all the different requests. When she next looked up, there was a queue of people at the door, and the diners already seated were looking around for Zoe. Olivia had never waited on tables before, but as Zoe was rushed off her feet, and she didn't want customers to be kept waiting, it was time for her to step up and learn.

She grabbed a pad and pen and went over to table four. 'Hello, welcome to the Bistro. Are you ready to place your order?' They already had drinks on the table and there were only two of them, so taking the order was quite straightforward. Olivia was soon off to the kitchen and passing the order on to Finn, in the way she'd seen Zoe do so many times. Finn flashed her a quick grin, but there was no time to stop and chat. She turned around and, at Zoe's gesture, hurried straight to another table.

The service flew by. Olivia managed to juggle making drinks, taking orders and serving food, just as Zoe did, including a number of orders for the lobster special – the dish Finn had been so secretive about earlier on. Once the first request came in for the bill, she went back to her normal routine, relieved not to have to wait on any more customers. After most of the tables had gone, Zoe came over with a subdued look on her face.

'What's the matter?'

'We've had a complaint.' Zoe looked mortified.

'Shall I get Finn to come out?'

'It's not about the food. It's about your service.'

Olivia flushed red. 'Which table is it?'

Zoe nodded discreetly towards a table in the corner, where an older couple were sitting. It was the first table Olivia had dealt with. The man had been a bit grumpy, but she didn't remember any issues. She took a deep breath and went over.

'Can I help, sir? My colleague said you weren't happy with my service.'

'That's right, young lady, I wasn't.' The man glared at her. 'You didn't listen to my order carefully enough and were less than polite when I corrected you about it. Then you still brought out the wrong dishes for our main courses. I'm very disappointed.'

Olivia stared at him in horror. She hadn't been impolite, no matter what he said. There had been some minor mistakes with their order, but this was due to some crossed wires in the kitchen, and she'd put it right straight away. She'd also gone out of her way to apologise. Still, there was nothing to be done about it now, and she would not criticise any other member of the team in front of her customer. She would just have to take the customer's unreasonable attitude on the chin.

'I'm sorry. What can I do to put things right?'

The man's demeanour changed at once, although he remained just as arrogant.

'Well, although they weren't what we ordered, the food was still excellent. We're happy to pay our bill, but this entire restaurant and its staff need to brush up their skills if you're all going to make a living from this job.' He turned back to his companion, dismissing Olivia from his presence.

'I am sorry. Let me go and get your bill.' Olivia turned and noticed Finn watching from the kitchen hatch. He'd no doubt seen and probably heard everything. He gave her a brief thumbs up.

When Olivia made up the bill, she took off the charge for the drinks, in the hope the gesture would be enough to pacify the customer. She put the bill on a dish and readied herself to take it over, but when she looked up, Finn was standing in front of her.

'I think you've had to put up with enough already. You've done a great job. Why don't you let me take it from here?'

'Thanks, Finn, but I'd rather see it through myself.'

The customer was pleased and left shortly afterwards. Olivia was proud of herself, but the whole event left her feeling unsettled about her ability to interact with customers, and wondering whether she was contributing anything worthwhile to the fortunes of the restaurant. She went back behind the bar to finish tidying up and to check her phone for any messages. There was one from Rupert.

Finn studied Olivia's face as she checked her phone. She closed her eyes and swayed, before grabbing the bar to steady herself. Her jaw was tight with tension and she seemed to be only just keeping things together. Thankfully, Zoe needed to get off quickly, and Jamie had already left. Zoe gave Olivia a quick hug before leaving, and then Finn turned off the lights.

'How are you holding up?' he asked.

Olivia didn't look up. 'About the complaint, you mean? Yes, I'm fine,' she said, a little too brightly.

He reached out to her and held her by the arms. 'Olivia, can you look at me?' He bent to look at her face.

When she finally lifted her head, he could see her eyes were full of unshed tears. He drew her to him.

'Hey, that guy was a grumpy-guts, looking for something to complain about. You dealt with him really well. Try not to take it to heart.'

'There's more, Finn. I had a text from Rupert to say La Riviera has been sold to Damian Carter. He's announced he's going to sell off all the indie restaurants including the bistro.'

Olivia leaned her head on his shoulder and let out her tears, soaking his chef's jacket in the process. Finn held her to him and let her get it all out, glad in one way to see her barriers breaking down. After a few minutes, she stopped crying and pulled back a little to wipe her eyes with the back of her hand.

'I... I'm sorry. That man was so pompous, and he reminded me of my father.' She looked under the bar counter for the box of tissues she kept there and pulled one out to blow her nose. 'This place is starting to mean so much to me and I felt like I was letting the side down.' She sniffled again.

'Don't think for one minute you're letting the side down. We've all had complaints over the years and as long as you deal with them fairly, which you did, it's all okay in the end.'

'But now we're also going to have to deal with Damian Carter and I have no idea how that's going to go.'

'No, we don't know, that's true, but we have a plan. All we can do is stick to it and be ready for the corporate execs when they come. Because they will.'

Olivia groaned. She'd known it was likely Damian would sell off the bistro, but the reality was hard to face. 'Hold me, please, Finn.'

Finn willingly put his arms round her again. Her body moulded against his and all of a sudden, the dynamic between them changed. She looked up at him and he smoothed a stray curl away from her face before bending to kiss her lightly on the lips. He studied her face, not wanting to overstep the mark. Olivia smiled tearfully, and snuggled closer. They stood locked in their embrace for a good while, neither one of them wanting to separate. Finn was the first to pull back. He looked gently down at her.

'Feeling better now?'

'A bit, yes. I must sound like such a spoilt brat to you. About the complaint, I mean.' She rolled her eyes in embarrassment.

'Just because you've had a different life to me doesn't make you spoilt,' Finn said, shaking his head at her.

'So you don't think I'm a bit of a daddy's girl?'

'You lost your mum when you were far too young, so it makes sense your dad would want to protect you from any further pain.'

'I suppose you're right, but as I've grown older, it's become stifling. It's difficult for me to deal with something as simple as a complaint.' She swiped at her tears with the tissue. 'As much as my father says he loves me, he's been so controlling all these years. He has no idea of the way the others at work hate me for being the boss's daughter. I didn't even tell him about Rupert, because I knew how furious he'd be.'

'So he still doesn't know that you and Rupert had a relationship?'

'I wouldn't even call it that, but no, my father doesn't know. And Rupert thinks he can control me too, but he's wrong about that.'

Finn stepped back so he could see her face. He gently moved another curl away from her cheek. 'You're one of the strongest people I've ever met. And you're standing up to your father and Rupert now, doing what you want to do. So don't put yourself down over one minor incident.'

She nodded. 'You're right. I need to keep some perspective.'

'You've handled everything life's thrown at you pretty well. You've come out quite nice, despite it all.' He winked at her to show he was joking and was surprised when she pulled away, affronted.

'Is that the best word you can think of to describe me? Nice?'

'Well, no,' he stuttered.

Olivia laughed. 'I should hope not.'

Finn didn't want to push his luck. 'I ought to start prepping for service tonight but we can talk about our business plans later.'

'Oh, of course, I'm sorry. I'll get out of the way.' She blushed, but he took her by the hand before she could run away.

'Don't be sorry. You don't have to go. You could always stay and help me again, if you like?'

'You know what my kitchen skills are like after the last time you set me loose on those poor vegetables.' She looked horrified at the thought of having to do it all again.

'It's all about practice, and it's about time you learned some skills, Miss Fuller.' And he led her off to the kitchen to make a start.

CHAPTER THIRTEEN

Olivia hated every minute of helping Finn to prep for the evening service. He had to show her how to do everything all over again, as if she was a hindrance rather than a help.

'These are young carrots, so all you have to do is top and tail them before giving them a light scrub under the tap.'

'Top and tail them?' she asked. Was this a new language he was speaking that only chefs could understand? Then he showed her and she was embarrassed not to have known what a simple instruction like that meant.

'Can you defrost a pot of fish stock next?' he asked.

She went to the freezer and took out a pot of his freshly made stock, easily identified by his neat label. Then she stared at it, biting her lip. She hated having to keep asking all the time.

'You defrost it by standing it in boiled water,' he explained, noting her hesitation and flicking the switch on the kettle.

Despite her lack of experience, Finn was patient with her and she enjoyed spending time with him, even though the work was hard. She'd never given much thought to the idea of cooking as she was growing up. That was something the housekeeper did for her and her father, not something she got involved with. Had her mum still been around, things might have been different.

Soon, Zoe and Jamie were arriving again and not long afterwards the restaurant was bustling. Thankfully, all the customers were happy this time, and Olivia was much more comfortable serving than she had been earlier in the day. Once everything was tidied up and the others had left, she grabbed her jacket and made her way through to the kitchen to look for Finn.

'Everything's sorted for the morning, so I'm going to make my way, okay?' she said, as he came out of the store cupboard.

His face fell. 'Okay.'

She took a step towards him and he reached out and gathered her gently into his arms, before kissing her deeply. When they pulled apart, she rested her forehead against his and sighed.

'I'm afraid of complicating our working relationship by getting involved with each other emotionally.'

'I understand that,' he said softly, stroking her hair. 'But sometimes, we don't get a choice where our emotions are concerned.'

Olivia looked up at him. 'Have you had similar doubts? You sound like you've given it some thought.'

He looped his arms around her waist. 'Along the same lines as you. But I don't want to hold back any more.'

'You don't?'

Instead of replying, he took her hand and led her to the kitchen door. He turned off the lights and then closed and locked the door behind them before leading Olivia upstairs to his flat. At his door, he stopped again.

'I don't want to push you into doing something you don't want to do. I need to be sure this is what you want, Olivia. I need to know you trust me and you won't be full of regrets afterwards.'

She studied his rugged face, pulling at one of her curls as she thought about what the consequences could be if she broke her golden rule. There was no doubt this could complicate things for their working relationship. But Finn was nothing like Rupert. And he was still interested in being with her, despite the fact her dad had lost his company and his wealth. She'd been over all these issues in her mind before now, but for the first time, she was sure of what she wanted. She'd worry about any consequences later.

'This is what I want, too, Finn.'

He unlocked the door and stood back to allow her to go in first. She looked around the small flat properly this time, taking in the open plan living, dining and kitchen area and Finn's tiny bedroom off to the left. For a moment she felt sorry for him having to live in such a cramped space, but then she remembered he spent most of his time in the kitchen anyway, and he was used to small spaces.

'It's not much, I know, but it suits me. It's probably not the sort of luxury you're used to, though,' he continued with a shrug.

She put down her jacket and reached out to him, taking his hands in hers. 'I'm not here for the décor, I'm here for you.' She smiled at him almost shyly, not wanting to sound too bold.

'I can't tell you how happy I am to hear that.' Finn let go of her hands so he could run his own down her arms. She shivered at his touch and he smiled as goosebumps appeared on her skin. He bent his head and kissed her just below her ear, and she released a small moan of delight. As he kissed his way down her neck, she plunged her fingers into his dark, curly hair, gently pulling him closer still. He worked his way round to the buttons on her blouse and began undoing them one by one.

'You're so beautiful, Olivia,' he said as he undid the final button and opened her blouse to reveal her creamy skin and breasts. Her skin heated under his appraisal, but his words made her feel better than anyone had ever made her feel before. She'd never thought of herself as beautiful and it was wonderful to know that's how he saw her.

He led her to the bedroom where he sat down to shed his shoes before pulling her down onto the bed next to him. She slipped her hands underneath his t-shirt, enjoying the warmth of his skin and the contour of his muscles. A second later, he pulled the t-shirt over his head and she marvelled at the sight of his chest, sprinkled with dark hair. She outlined his pecs with her fingers, making him shiver this time, before placing a soft kiss right in the middle of his breastbone.

'One of us still has too many clothes on,' he whispered in her ear and in a matter of moments, he'd removed all her clothes, and they were skin to skin at last.

Finn ran his hands down Olivia's back, delighting in every inch of her skin while enjoying the taste of her kisses – and loving the passion she was sharing with him. It was as if the floodgates had been opened for them to express their feelings with no restraint and Finn embraced the moment, holding nothing back.

'Why did it take us so long?' Olivia cried when their bodies joined as one. Finn couldn't speak for the pleasure building inside him. His thoughts were on the same wavelength as hers and he wanted to savour every minute of this first time together. They both reached their release and tumbled back onto the pillows panting.

'God, Olivia, my heart's pounding,' Finn told her when he'd got his breath back.

She reached out to place her hand over his heart and gave a sweet smile, and he knew she understood what he was saying was true. He hoped she felt the same. They lay there side by side for some time, hardly saying anything, just enjoying being together. After a while, Finn reached out for Olivia and pulled her towards him so he could look at her face.

'You are so gorgeous, you know.' He kissed her tenderly on the lips, unable to resist the taste.

She rested her head against his chest and he could have stayed with her like that forever. When a few more minutes of silence passed, he began to worry.

'Is everything okay? You're very quiet,' he said gently.

'I'm just enjoying this time together,' she said.

He wanted her to tell him she had no regrets, but then he chided himself for being paranoid. She'd tell him in her own time. 'Me too,' he replied instead, pulling her closer. 'I am starving, though. How about you?'

'Peckish, maybe. It must be getting late now.' Olivia reached over to look at her watch. 'It's nearly one o'clock. Should I be getting back to the hotel?'

'I was hoping you'd stay here.'

'I'd much prefer that.'

'Right. Let's make some toast.'

Olivia laughed but jumped up to help him. She pulled on Finn's t-shirt, which nearly drowned her, and followed him to the kitchen where he put freshly cut slices of bread in the toaster. Even though his flat was small, everything had its own place, and he made good use of it.

Olivia curled her arms around Finn's waist while they waited for the toast. 'Mmm, I can't decide whether the smell of your skin or the toast is more inviting. It's a wonderful dilemma to be in.' She chuckled and Finn's face lit up.

When the toast came up, Finn set about buttering it. Olivia groaned with delight as she bit into the first buttery piece, and this time he laughed. There was no better comfort food than toast, especially after sex.

They fell back into bed after their toast was finished and snuggled under the duvet together, arms wrapped around each other. Within minutes, Olivia was asleep, leaving Finn to think about where they went from here. He couldn't remember his last girlfriend. It had been so long since anyone had got past his love for his job. Olivia was different. She loved the restaurant as much as he did, and now she was gradually letting her guard down, allowing him to see the real her, he was ready to open his heart. As that thought registered in his brain, he fell asleep too.

Finn woke first, dazzled by the sunshine streaming in through the window in his bedroom. He turned on his side to study Olivia, taking in her tangled, curly hair, her slender, freckled arm thrown over her head and her creamy skin. She stirred and her blue eyes flickered open. For a brief moment, confusion reigned in her expression as she tried to remember where she was. Then her leg brushed against his thigh and Finn smiled as everything came back to her in a rush.

'Morning,' she said, moving closer and slipping her arms round his waist.

He kissed her tenderly and stroked her cheek. 'I can't tell you how many times I've dreamed about us waking up together like this.'

'Really?' She pulled back, surprised.

'Yes, really,' he replied, drawing her gently back towards him. 'And the real thing is even better than the dream.'

Olivia retreated into her thoughts. Finn studied her face, wishing he knew how to encourage her to share what she was thinking. Usually when he asked, she shut down. A stab of anxiety shot through him as he worried whether she was changing her mind about getting together with him.

'Everything okay? You look deep in thought.'

'I was just thinking about spending the coming months here in this little seaside village with you. I'm looking forward to that.'

Finn beamed, delighted she'd shared some of her thoughts.

'I suppose we ought to be getting up.' Olivia yawned and stretched like a cat.

Finn was tempted to keep her in bed all day, but conscious of the day ahead, he asked, 'What is the time anyway?'

Olivia reached for her watch again. 'Oh hell, it's nine o'clock. We'd better get a move on, or Zoe and Jamie will find us here in bed.'

The rest of the week was busy and there was no time for Olivia to dwell on her growing feelings for Finn. The situation with the restaurant was urgent. They would have to persuade Damian to sell to them and although he had offered her a job before, she didn't know what made him tick. It was only a matter of time before he sent some of his staff down to assess the situation, and she wanted to have a plan of attack before they came. By the time she left once again for the bistro on the Saturday morning, she was no further forward.

She was planning to work on the accounts before their lunchtime service; it would take her mind off the immediate threat facing them. She'd cleared the whole office and introduced a simple filing system which made working there much more enjoyable. She opened her laptop and the accounts spreadsheet she'd set up, but had only just got to work on it when Zoe appeared at the office door.

'Is everything all right? You look out of breath.' She stared at Zoe, hoping it wasn't any more bad news.

'I have some great news.' She sucked in a huge breath and held her chest, willing it to calm down. 'I just came from having breakfast with my friend, Esme. You know, the artist?'

'The one who provided us with the paintings for the bistro?'

'Yes, that's right. She needs somewhere to launch her exhibition, because her venue has cancelled. And I thought we could do it. We've got plenty of room for the numbers she was talking about. What do you think?'

Olivia tapped her chin with her pencil. 'What sort of thing does she want? Do you know?'

'She needs somewhere to display her paintings, obviously, and she was going to organise some canapés and drinks. We could do that easily. And we could do it on a Sunday or Monday evening when we'd normally be closed, so we wouldn't lose any business.'

'That sounds like a great idea, Zoe. We'll have to run it past Finn and do the costings, but I think you're right, we could definitely do it.'

'It would be good publicity for us and would maybe lead to other events along the same lines.'

'That sounds fantastic. If we go ahead, I could advertise it through the website and social media. Could you give Finn a shout? Let's talk to him now about it.'

When Finn joined them a moment later, Zoe explained it all to him.

'That sounds brilliant, Zoe, and exactly the sort of thing we'd be looking to do in the future. Why don't you suggest to Esme that we meet up with her here on Monday to talk about it in more detail?'

Finn beamed at Zoe and then at Olivia, knowing this could be the first of many hospitality events for the bistro and a great source of income. Zoe went off to call Esme and let her know. Finn sat down in the chair across the desk from Olivia.

'I've had another idea, too,' he told her.

Her eyes widened. 'Go on then, tell me.'

'I want to show you instead. Come with me on a trip along the coast tomorrow.' He gave her one of his intoxicating smiles and that was all she needed. She was also desperate to know more.

'Can't you give me any clues?'

'No. It will be more fun this way.'

'Okay, what time do you want me here in the morning? Or will you pick me up?' Olivia shook her head to move her hair out of her eyes, surprised at how long it had been since she'd had a haircut.

Finn had quite a different reaction to that action. 'You have no idea what you do to me, Olivia,' he said, smiling at the blush that crept up her cheeks.

'That wasn't quite the answer I was expecting,' she said with a shy smile.

'Would you like to stay here tonight? Then we could make an early start in the morning.'

'That would be great,' she said.

They both stood and came together as one.

'I wish we could go upstairs now,' Finn whispered in her ear.

'I'd like that too. But we can't.' She pulled back a little, and when she saw his face, she was sure her own expression had to be a mirror of his. They kissed, softly at first, and then more passionately, telling each other how they felt without needing to say the words. Their embrace was interrupted by the sound of Olivia's email notifications pinging. They stared at each other, neither one of them wanting to be the first to break away and face whatever the email contained. In the end, Olivia twisted round without letting Finn go.

'It's from Rupert.'

'He never lets up, does he?' Finn let Olivia go.

Her eyes scanned the message quickly. 'Oh, my God. He's been taken on by Damian Carter and his first job is to come and assess us.'

When Olivia joined Finn in the kitchen after the evening service, he removed his apron and turned to take her into his arms.

'Do you want to talk about Rupert?' she asked.

'Shhh, no. Let's leave all that until tomorrow.'

He kissed her before taking her by the hand and leading the way upstairs.

'Would you like a glass of wine?' he asked, as Olivia sat down in the armchair and removed her shoes.

'That sounds like heaven.' She rubbed her feet, groaning at the relief it was giving her. Finn had grown used to spending so many hours a day on his feet, but he could appreciate how hard it must be for Olivia, who had never done this kind of work before. He returned with the two glasses of wine, setting them on the table between the chair and the sofa. Olivia had closed her eyes.

He glanced round his shabby flat. 'Are you asleep?' he asked.

'No, just resting my eyes,' she replied, smiling. She opened them then to look at him and their brilliant blue drew him in as always, making him catch his breath.

'I was wondering if we should have gone to the hotel instead. It's so grotty here.' He shrugged, disappointed he could offer her so little.

'It's fine here. I know it's a bit rundown, but it's clean, and that's all that matters.' She came and sat next to him on the sofa. He put his arm round her shoulders and she tucked her feet up underneath her and leaned against him. 'To be honest, I probably can't afford to stay at the hotel much longer now La Riviera's not paying the bill any more. My salary will run out pretty soon, and this month will probably be my final one.'

'I hadn't even thought of that. I'm sorry. You could always move in here with me. I know it would be cramped, but that wouldn't matter to me. Just to have you here would be wonderful.'

Olivia set her feet down on the floor and turned to look at him. 'It doesn't matter to me either, if we're short on space, and I would like to move in, but...'

'Oh, there's a "but".' Finn looked down at his wine.

'Hang on a minute, you didn't let me finish,' she insisted.

He met her gaze. 'Sorry, go on.'

'If we move in together, we're taking the next step, aren't we? I just want to know if you're ready.' Her voice dropped, and Finn sensed she was as afraid as he was of rejection. He put his wine glass down next to hers and took her hands in his.

'Olivia, I haven't had a relationship with anyone for a long time, but you give me hope for the future.'

Tears sprang to her eyes and she threw her arms round him. 'I don't know what I'm going to do when the time comes for me to leave.'

'I want to be with you, Olivia and if I have to spend the next few months convincing you to stay here with me, then that's what I'll do. I don't want you to go, I can't lie, but I hope you'll reach the same conclusion on your own and decide to stay of your own accord.'

'I can't believe you're being so generous about it. There doesn't seem to be much in this for you.'

'Oh, I think there's a heck of a lot in it for me.' He shifted closer to her and kissed her neck and was rewarded with a sigh. He trailed light kisses along her jaw before finally kissing her on the lips, leaning the full weight of his body over hers. She stretched out beneath him and he revelled in the touch of her body where it met his. She ran her hands up and down his back, and he flexed his muscles at her touch.

They moved to the bedroom a little later, removing each other's clothes on the way and were soon delighting in showing their earlier passion to one another in the freedom of their own space. By the time their bodies connected together, Finn thought his pleasure might overwhelm him. Each time they'd made love, he'd experienced the same feeling of being so lucky to have met Olivia. As they reached their release, he poured all the love he felt for her into his final caresses.

'I love you, Olivia,' he whispered, lying down again by her side. He took hold of her hand and squeezed it gently. When she didn't say anything, he turned his head on the pillow to look at her, only to find a tear rolling down her beautiful face. He turned on his side at once and wiped the tear tenderly away.

'What's the matter? Did I hurt you?'

She shook her head vigorously. 'No. It's just no-one's ever said that to me before. I feel so lucky.'

He embraced her, keen to show her how much he agreed with that sentiment. Now all he had to do was to persuade her they belonged together forever, side by side. He just hoped he was up to the challenge.

CHAPTER FOURTEEN

Early next morning, they set off for their trip along the coast. Olivia didn't know why they'd had to get up quite so early, but she trusted Finn to know what he was doing. She'd borrowed a pair of his wellies, on his advice, but was feeling awkward in them because they were so big. She crossed her ankles in the footwell in front of the passenger seat and tried to ignore the boots. The atmosphere between them seemed different this morning – in a good way. It was as though stating their commitment to each other had made it more real for both of them. She glanced over at Finn, and from the smile on his face, she was sure he felt the same as she did.

'Are you going to tell me where we're going?' she asked, knowing full well what his reply would be.

'All you need to know is we're going to the seaside.'

She laughed. '"The seaside" sounds so quaint. To be honest, I don't think I've ever been.'

'What? That can't be right.' Finn looked aghast.

'I tried to remember if we'd ever been with my mum, but I couldn't think of a time. I know for sure my dad has never taken me.'

'Well, I'm delighted to have the honour of being the first person to take you to the seaside. It might not be the best day for it today, though.'

Olivia looked out at the cloudy sky and the low-lying mist over the fields. The weather could change at any moment, so she didn't worry too much about it. She just hoped it didn't rain.

'We ought to talk about Rupert, I suppose.' Finn interrupted her thoughts.

'I know. I've been thinking about it, but I can't come up with a way to persuade him to advise Damian to sell the restaurant back to us, rather than selling it on to someone else.'

'We do own the lease, don't forget.'

'That's true, but I'm not sure it's going to be enough. I'm worried if we use that to negotiate, it will only get their backs up, and they might decide not to sell at all. They'll want a lot more money than we're able to pay.'

'I think it's a risk we'll have to take. We don't have any other options.'

They both fell silent. Olivia stared out of the window again, able to see so much more now the sun was rising. They hadn't followed the coastal road, as she'd been expecting, but had driven inland instead. She assumed the coastal path continued west from the part they'd walked the other day, and she was glad the sea views were reserved for walkers rather than cars.

Before long, they arrived at a small seaside village. There was hardly anyone about as it was early on a cloudy Sunday morning. Perhaps they'd even have the beach to themselves. Finn parked in a car park opposite a path that had a sign next to it pointing to the beach. The tide was out when they reached the deserted sands. Olivia stopped to appreciate the fresh, sea breeze blowing through her hair and the scrunch of the sand underneath her feet.

'How does it feel?' Finn asked with a grin.

Olivia realised how much she'd changed since he'd first met her, although she still didn't always get her clothes choices right for every situation. 'Wonderful. And it smells so unique. I wish I could take my boots off and dip my toes in the water.'

Finn took her hand. 'I know. It's a lovely feeling, however old you are, but the water would be freezing today. We'll come back in the summer, I promise. Come on. I want to show you what we came for, and we don't have a lot of time.'

They walked further down the beach. All of a sudden, the sand became mud.

'Ew! Thank goodness you lent me these wellies. This is yucky.' Olivia stepped gingerly, worried she might get stuck. 'Why is it all muddy like this?'

'These are called mudflats. They're only uncovered at low tide, and when they are, you find some special ingredients.'

'Ingredients? What kind of ingredients? Not ones you eat, surely?'

Finn laughed at the obvious look of distaste on Olivia's face. He led her towards the little rock pools nearer the sea at the bottom of the cliffs. Then he let go of her hand. There were plants growing among the rocks, and he bent down to study them more closely. A few minutes later, he picked off what looked like a small clump of asparagus spears and held it out to her.

'Finn! I don't want to touch that. What is it? It looks like a bunch of little alien fingers.'

'This is samphire. Please, take a closer look. It's actually beautiful.'

Reluctantly, Olivia moved closer and took the sprig of plant he was holding. It looked like a cross between asparagus and wild rosemary, but it had no particular smell other than a saltiness straight from the sea.

'Why have you brought me here to show me this? Don't you buy it from your veg supplier normally?'

'I do, but demand is outstripping supply. And this here is rock samphire, which is a bit different and not available commercially. I thought if we could forage for it here every once in a while, it might add something distinctive to our menu and allow us to promote our use of local ingredients.'

'Okay, I see what you're getting at. But wouldn't it be hard work coming to harvest this here at low tide?'

'It would, that's true, but we could also pickle it to use later, which would make for some interesting recipes through the winter.'

'And have you got any recipes using pickled rock samphire?'

'It just so happens I have, Miss Fuller. So you can stop being so cheeky with me.'

Olivia gave him a wounded, innocent look and he slapped her playfully on the arm.

'Shall we take some home with us today?' she asked. 'It would seem a shame to have come all this way and not take any home.'

Finn pulled a food bag from his pocket and waved it in front of her with relish. Olivia rolled her eyes at him.

'See how organised I am?' he said. 'Come on, let's take a handful before the tide comes in and then go and get a hot chocolate somewhere.'

Olivia woke before the alarm again the following day, excited about their meeting with Esme. As she stood in the shower, she decided it must be the sea air that was waking her so early these days. That and how happy she was here in Devon, running the restaurant with Finn. If only they could sort the mess out with Rupert and get the restaurant back, everything would be perfect.

Olivia turned the water off and reached for the towel from the rail, wrapping it quickly around herself with a sigh. She couldn't let her thoughts run too far ahead when everything in her dad's life was so unsettled. She had no idea what he was going to do once he left the company and sold the house, but she was sure he would be depending on her, like he always had done. As she went back to the bedroom, she heard Finn in the kitchen. She was heartened by the

THE BISTRO BY WATERSMEET BRIDGE 163

thought of him making breakfast for them both. Dressing in her new uniform of jeans and t-shirt, she made her way out.

'Hey, beautiful.' Finn gave her the biggest smile before delivering scrambled eggs onto slices of buttered toast.

'Morning. Thank you for spoiling me like this. I should cook for you since you spend all your time in the kitchen.'

'Why? I like cooking even on my day off, and your pleasure makes me happy.' He gave her a quick kiss before sitting down at the small table in the corner of the lounge and tucking in.

'What have you come up with as a menu for Esme's exhibition?' Olivia asked.

'Well, I've had some ideas for canapés that I think could work, but I'd like to wait to hear what she has to say when we meet her. Canapés can be boring, and there's always the struggle to juggle your food and drink, let alone make any notes about purchases.'

'Yes, good point. We must cost it out properly when we know what she wants. We have to make a profit from this if it's to be worth our while.' She gave him a warm smile to soften the blow she was delivering. He understood the need to rein in their expenditure so much better now.

'I'm learning, slowly but surely. But that's where you come in, to keep me on track. Come on, we'd best make our way downstairs. She'll be here soon.'

They'd just turned the lights on in the bistro when Esme arrived.

'I'm Olivia, as you've probably gathered, and this is Finn. We... er... run the restaurant together.' She glanced at Finn, hoping she hadn't offended him with her stumbling description of their new status.

'Hi, Esme, great to meet you. Come and have a seat.' He gestured towards the table he'd set with a tray. 'Would you like a coffee?' He poured out three cups and then sat down next to Olivia. 'Why don't we start with the sort of thing you're looking for?' he began.

'I'm going to take notes, if that's okay so we don't forget anything later on.' Olivia opened a new note on her iPad.

'I usually have the standard canapés and drinks affair.' Esme pulled a face. Even so, with her long black hair and green eyes, she was a striking woman.

'I'm guessing you don't like that arrangement?' Finn laughed.

'That obvious, huh? Yeah, I'd like something a bit different.' Esme glanced around the bistro, indicating her paintings. 'It'd be great if the food and drink could reflect the changing nature of the sea, as my art does.'

'I had seafood and fish in mind when I was thinking of ideas, so I'll give it some more thought. How many people would you expect to attend?'

'I have firm replies from thirty people. That might increase to forty, depending on the date.'

'A Monday evening might be best, but we can be flexible. Forty people is our maximum, given we can seat twenty people normally. We want your guests to feel comfortable.'

'That sounds great. And about drinks. I'd like to have some Prosecco or similar sparkling wine, and also some interesting soft drinks.'

'No still white wine, or rosé?'

'Well, it's the cost factor.'

Finn was impressed by Esme's business sense. 'We have an excellent wine supplier in Barnstaple. He has some super local sparkling wines, as well as still whites and rosés that would go so well with our food. He also sells some great soft drinks. Our arrangement with him is exclusive so it could all be based on what we sell.'

'Brilliant, thank you. The only other thing is that I'd rather not have staff brought in. They tend to get in the way and to distract from the exhibition. Perhaps you could serve the food in stages for people to help themselves, and then do a few rounds of drinks.'

'That all sounds fine. Do you have a date in mind?' Finn asked, as they stood up, drawing the meeting to an end.

'Could we go for your first free Monday in May, please? I look forward to hearing from you with your quote.'

They shook hands and said goodbye, with Finn promising to get back to Esme as soon as possible. Once Esme had gone, Olivia sank against Finn, slightly overwhelmed but also excited about the prospect of this new venture, as long as they could make the figures work.

———

Finn had planned an early trip to his suppliers to get some costings for some of his canapé ideas, and he was on his way back to the bistro well before ten. He'd wound the window down and was enjoying the wind blowing through his hair when his mobile beeped. It was in his bag on the back seat, but the thought it might be something urgent nagged at him for the rest of the drive back home.

He jumped out of the car as soon as he'd parked and retrieved his phone. The message had been from Olivia. Without bothering to look at it, he made his way quickly inside.

'Olivia?'

'Oh, Finn.' She came running down the stairs at the sound of his voice, an anguished look on her face.

'What's happened?'

'We've had a call from Mr Stephens. There's only bad news, I'm afraid. The first bit is that the bank still hasn't made up its mind whether to lend us the money. He says most of the board members are reluctant to give their approval.'

'Well, while they're still undecided, there's hope, I guess. And the rest?'

'The corporate bloodsuckers are here and they want to see us.'

Finn smiled at her terminology. 'So Rupert wasn't brave enough to come on his own. And when you say here...?'

'They're staying in Barnstaple and want to come and see us this morning.'

'Well, that's a "no". We have to get ready for service, and we won't have time. What did you say?'

'I said exactly that and suggested they come at three o'clock instead. I hope that's okay?'

'Of course, that's what I would have done. How did you leave it with Mr Stephens?'

'He's calling back to confirm.'

'We should expect a call soon, then.' Finn took off his jacket. He was just hanging it up when Olivia's phone rang.

'Hello? Oh, Mr Stephens. Thanks for calling back. What did they say?' She glanced hastily at Finn. 'Really? Well, I'll have to check our bookings. Could you hold on a minute, please?'

'What the hell? They want to eat here before telling us they're selling our restaurant?' Finn raked his fingers through his hair, trying to keep calm. He opened the bookings system.

'How many of them are there, Mr Stephens?' Olivia asked. 'Four? Seems like they're using a sledgehammer to crack a nut to me.'

Finn raised his eyebrows but nodded, his lips tight.

'Yes, it appears we do have space. Shall we say 12.30? Oh, that sounds like a good idea. Hold on again, sorry.' She put the phone against her chest. 'Mr Stephens wants to come too. Is that okay? He could keep an eye on them,' she whispered.

'Yep, we can do that at 12.30.' Finn ran his hands over his face, wondering what the day's service would be like with this new development.

'Yes, that's all fine. Thank you so much. We'll see you later.'

Olivia blew out a long breath after disconnecting the call. 'We've got our work cut out to plan what we're going to say when we meet them.'

'Come with me to the kitchen and we can talk while we prep together.'

Olivia had no complaints about helping Finn prep this time. He set her prepping leeks, fennel and carrots in a fine julienne to go with some sole he'd purchased that morning for the special.

'We have to remember what we want,' he said, 'which is to buy the restaurant from them for the same price they paid for it.'

'And obviously they'll say "no" to that, because they're greedy, money-grabbing... well, there's no other word for it. They're bastards.'

Finn stared at Olivia. 'That's the first time I've heard you swear. Ever.'

She blushed. 'Sorry. I feel so strongly about this.'

'Don't be sorry. I know you're passionate about the bistro. We both are, because it's our restaurant. When they say "no" – which they will – that's when we'll counter with the secret news that we own the lease, and that we hope that's enough to make them realise they'll never sell it to anyone else but us.'

'When they agree – fingers crossed – that's when we'll say we need some time to raise the money.'

'That's right. We need to be careful not to give them the impression we're doing too well here. They might work out the business is worth more than what we want to pay for it.'

Finn finished filleting the fish and put it back in the fridge in a covered container, ready for later. He was at the sink washing his hands, just as Jamie's friend, Harry, came in to do his shift.

'Hey, all.' Harry grinned. 'What's cooking today?' His youthful cheeriness was infectious and just what they needed. Finn set Harry to work and then followed Olivia back to the dining area. He helped her lay the tables with new cutlery and serviettes as they both pondered their earlier discussion. Then Olivia stopped, right in the middle of folding a serviette.

'I've just had an awful thought. There are four men coming from the new company. One of them is obviously Rupert, but the other three will most likely be from the acquisitions team. The same one I used to work for myself. If there are three of them, that can mean only one thing – the vultures have landed.'

***

Olivia saw them appear outside the door to the restaurant and was relieved when Zoe went to greet them. She was rooted to the spot behind the bar, her mouth suddenly dry. She could only see her three former colleagues. Where was Rupert? She looked down as they came inside, hoping none of them would see her before they sat down. She was filled with dread at the thought of having to talk to them in a civil manner, but then her heart rate quickened. She would have no choice. If she and Finn were to succeed, she would have to try and charm them. She ground her teeth together and pasted on a smile.

When she looked up, Zoe was standing in front of her, ready to give her their drinks order.

'Are you okay, Olivia? You've gone pale.'

'I'll be all right,' she said quietly. 'It's just that I used to work with those... those men over there, and I was hoping I might never have to see them again.'

'Oh, shit. Yes, they've been quite annoying already. One of them keeps braying like a donkey, as though he's the only customer deserving my attention. I'll take their table, so you can keep out of their way.'

Olivia gave her a grateful smile and set to work on their drinks order. She was surprised to see they'd ordered a bottle of wine. They were supposed to be working. They'd catch it from Rupert when he arrived. She glanced over at their table in the window to find Jake staring at her intensely. She ignored him and went to take orders from the tables on the other side of the restaurant, still vaguely wondering where Rupert had got to and irritated there was no-one for her to ask.

Zoe collected their drinks and made her way back to their table. When Jake said something to her, she shook her head, gesturing at the busy restaurant. Olivia hoped she'd managed to put him off, whatever request he was making. She made her way to the kitchen hatch to pass her orders over.

'How's it going out there, Olivia? Are they here yet?' Finn looked as worried as she was.

'Yes, they're here, and as I thought, it's the men I used to work with. Zoe's managing their table, thank goodness. There's no sign of Rupert.'

'Are you okay? You look a bit pasty.'

She rolled her eyes. 'Honestly, you and Zoe are going all out to shower me with compliments today.'

Finn touched her cheek lightly. 'I'm sorry. I don't want them to upset you, that's all.'

'I know. I'm sorry for snapping at you. It's unnerved me seeing them again and I'm on edge, waiting to see if they'll do anything, but I'm not going to let them get the better of me any more. Anyway, I must go.' She gave him a tight smile before returning to the dining area.

She kept herself busy with drinks and food orders and began to relax as the end of service approached.

'Have you been avoiding us, Olivia?' She looked up and froze. Jake was blocking her exit from the bar area, and she cursed herself for having given him the opportunity.

'Not at all,' she replied smoothly. 'As you can see, it's been a busy service this lunch-time. Did Rupert change his mind about coming?' She had to ask, even though it prolonged the conversation.

'He was called back to the office at the last minute,' Jake replied with a smirk.

She made to go past him, but he didn't budge.

'Excuse me, I need to take this bill to a customer.' She waited until he'd moved completely out of the way, keeping eye contact with him until he did. She didn't say another word as she passed through the gap, but she sensed a sheen of perspiration on her lip as she walked away from him. She was certain he was staring at her as she went, and her old resentment of the way they had all treated her resurfaced with a bang.

When she'd given the customer their bill, she went straight to the kitchen.

'Finn, could you come out and circulate? I'd feel more comfortable if you were there.'

'Of course. We're about done back here. Has something happened?'

She shook her head. 'No, but it's only a matter of time. Rupert was apparently called back to the office.'

Finn gave her a look of disbelief before coming out to wander around the tables. He finally ended up at the table Olivia had been avoiding all lunch-time. He glanced fleetingly at the three men but reserved his handshake for Mr Stephens.

Goodness only knows what the poor man's lunch had been like, Olivia thought. She felt sorry then for not going over and talking to him. She was wondering whether to approach the table when he stood up and came her way.

'Olivia, how are you?'

'Not too bad, Mr Stephens. How was your lunch?' She tried not to grimace but wasn't sure she managed to pull it off.

'The food was excellent, as I expected. The company, sadly, not so much.' His eyes twinkled and she marvelled at his restraint.

'I hope they didn't spoil your lunch,' she said under her breath.

'Not at all. The wine loosened their tongues in a way that was most instructive. I don't think I'd have got that much out of them if their boss had been there.' He raised his eyebrows a smidgen and she smiled. He was a wily, old fox.

'Perhaps I'd better put on a strong pot of coffee for our meeting.'

'I'd leave it a while, my dear, perhaps until the main business has been concluded?'

She nodded, understanding his meaning. She glanced round to see that most customers had now left.

'Excuse me, I must see to the remaining customers but I'll see you again shortly.'

Ten minutes later, when everyone had gone, Finn marshalled the vultures to a large table in the middle of the restaurant. He sat Olivia between himself and Mr Stephens and gestured to the others to take the remaining seats.

'Shall we make a start?' Mr Stephens suggested.

Olivia swallowed nervously and hoped the three buffoons had the power to make decisions without Rupert.

CHAPTER FIFTEEN

Mr Stephens opened the proceedings. 'If you are all in agreement, I think it might be best if I act as a sort of impartial chairperson of this meeting.'

'That's fine by me. Olivia?' Finn gave Olivia a nod, letting the other three know they were equal partners in this.

'Yes, of course.'

Mr Stephens turned his attention to the others. 'Is there someone who is speaking for you as a group?'

'Yes, that's me,' Jake jumped in, folding his arms.

'That's not true,' Marcus said. 'That was never agreed before we left the office. We are all equals in this.' He looked first at Mr Stephens and then at Olivia and Finn, raising his chin.

'You are representing your company,' Mr Stephens said, 'and I presume that means you're all at least agreed on what the company is expecting to get out of this meeting.'

'Can we get on with it? We have a train to catch.' Ryan threw an irritated look at his colleagues.

'Perhaps you'd like to begin by telling us what it is your company is hoping to achieve?'

Finn marvelled at Mr Stephens' politeness in front of these three oafs.

'That's simple. We want to sell this restaurant to recoup our losses.' Ryan smirked at Olivia but she didn't bite. She glanced at Finn, and he gave her a look of admiration. He was beginning to understand where her mistrust of men might have come from.

'Of course,' said Mr Stephens. 'And what price are you planning to put it on the market for?'

'It's going back on for £100,000, as it was when old man Fuller first showed an interest in it,' replied Jake. 'You got a good valuation on it, at least.'

The dig was directed at Finn this time, and, following Olivia's lead, he didn't bite.

'I should remind you we didn't have any interested buyers in it before Mr Fuller came along.' Mr Stephens emphasised the "Mr", gently admonishing the younger man. 'What makes you think you will be able to get that amount for the restaurant now?'

'The high street location and the valuable lease make this place worth every penny of that price,' Marcus argued.

'Ah yes. Are you aware the lease actually belongs to Mr Anderson?'

Silence fell. It took Finn all his power not to smirk at them now. Then Olivia reached out and squeezed his thigh gently, increasing his need for superhuman control even further.

Ryan regained the power of speech first. 'We weren't aware of that fact, no,' he said in a strangled voice. 'Well, we need the lease from you if we're to sell the restaurant at a profit.'

'We have another proposition for you, gentlemen,' Finn said. 'We will buy the restaurant from you, but we're only prepared to pay you what Mr Fuller paid for it. That's to say, £50,000.'

'You have got to be kidding me,' Marcus cried, unable to help himself.

Olivia had to stifle a laugh.

'That's a fair price when we have the lease, and what's more, we're the ones running the restaurant, so we deserve to reap any rewards that might be coming our way.' She smiled sweetly at all three of them. Finn was glad to see her new-found confidence was giving her the strength to stand up to them at last.

'You'll be lucky if you get any rewards out of this dump,' sneered Jake.

'If you think it's a dump, then maybe we should offer you less?' suggested Finn.

'No, no,' said Ryan. 'Look, we'll have to consult with the office and come back to you. Is there somewhere we could go to make some calls?'

'There's a coffee shop along the high street. We'll see you shortly.'

Finn, Olivia and Mr Stephens watched as the trio disappeared out of the bistro, all previous traces of arrogance gone.

Finn shook Mr Stephens' hand. 'Thanks for all your help,' he said.

'Not at all. You did it all by yourselves.'

Olivia gave him a spontaneous hug. 'I'm going to put that coffee on now. I don't think they'll be long.'

Sure enough, she had just put the coffee pot on the table when she heard the doorbell go. Finn disappeared into the kitchen to fetch a tray of cups, returning a moment later to find them all seated again, looking sorry for themselves.

Olivia poured cups of coffee for everyone.

Ryan took a sip of his black coffee and cleared his throat.

'We've spoken to the office and he's... er... they've instructed me to tell you they're not happy with that price at all. They still want to put the restaurant back on the market for £100,000.'

Olivia narrowed her eyes. Finn imagined she was thinking the same as him – that they'd just spoken to Rupert, who was the one pulling the strings here. Perhaps he'd decided not to come on purpose.

'Did you tell them about the lease?' Finn asked.

'Yes, of course, but they won't budge.'

'Well, thank you for your time. I think we can call an end to this meeting now, everyone.' Mr Stephens stood up, with a sigh.

'Wait a minute, there's something else,' Ryan said.

'What is it?'

Even Mr Stephens looked annoyed now, Finn thought.

'They'll pay you a further £25,000 for the lease if you'll hand it over right now. If we leave today without an answer, that offer gets taken off the table.'

'That's ridiculous.' Finn jumped to his feet. Olivia reached out and touched his arm, something which didn't go unnoticed by all three of her former colleagues.

'I think you ought to leave now,' Olivia told them. 'The lease is not for sale, but our offer of £50,000 for the restaurant remains. We would also appreciate a quick answer. You might like to tell your new boss that we have the cash, so there would be no delay.' They didn't need to know the money wasn't quite in their hands yet.

The three men stood up. No-one extended a hand to them and that seemed to suit all parties. Finn led the way to the door and held it open, eager for them to be gone now he understood what a tough time they'd given Olivia in the past. They shuffled out without a further word.

The season proper had got underway with the start of the Easter holidays, and both Finn and Olivia were exhausted. A long lie-in on the Sunday morning was what they both needed.

'I'm dreading this trip, you know,' Olivia admitted.

Finn tightened his embrace and kissed her shoulder, sensing she'd already spent a long time thinking about it in bed. 'I know you are, but I'll be with you and I promise I'll do my best to be there for you.'

She turned and kissed him on the lips. 'I'm glad you'll be there with me,' she said after a few moments. 'I have no idea how my dad's going to be – elated to have got the hell out of the company, or depressed at the way they manipulated his departure. Not only that, but if we sort out Mum's things, it's going to be emotional.'

'We don't have to do everything this weekend. We can go back another time if we need to.'

She pressed her warm body against his. 'Have I told you I think I'm falling for you, Mr Anderson?' she whispered against his lips.

'I think you might have mentioned it once or twice.' He claimed her lips in another passionate kiss, slipping his arms underneath the duvet so he could pay full attention to her beautiful body. She arched her back with pleasure. It was a lot later than they'd expected when they finally climbed out of bed.

It was lunch-time by the time they reached Bridgwater so they stopped at a pub for a sandwich and a beer before continuing on towards Bristol. As the journey passed, Finn sensed Olivia's agitation increase, and wondered how to distract her.

'You know, I've never told you what happened between me and my family. Maybe now would be a good time for me to tell you that sorry story.' He laughed, but his laughter sounded hollow, even to his ears.

'I'd like to know what happened.' Olivia angled her body slightly to see his face more closely.

Finn tried to calm himself. He'd never told anyone what had happened before, but he wanted Olivia to know. 'When we were growing up, Declan, my older brother, was always the golden boy. We were close, but I hated the way he could do no wrong, whereas I was always in trouble. And when enough people keep telling you you're no good, that you'll never make anything of your life, you start to believe them.'

Olivia reached out and touched his forearm. He glanced at her before returning his eyes to the road.

'When I turned fifteen, I got a job in the restaurant kitchen doing the washing up. I went to school nearby, so it was easy to go on to after school ended each day. I loved the environment from the first minute and Bob was happy to show me everything he did as chef.

Pretty soon I was working all the hours I could, just to learn every-thing. So many sous chefs came and went, all leaving in the end to go on to greater things, but all I wanted to do was work there. I kept my head down at school, but as soon as I could, I left to work at the bistro as a kitchen apprentice.'

'What did your mum and dad say about that?'

'I didn't tell them. I pretended I was going to college and still working at the restaurant in the evenings. When my dad found out, he was furious. He never wasted an opportunity after that to compare my lowly status to that of my brother. Declan had always been much more of an academic than me, and so it came as no surprise when he decided to apply for university. He went on to do an MA and a PhD, and I was glad for him. Even though the path he had chosen was so different from mine, he understood I had a passion for cooking, in a way my dad never could.'

He fell silent and Olivia was sorry she couldn't comfort him.

'Eventually, I worked my way up to sous chef, and Bob started talking more and more about me replacing him as chef when he and Jen retired. To me, that was years away, so I carried on with cooking and learning my trade. Then one day Bob had a mild heart attack, and it was time to go. They offered me the restaurant for £60,000, which was much less than it was worth, but they wanted me to have it.'

'What did you do to get the money?'

'I made the mistake of asking my parents if they would help me by lending me half the money. I thought the bank would be happier then about lending me the rest. But my dad refused flat out, espe-cially after I'd lied to him for so long. Then he laid into me with all the built-up resentment he'd been harbouring, telling me he wished I was more like my brother, that he was so proud of him but not of me. That really stung.'

'Of course it would. I can't believe he said that to you. Did you go to the bank for the full amount?'

'Yes, and I was lucky, because Bob spoke up for me as my father should have done, and they decided to take a risk. I moved into the flat and I moved on. The next contact I had with them was when my dad got in touch to tell me my mum was in the hospice.'

'Oh Finn, I'm so sorry. Where does your brother live? Does he live with your dad?'

'No, no, he's living abroad now and has been for a while.'

'Do you miss him?'

'Yeah, I was close to Declan and I do miss him. We've drifted apart with the distance, you know. And I also said some things in the heat of the moment that I really shouldn't have.'

'And what about your dad?'

'We've been in touch recently, and I asked him to come and visit, but it hasn't happened yet. Maybe it never will.'

They both fell silent after that, each lost in their own thoughts. A short while later, the Clifton Suspension Bridge appeared in the distance. It wasn't far to go now.

Finn hoped it wasn't too late for Olivia to be reconciled with her dad, and that one day soon, maybe he and his family might overcome their differences, too.

As Finn pulled up in front of the house, Olivia could see her father pacing up and down in the drawing room, which looked onto the main street. She didn't get out of the car straight away. Ever since she'd called to say they were nearly there, she'd found herself becoming more and more anxious about how things would go. Her father had sounded distant on the phone. She was going to have her work cut out this weekend, trying to repair their relationship after all that had happened.

'Are you okay, Olivia?' Finn asked.

'I'm worried, that's all.'

Finn took her hand and gave it a squeeze before getting out of the car to gather their bags.

A moment later, Olivia rapped on the door. She tried to relax as she waited for her father to let them in.

'Hi Dad.' She smiled uncertainly at him.

'Hello, sweetheart, Finn. Come on in.'

Olivia crossed the threshold and extended her arms. They embraced in their usual way, with a kiss on both cheeks. Her father then shook hands with Finn and took one of the suitcases from him, setting it down in the hallway.

'Shall I make us all a drink?' They both nodded and he led the way along the hallway to the kitchen at the back of the house, overlooking the long garden. Olivia went straight outside and Finn followed, eyes widening. Blooming spring flowers filled every available space. Tulips and hyacinths created a riot of colour in the borders. The fragrant smell of honeysuckle filled the air from the trellises along the edge of the patio. Olivia breathed it all in.

'My wife, Marianne, loved the garden,' her father told Finn. 'So does every visitor we've ever had to the house.'

'I'm going to miss it, Dad. I'm sure you will too.'

'Of course. I feel guilty about leaving your mother's garden behind.'

He sighed and disappeared into the kitchen to make some tea, reappearing a few minutes later with a tray. He'd always been so fastidious about even the smallest things, Olivia thought, as she watched him assemble the jug of milk, pot of sugar, with spoon, and cups and saucers on the outside table.

Olivia sat down and stirred the tea in the pot before pouring out three cups.

'How are you, Dad? How did it go when you left the office?'

'To be honest, it wasn't that bad. I was well prepared, and I didn't let them get away with anything.'

'They've already sent the acquisitions team down to tell us they want us to sell up. Did you know?' She stirred her tea, remembering that awful day. Finn sat down beside her and took her hand, as though reading her thoughts.

'No, although I knew they wouldn't waste any time. Did you use the lease as your ammunition?' He looked between the two of them.

Finn filled him in on what had happened, and her dad tutted before taking a sip of his tea. 'No disrespect but they will never get £100,000 for it. You need to be patient and they'll come round.'

'Can I ask you why you think that, Mr Fuller?' Finn looked curious, not annoyed.

'I thought I asked you to call me George. But to answer your question, your restaurant is in a good location, but it's a seaside village with little business in the winter months. This makes it less valuable than a site on a high street that's steady all year round. Your cooking is excellent, and you two do make a good team, but as you know, Finn, if anything changes in that equation, the whole success of the restaurant could drain away.'

Finn nodded. 'The bank still haven't agreed to lend us the money, but it hardly matters since we still need the company to accept we're the best buyers.'

'Which team did they send down to negotiate?'

Olivia rolled her eyes. 'My old team, the three musketeers. They were so awful, even Mr Stephens got fed up with them.'

'Hmm. I don't know why I kept them on so long. Rupert seemed to think they had something to offer the company but I'm not sure what exactly. Still, that could be to your advantage. Let me have a think about it and we'll see if we can come up with a plan of action together. That's if you don't mind me making suggestions?' He looked nervously from one to the other.

'I think we'd both appreciate any help you could offer, Dad.' Olivia smiled at him. His face relaxed, and she was glad they'd overcome the first hurdle.

'I wanted to talk to you about something else, Olivia, and I hope you won't mind me mentioning it in front of Finn.'

She shook her head, glancing briefly at Finn.

'When I met the board the other day, Damian Carter led the meeting. He asked if you would be going to work with him at Café

Express now. I said I thought not, but he mentioned that he was the one who had offered you a job before. Is that right?'

'Yes, Dad, it is. I was flattered by the offer even though there was history between you. And that was the job I would have taken if you hadn't sent me down to Finn's.'

'Hmm. I must have hurt you very much if you'd consider going to work for Damian.'

'Oh, Dad. I wasn't hurt, just frustrated. I'd done reports for long enough and you didn't seem to want to give me a chance. Rupert was always there one step ahead of me.'

Finn coughed awkwardly, clearly hating being in the middle of this personal conversation.

Her dad glanced at him, acknowledging his discomfort. 'Well, Damian said he would get in touch with you directly, so be warned and be prepared.'

'I will, Dad, thanks for the heads up.' Her heart sank at the news. This was all she needed. 'Did you know Rupert is working for Damian now?' She watched her dad closely for his reaction.

'Damian delighted in telling me that, too. I'm disappointed in Rupert, but he's always been ambitious, so it wasn't entirely unexpected.'

'It's going to be even more difficult trying to convince him to let us keep the restaurant now.'

'It won't be easy, but I know a thing or two about Rupert that we might be able to use to our advantage if we need to. So, as I said, leave it with me and I'll see what I can come up with.'

They all fell silent for a moment. Then her father changed the subject.

'And the other thing is, you know I told you about my feelings for Valerie?'

Olivia nodded, looking a little embarrassed at having this sort of conversation with her dad.

'Well, it turns out she feels the same way for me, and she's taken early retirement from the company as well.'

'Has she? Goodness! What are you going to do next?'

'When both our houses are sold, we're going to buy a camper van and travel the country for a while.'

Olivia couldn't help but laugh. 'Dad, I never imagined you behind the steering wheel of a camper van, of all things. But I'm pleased for you both. You deserve to have the freedom to enjoy life.' She reached out and patted his hand.

'We thought we might start with a trip to Devon. What do you think?'

Finn swallowed a larger than expected mouthful of tea and started coughing.

'That would be lovely, Dad.' Olivia stared pointedly at Finn, but she couldn't help herself from letting a small smile escape, too.

Olivia made herself a coffee the following morning and went outside to drink it in the garden. It had been a long time since she'd sat on the patio like this, listening to the birds and the early morning sounds of people waking up to a new day. As she sat there, an image came to her of her mother gardening on a Sunday afternoon. She closed her eyes, savouring the rare memory. She could see her in her mind's eye, a battered straw hat on her head and a floral apron over her clothes. The vision was so clear, it made her smile. But the memory was only fleeting and as suddenly as it had come, it was gone. A lone tear fell down her face. She opened her eyes and wiped it away.

It was then she noticed her father sitting quietly across the wrought-iron table from her.

'Morning, Olivia. Did you sleep well?' he asked softly.

'Yes, thanks. How about you?'

Maybe he hadn't seen her crying. She was sure he would have mentioned it if he had.

'Yes, not too badly.' His smile was brief. 'It hurts me as much as you to think of leaving all the memories of your mother behind, but the reality is that your mum has been gone a long time now. It's time for me to move on with my life, just as you are moving on with yours.' He paused to see if she would say something, but she couldn't argue with his words. 'Would you like to make a start on sorting out your mother's things today?'

'I'd like to enjoy being in this house one last time before I get on to the real packing up.'

'There's no real rush. Although the house is now sold, it will be another few weeks until everything is sorted out. But I have done a first sort of your mother's things to make it easier for you whenever you feel ready to take a look.'

'You have?' Her eyes widened. He might have already thrown out something precious.

'Don't worry, my dear. I meant I've put everything into the spare room for you to look at all in one place.'

'Okay. Well, I might take a look later.' She wasn't ready yet. She'd need to build herself up to it.

They both looked out at the garden once again.

'It's a young family that have bought the house,' her father told her a few minutes later.

'I'm glad. It's the sort of house that needs a family.'

'Yes, I agree. I think they'll be happy here. Your mother fell pregnant with you just after we moved in, so it feels right that another family will now take our place.'

'And how do you feel about moving after all these years?'

'I will be sad on the day I leave, but a house is only as happy as the people living in it. I have no need of this big house any more, so even if I didn't have to leave, I'd probably be thinking about doing so soon anyway.' He looked content with the prospect, but she could sense his sadness.

'I am glad for you and Valerie, Dad. This is a new start and a new phase in your life. I hope you'll be very happy together.'

'Thank you, I appreciate that. I only wish we'd declared our feelings sooner and not wasted all this time.'

'You didn't waste it though, did you? You were together every day. And now you can make the most of your retirement.'

He laughed. 'Yes, indeed. We must think of the positives.'

In that moment, Olivia understood her dad no longer depended on her. He had moved on, and so could she. They both turned at the sound of the kitchen door opening. Finn emerged, his tousled hair still damp from the shower. His eyes locked onto Olivia's, and her heart soared at the grin he gave her.

'Morning. What a lovely day and a beautiful spot to enjoy it in.'

He kissed Olivia softly on the cheek and sat down beside her.

'What's for breakfast?' he asked, rubbing his hands together.

Olivia laughed and her father joined her. She was glad they'd come together. Now she would have memories of being with Finn at this house, as well. They all went back inside and Finn went straight to the fridge to see what he could rustle up. After a few minutes, he turned around.

'I'm sorry, Mr... er, George, I'm being so rude. I should have asked before rummaging round in your fridge.' Finn looked so awkward, Olivia had to stifle a laugh for fear of upsetting him further.

'Don't be daft,' her father replied, in his usual forthright way. 'I'm not going to turn down your offer to make me breakfast. I'd have to be mad. No, you go ahead, Finn, and I'll look forward to whatever you come up with.'

Olivia put another pot of coffee on and her father poured out three glasses of orange juice. They sat watching Finn as he made light work of whisking up some eggs before slicing an onion, a pepper and some new potatoes in what seemed like a matter of moments. He pulled out a cast-iron frying pan and set it on the range. Olivia glanced at her father and was surprised to see tears in his eyes.

'You've both gone quiet behind me. Is everything all right?' Finn asked, without turning round.

Olivia reached out and squeezed her dad's hand. 'Yes, we're both entranced by watching your prep. My mouth's salivating at the thought of how wonderful this is going to taste.'

Her dad gave her a grateful smile and again, she patted his hand. That pan had been one of her parents' wedding presents, but Finn wasn't to know that. As far as she was concerned, it was good to see it being used. Deep down, she was sure that's what her father felt too – it had just been emotional to see it.

Then Finn was in front of them serving up his delicious breakfast dish, oblivious to the emotional upheaval that had gone on while he was cooking.

'Hmm, This is delicious, Finn, thank you.' Her dad gave Finn a genuine smile. They all tucked in and Olivia decided her mum would have liked Finn very much – so much, in fact, she would have wanted him to have that pan and use it in the way that it was intended to be used. She'd been right about it being difficult to come home. The memories were all around, and it was only going to get harder the longer they stayed.

CHAPTER SIXTEEN

Olivia spent the rest of the morning working her way through the spare room where her dad had placed all her mother's things. Most of it was stuff she didn't remember, but when she picked up a little wooden house, something stirred within her. She blew off the light covering of dust and gently lifted the lid. The old hinges creaked.

All at once, music filled the air, transporting her back to her mother's lap. As she listened to the music box tinkling out its tune, she remembered how her mother would play it every night as she dried Olivia with a big, fluffy towel after her bath. The memory was crystal clear, but it had taken the sound of the music to revive it for her. Curiously, she wasn't upset; she was happy at the number of memories of her mother that were now coming back to her. She put the music box on the shelf where she had been gathering the precious things she wanted to keep.

After breakfast, she'd asked her dad if Finn could keep the cast-iron pan and anything else he could use in the restaurant. Her father had agreed to sort out the kitchen items he didn't need himself before giving Finn free rein to take what he wanted.

Olivia carried on sifting through her mother's things and had almost finished when she found another, bigger wooden box filled with letters. As she examined them more closely, she saw they were all addressed to her father. She took out one envelope and stroked the cream-coloured paper just the once before putting it back in the box.

'I don't mind if you want to read them, you know.' Her father's voice sounded from the door and she jumped.

'No, Dad. They're private, but it's lovely to see you wrote each other letters.'

'She wrote me those when we were first courting. I only ever managed to read them once after her death.' He cleared his throat and looked away.

'It makes me so happy to know how much you loved each other, Dad.'

He met her gaze, his eyes full of unshed tears. 'I loved your mother very much, Olivia, and I missed her so much when she died. I tried to protect you from all the hurt, but there came a point when I knew I couldn't protect you any longer.' He paused as if deciding whether to continue. 'When you were seeing Rupert, I wanted so much to step in and give you the benefit of my advice, but I knew that was the last thing you would have wanted.'

'Wait, you knew about Rupert?'

'He told me, Olivia. He didn't want it to be a problem for him at work. I didn't want him to start seeing you, because I was sure you weren't right for each other, but that wasn't my decision to make.'

'Well, you were probably glad to be proved right when it all came to a horrible end.' Olivia couldn't keep the bitterness out of her voice.

'You couldn't be more wrong. I was very upset for you.'

'I wish you'd said something at the time. He was arrogant and abusive. He treated me like a plaything, and all he wanted was to get into your good books so you would promote him.'

'I didn't know any of that, Olivia, you have to believe me.' The pained expression on her father's face proved he was telling the truth. 'But I knew he was only trying to promote himself. I was never fooled by his ambition. I was so proud of you when you left him all on your own.'

'Well, thanks to Rupert, I stayed right away from any more relationships with men after that. He took away all my self-esteem and confidence. It's only since meeting Finn that I've started to get any of that back.'

'I'm so sorry, Olivia, I really am.'

Olivia couldn't think of anything to say in response. There was no point in holding on to her anger, but she would need some time to recover from this latest revelation from her father. She stood up, desperate to move on from the subject, and went to the window ledge to collect the music box, along with the photos and other bits and pieces she wanted to keep. She went to show her father.

'Is it all right if I keep these things, Dad?'

He looked over what she had in her arms and smiled as she opened the lid of the music box once again.

'Of course. Have you looked through everything?'

'Yes, and this is all I want. Just a few mementos.'

'Valerie's arrived and she's busy making lunch with Finn. That man loves to cook, I'll say that for him.'

'Just as well, otherwise we'd be stuffed.'

They both laughed, breaking the earlier tension. To her surprise, her father put his arm round her and hugged her to him. She relaxed into his embrace, enjoying the new closeness they were sharing. It was going to take time for them to rebuild their relationship, but she was doing her best.

They found Finn and Valerie in full chef mode in the kitchen and decided to escape to the garden rather than getting in their way.

Valerie appeared a moment later, giving Olivia a kiss on both cheeks, followed by a quick kiss for her dad, before sitting down next to him.

'I'm glad to hear about your plans to travel the country together, Valerie,' Olivia began. 'I'm happy for you both.'

'That's lovely of you, Olivia. I'm sorry we've not got to know one another properly after all these years.'

Her father blushed.

'I've been a foolish old man for far too long, and I'm sorry to have kept you both at arm's length with my stupid rules.'

Valerie patted his hand. 'It's all water under the bridge now. I'm sure you feel the same, Olivia.'

'I don't know that I do yet. I'll need more time, I think. I just hope there are no more secrets to be revealed.'

Her dad shook his head but didn't say anything. They descended into an uncomfortable silence. Thankfully, Finn started bringing food out, and so Olivia went to give him a hand. In the kitchen, he pulled her to him and sneaked a kiss. Although it was only a brief touch of the lips, it left her breathless nevertheless with the strength of his passion for her.

'I've missed you this morning,' he said, passing her a bowl of salad to take outside.

'What did you get up to apart from cooking?'

'Your dad showed me loads of old cookbooks and I spent a good long time poring over them. Then I pottered about in the kitchen, seeing what equipment there was, before deciding on what to make for lunch.'

'Sounds like you had a fine time. Come on, let's take this lovely meal outside.'

Finn followed with a bottle of chilled French rosé and a basket of bread.

'I've prepared a squid and chorizo dish for you with salad and bread to go with it. Thanks for all your help, Valerie. Now, please tuck in.'

They all helped themselves, and the conversation halted for a while as they enjoyed the combination of smoky flavours in the dish.

'What's the verdict?' Finn looked round the table, but they were all busy eating.

'This is fabulous, Finn,' Olivia managed to say at last. 'We should make this a regular on the menu. You know, we could maybe even have a canapé for Esme's do using these ingredients.'

Finn nodded thoughtfully. 'That would go down a treat, and it would be unusual, wouldn't it?'

'What's this?' her dad asked, finishing his mouthful.

Olivia proceeded to tell them both about their plans to host Esme's gathering for her art exhibition.

It was Monday, the day of the art exhibition, and Esme was due in the afternoon to put all the finishing touches in place. Finn had gone through his checklist a dozen times but still felt on edge about missing an important detail.

'Hello!'

He heard Olivia's voice calling from downstairs. She'd just been to the bakery to get them a breakfast treat as it was going to be a busy couple of days. He went to greet her at the top of the stairs. When she appeared, she was grinning all over her face.

'Hey, you look happy. What's happened?'

'Rosie's had the baby. It's a girl, and everything went really well.'

'Oh, that is good news and a great way to start the day.'

'I told everyone in the bakery, including Ed, about our new venture. He promised to have a think and come back to us with any ideas.'

'I haven't caught up with Ed for a while. I must try and pop into the pub some time soon. At the least, we owe him a good meal.'

They sat down with warm croissants and coffee and Olivia pulled up her checklist to compare it with Finn's.

'Do you want to start, or shall I?'

'You start,' Finn replied. 'I've looked at my list so many times this morning, it's starting to do my head in.'

'Okay. We've reached the maximum of forty tickets through website sales, which is great news. All those tickets have been paid for online. And Esme said she's happy for us to take those funds, which will cover our costs, while she takes the profits from the sales of her paintings. Zoe has organised everything we need for the event to be delivered here first thing tomorrow morning, and I've also organised for the drinks to be delivered then, including some bottles of that local sparkling wine you mentioned. The only thing I have left to do is the programme.'

'Is that everything on your list then?'

'Yes, I think so. Shall we have a look at yours?'

Finn went through his list of different, mouth-watering canapés, including the squid and chorizo one inspired by their trip to Bristol.

'Sounds perfect.'

'Didn't you say you were going to contact the press?'

'I did, and someone's coming from the *Gazette*.'

Finn smiled at Olivia. She'd put so much in place already, and they worked so well together. He just hoped nothing would go wrong for their first event. So much was riding on it and he wanted to make sure it was a success.

The afternoon passed in a blur of activity, with everyone working on transforming the restaurant for Esme's art exhibition, and Finn, Jamie and Harry cooking up a storm in the kitchen. Esme had called her exhibition, 'A Taste of the Sea'. As she worked to put each painting in its right place, the bistro took on a completely different air.

'That bunting is the icing on the cake. Thank you,' Esme told Zoe, who was pinning the last strip to the wall. Zoe had found some bunting that had wooden seagulls alternating with seashells and jellyfish along a coil of rope; their pastel colours fit right in with the bistro's design.

Soon they were all gathering in the main dining area ready to welcome Esme's guests. Zoe stood just inside the entrance with glasses of freshly poured sparkling wine and orange juice, while Olivia waited at the door ready to take tickets and give out programmes. Jamie stayed in the kitchen to keep an eye on the final cooking, and Finn had changed into a new set of chef's whites so he was presentable. The look Olivia gave him when he appeared from the kitchen conveyed that he looked even better than presentable, and he gave her a cheeky wink.

The guests began to arrive a few minutes later and the bistro was soon filled with chattering, art-loving guests. Finn delivered the first platter of canapés twenty minutes in and the sounds changed to ones of appreciation. Olivia was wandering round taking some photos to put up on their website, and he took a minute to appreciate how everything was under control.

Esme waited until the photographer from the *Gazette* arrived before giving her speech. He got some great shots of her and stayed to mingle afterwards, taking more photos inside and outside the bistro before taking his leave. Finn couldn't have been more proud.

Finn went back to the kitchen, confident Olivia had everything under control in the restaurant itself.

'Everything okay, Jamie?'

'I'm worried we won't have enough canapés to satisfy everyone. The first lot went in seconds. We're about to serve the second round, but after that, we only have the one lot left.'

'Okay, let me have a look in the fridge and see what else we can come up with.'

Finn was annoyed with himself for not having calculated the amount of food needed correctly, but he had some shell-on prawns he'd been planning to use the following day. They'd need to prep some vegetables, and they could pan fry the prawns in no time.

'Harry, can you cut up some garlic, please?'

He placed the box of prawns on the worktop, grabbed his favourite knife from the magnetic bar above, and began to cut up some red chillies. When Jamie came back, he started on the cooking. They worked silently, concentrating on getting the prawns ready in time, and they breathed a collective sigh of relief when the tray was ready to be taken out.

It seemed like only a few minutes later that Olivia was poking her head through the hatch and they were cleaning up.

'Well done tonight, guys. Everyone seemed to love the food and the timing was excellent. One of the guests said the prawns were particularly good.'

'Thank you,' Finn replied. 'It was a real team effort in here. It looked like it was a success from your end, too.' He came towards the hatch, wiping his hands on his now well-used apron.

'Yes, I think it was. I've just been speaking with Esme's designer friend, Amy, who'd like to hold her hen do here.'

Finn couldn't help the look of horror that sprang to his face.

'It's okay, I think it will be quite a sedate affair.' Olivia giggled, making Finn laugh in return.

He beckoned to Jamie and Harry. 'Shall we go and see Esme?'

Zoe was just seeing the last guests out. After they'd gone, she locked the door and pulled down the blind.

'How did you feel it went, Esme?' Olivia asked as they found themselves on their own again.

'I sold all my paintings,' she cried, beaming. 'I can't tell you how grateful I am to you for letting me hold my exhibition here and for the fantastic job you've all done on my behalf.'

'That's wonderful news. It was our pleasure. Thank you for being such a wonderful customer to work with,' Olivia replied.

With that, Zoe, Jamie and Harry all yawned. 'Off you go, guys, we'll finish the rest,' Finn said. 'Thanks to all of you for working tonight, and for making it such a great event.' When he'd waved them off and Esme had left with her friend, Finn took Olivia's hand.

'Come on, let's leave everything else till tomorrow. We've earned an early night,' he said, and they wound their way slowly but surely up the stairs.

The week after the art exhibition passed slowly, and by the weekend, they were all exhausted. Olivia was glad Finn had persuaded her to move her stuff from the hotel into his flat before the exhibition. Now all she would have to do was make her way up a short flight of stairs before she could fall into bed.

'I'm looking forward to sleeping for the next two days,' Zoe told Olivia as they saw the last few customers out on the Saturday evening.

'I can't believe Finn's going to spend the morning looking for samphire with Harry and Jamie again.' Olivia groaned. 'He'll have to get up so early.'

When Olivia woke the following morning, Finn had already left. She hadn't heard a thing. She reached for her phone to see what the time was. Eight o'clock. She rolled over in disgust. Now she was awake, her mind was starting to buzz with all the things she could be getting on with in his absence.

Gavin, the photographer from the *Gazette*, had sent through some fantastic photos with permission for her to use them on their website. He'd also mentioned he would be interested in booking the restaurant for his wedding reception in June. What with Amy's request for a hen do, they now had a lot to get on with in the coming months. Finn agreed they should limit themselves to only one extra event a month. Their normal work in the restaurant was tiring enough as it was.

Olivia was keen to bring the accounts up-to-date that day, so she could see how well they were progressing towards their target of £50,000. They'd heard nothing back from the vultures, or from anyone else, but it would only be a matter of time.

She hauled herself out of bed, determined to make the most of her day. She was going to see Rosie and her new baby, Lily, in the afternoon, so she needed to get started. She spent the morning on the paperwork and she was pleased to see it was looking like their profits would be double the previous month's.

Once she'd uploaded the photos from the *Gazette* to the website, she had a quick bite to eat and then made her way along the high street to the bakery.

'Hello, Olivia, come on in.' Ewan greeted her at the door and she followed him into the living room. Here she found Rosie seated in an armchair with her new baby in her arms. Olivia was overwhelmed with how happy she looked.

'Olivia, how lovely to see you. Come and meet Lily.' Rosie looked tired but glowing at the same time. Olivia had never been around any babies or new mothers, so she'd had no idea what to expect, but she was enchanted. She leaned in and kissed Rosie on the cheek, before sneaking a peek at the little baby hiding underneath a mass of dark hair.

'You must both be so proud. She's beautiful.'

She stayed for an hour chatting with them both before taking her leave. With a newborn baby and a toddler as well, they would be too worn out for long visits.

After saying her goodbyes, she wandered back towards the bistro, sighing wistfully about motherhood and the gorgeous baby she'd just met. She was so deep in thought, she didn't notice the people waiting for her at the back door until she was almost upon them.

'Hello, Olivia. Long time no see.'

She looked up straight into the face of Damian Carter and almost jumped in surprise. And he had Rupert with him, too. She gave him a look of disgust and was rewarded with a smirk.

'Mr Carter. What are you doing here?' She was polite but no more, considering all he'd done to her father.

'I've come to talk to you about this little restaurant of yours. Why don't we go inside where we can talk more privately?'

She turned to unlock the kitchen door, her mind racing ahead. She reminded herself of how far she'd come since she started working at the bistro. She could handle this.

'You can go on through to the dining room and I'll make some coffee,' she said. She waited until they'd gone past her before taking her phone out of her bag and sending off a quick text to Finn.

'Carter + Rupert here. Come quickly.'

She thrust her phone hurriedly away again, and carried on making the coffee. When she took the pot and cups through, Damian and Rupert were whispering conspiratorially. She had no doubt they were up to no good.

'Olivia, my dear, how are you? I can't believe you've stayed this long in this tedious little backwater.' Carter leaned back in his chair, his hooded eyes watching her.

'Why don't you come to the point, Mr Carter? You know Finn and I want to buy the restaurant back from you, and you know the price we're offering.'

'Oh yes, Olivia, I know exactly what you want. However, there's something I want, as well.'

She folded her arms and glanced at the clock, willing Finn to arrive.

'Rupert, go and wait for me in the car,' Damian barked without taking his eyes off Olivia. Rupert's face dropped, and Olivia felt momentarily sorry for him at this slap down by his boss.

As soon as he'd left, Carter finally got straight to the point.

'I offered you a job a few months ago, but you turned me down. I understand that a lot of things have happened recently. However, my job offer still stands. I need someone to help me streamline your father's old company, to get rid of all the dead wood, including the restaurants that aren't pulling their weight. I think you would fit the role perfectly. With you and Rupert working for me, I know we can turn the company around.'

'But I don't want to work for you, Mr Carter.'

'Ah, but if I agreed to let your chef buy the restaurant at the price you've specified, I think you might be persuaded to change your mind. He'd get what he wants and so would I.'

Olivia swallowed. He had her right where he wanted her. She heard the kitchen door open and, suddenly, Finn was standing at her side. He put his hand on her shoulder.

'What's going on here?'

Finn looked from the oily-looking businessman to Olivia. This man must be Carter, and he already had a bad feeling about him. Still, he was sure Olivia had been able to stand up for herself.

'Ah, you must be the chef.' Carter extended his hand and, reluctantly, Finn took it. He didn't like the look of him one bit.

'I'll leave Olivia to explain our conversation. My offer won't be there for long, Olivia. I'll be waiting to hear from you.' He slipped away through the kitchen, leaving the two of them alone.

Finn sank into the chair Carter had vacated, waiting for her to tell him what was going on.

'So that was the famous Damian Carter,' she said. 'The man who pushed my father out of the company and will be taking over in his place.'

'I guessed as much. Your dad was right, then, when he said he'd get in touch with you. What did he want?'

Olivia sighed, biting her lip. Finn took her hands in his.

'Please, Olivia, tell me. Whatever it is, it's better if we work it out together.' When she didn't reply, an icy feeling gripped him. 'Did he come here to offer you the job again?' Finn frowned.

Olivia pulled her hands away from his and started clenching and unclenching them. 'Yes, and of course, I said no, but then he told me if I took the job with him, he would let you have the restaurant for the price we want.'

'Oh, shit.' Finn closed his eyes.

'So now we're trapped. I can't see any way for us to come out of this on the winning side.'

'Let's not do anything hasty. I think we should call your dad and see what he has to say.'

'I don't think that would be a good idea right now, given his history with Damian.' She stood up and began pacing back and forth.

'Look, I have to go back and get the boys. Come with me and we can talk more on the way.'

'No, I'm fine. I'll stay here and think about what to do.'

Finn stood up and closed the gap between them, drawing Olivia gently into his arms.

'You know I would rather have you than the restaurant if I have to make a choice, Olivia.'

She leaned her head on his shoulder and hugged him tight but didn't say anything. She stepped back a few minutes later and looked deep into his eyes.

'I want to find a way out of this, Finn. A way that works for everyone.'

Finn set off to pick up the boys from the beach, where they'd been merrily collecting samphire until Olivia's text had come through. He'd been concerned about having to leave them, and now he was just as worried about having to leave Olivia.

He arrived back at the beach twenty minutes later to find the boys tired but safe. After loading their buckets into the back of the car, he headed straight back to the restaurant, praying Olivia would still be there. It was getting on for an hour now since he'd left her, and he had a nagging feeling she might have taken things into her own hands.

Jamie and Harry helped him to take the buckets into the kitchen and fill them with fresh water to rinse the samphire, and then they headed off. Five minutes later, Finn checked the dining room for Olivia. There was no sign of her, and so he rushed upstairs to his flat. He was met with silence when he opened the front door. His heart sank. The door of the bedroom was ajar so he went to check there. The room was empty. He glanced around. Olivia's Kindle was gone from the bedside table. *Please God, no.* He went to the wardrobe, yanking the door open in his hurry. Her clothes were gone. She must have packed really quickly to have got away already. He looked out of the window but there was no sign of her. He sank down on the bed, hardly able to believe she would do this.

Finn took out his phone. If he called her and spoke to her, maybe he could make her see sense. The phone rang and rang at the other end, but she didn't pick up. He couldn't bring himself to leave her a message. What could he say that would make any difference?

He loved her so much, and even if he did get the restaurant back, it would be a hollow victory if she wasn't going to be there to share it with him.

CHAPTER SEVENTEEN

The following morning, after an overnight stay in Barnstaple, Olivia took her seat on the train back to Exeter, feeling numb from her actions. She could only imagine the hurt she must have caused Finn by leaving, but she had no other option. She had to take Damian Carter up on his offer. If she'd stayed, Finn would only have talked her round – and if he'd stopped her from leaving, there was no doubt he would lose the restaurant. Mr Stephens had finally emailed that morning to say the bank would lend them the money, and together with the lease, everything was now in place for Finn to buy back his beloved bistro. Olivia was the only remaining piece in the puzzle. All she had to do was to give up the man she loved, in order for him to gain the one thing he wanted more than anything. When she thought about how much she loved Finn, her heart broke a little bit more, but it was too late. He'd never forgive her for leaving him. She'd broken his already fragile trust, and there was no way back.

After a quick change in Exeter, she was on her way to Bristol. It was nearly lunch-time by the time the train pulled in to the station. She planned to make her way to Café Express's HQ to tell Damian Carter she was ready to start working for him after all, as long as he kept his word and let her arrange for the ownership of the bistro to be transferred back to Finn. She also wanted to make it clear that she expected to report directly to him and not to Rupert. Olivia wanted no more to do with her ex than was absolutely necessary.

She joined the queue outside the station for a taxi and had just got settled in a cab when her mobile rang. She was expecting it to be Finn, but the screen flashed up her dad's name. She hesitated for a long moment, then accepted the call.

'Hi, Dad, how are you?' Did he already know of her betrayal?

'I'm fine, sweetheart. I was ringing to let you know the house sale has gone through, so Valerie and I were thinking of coming to see you and Finn down in Devon as the first stop on our travels. What do you think?' He sounded so happy, Olivia hated herself for the unhappiness she was going to cause him.

'Dad, I... I'm in Bristol. I'm not down in Devon any more.'

'Are you coming to visit me? How long will you be staying?'

'No, Dad. I'm on my way to see Damian Carter.' She closed her eyes in anticipation of his fury.

'What for?' Her dad fell silent, and she imagined him at the other end of the phone as he worked out all the possible reasons. 'Olivia, please don't tell me you're going to work for him after all. What about Finn and the bistro?' He didn't sound cross, just disappointed which was somehow worse.

'Dad, I had no choice.' She explained the dilemma Damian had presented her with, and how she had made her decision to leave.

'And you'd give Finn up for that? Did Finn ask you to do it?'

'No. He told me I meant more to him than the bistro, but I know that's not true. The bistro is all he's ever wanted and I... I can't be the one to deny him that.'

'You're making a huge mistake here, Olivia. You love Finn and he feels the same way. That's worth more than bricks and mortar. Go back to him before it's too late. Please!'

'I can't, Dad. Look I'm here now. I have to go.' She hung up and switched her phone to silent, before paying the cab driver and stepping out onto the pavement. The Café Express head office stretched high into the sky, just like her father's old company building, heralding her return to the corporate world. There wasn't one tiny bit of her that was excited about the prospect. Damian had left her little choice but to take this job, and she would be working alongside Rupert, who she detested. So much for all her ambition.

'I'm here to see Damian Carter, please,' she announced to the receptionist a few minutes later.

'Is he expecting you?'

'No. But he'll want to see me.'

The receptionist called Damian's office, a sceptical look on his face, as if no-one got through to the top man without an appointment. She waited to see his reaction, and had to suppress a smile when he was clearly told in no uncertain terms that Olivia's arrival was keenly anticipated.

'Please go up to the executive suite, Miss Fuller. You can use the last bank of lifts and someone will meet you up there.'

She gave him a dazzling smile, even though her stomach was churning at the thought of what she was about to do. She joined the throng of people waiting for the lift, noticing how no-one was speaking to each other, just like at La Riviera. For the first time in a long time, she wondered whether this was really the life for her. She missed Lynford so much already, and the quiet life in the community she had come to love in recent weeks. She wasn't sure she could slot back in to this cut-throat business world, where no-one even seemed to like each other.

The lift was soon speeding up to the top floor, giving her little time to think about whether she was doing the right thing. When the doors eventually opened, she was surprised to see Rupert waiting for her.

'Ah, Olivia, so glad to see you made the right decision.' He gave her a smug look of satisfaction before taking a step towards her, presumably to kiss her on the cheek. She took a decisive step to the side to stop him from doing any such thing. The terms of their future relationship were going to be clear from the start this time.

'I'm here to see Damian, Rupert, if you'd care to lead the way.'

Finn was surprised to receive a call from George Fuller saying he wanted to meet with him at the restaurant as soon as possible. With Olivia gone and La Riviera no longer owning the bistro, he had no reason to talk to her father now, but he was curious about what her dad might have to say. When Mr Stephens had called too, to let him know the bank had approved the loan, he had experienced none of the elation he'd been expecting to, but he decided to ask him to join them. Together, they might all be able to come up with a way forward.

George arrived in a taxi at ten on the Tuesday morning. Valerie was with him and they were both carrying small travel bags. A few minutes later, Mr Stephens pulled up in his car. Finn watched them all greet one another before realising he ought to go out and make an appearance.

'Hello, George, Valerie,' he greeted them warmly. 'Mr Stephens. Good to see you again, too.'

They followed him through the kitchen to the dining area where he gestured to a table and waited while they took their seats.

'Will Olivia be joining us, Finn?' Mr Stephens came straight to the point.

'No, umm... Olivia's in Bristol. Damian Carter persuaded her to go and work for him in exchange for selling me the restaurant at the price George paid for it.'

Mr Stephens' face fell. 'Oh, I knew they were up to no good when they came to see me last week. I'm so sorry, Finn. I tried to keep them on side so I'd know what they were doing, but I had no idea this was what they were planning.'

'No, of course not. None of us did. But they're cunning, and now they've got exactly what they want. And I still can't believe Olivia took that option.'

With that, he disappeared off to the kitchen, returning a few minutes later with a pot of coffee and cups on a tray. The others were all talking quietly but fell silent when he put the tray down.

'So, Finn, I know you're upset about what's happened, but after speaking to Olivia myself yesterday, I want to try and work out a way forward for you both from here.'

'I don't see how there can be a way forward for us both. The bank has lent me the money. Now I need to see whether Olivia can get Carter to stick to his side of the deal. If she does, I'll have to move on without her... and the same if she doesn't really.' He sank onto a chair and let his head drop into his hands.

'Do you love Olivia, Finn?' Valerie's soft voice cut through the incessant thoughts in his head.

'I do, but none of that matters if she doesn't feel the same way,' Finn replied, glancing up.

'I'm absolutely sure she feels the same way, otherwise, she wouldn't have gone to these lengths to give you what you want most of all,' George said, with a hint of reproach.

And suddenly, Finn was ashamed. George was right – Olivia was sacrificing everything for him, and all he was doing was feeling sorry for himself. He sat up straighter in the chair.

'Tell me what I can do to get her back, George. I want her here by my side, running our restaurant together. She's turned its fortunes round and helped me make a success of things. I don't want to lose her, but I don't know how to persuade her to come back. Worst of all, I'm no match for men like Rupert and Carter.'

Mr Stephens cleared his throat and everyone looked his way. 'Well, Olivia has accepted his job on the basis she will be the one negotiating the sale of the restaurant back to you. I imagine she'll want to get on to that right away, especially as she knows you now have the money to buy it back. Once she's done that, and every-thing is in your name again, what's to stop her from leaving

Carter's company and coming back? Do we know what's in her contract?'

Finn threw up his hands. 'She'd gone by the time I came back. I have no idea what her contract involves.'

'This could be a way of getting our cake and eating it,' said George thoughtfully.

'Someone needs to talk to Olivia and to make her listen,' said Valerie.

This time, all eyes swivelled to Finn.

'How can I do that? I don't even know where she's staying and she won't answer my calls. And even if I could get through to her, how could I spare time from running the restaurant, unless I want everything to fail again?' Finn groaned in despair.

'What about if I try calling her? Do you think she would answer my call?' Valerie looked between the three men's faces, which were all etched with concern.

'I think that could work. It's worth a try, anyway.' George smiled at her, and the other two men nodded their agreement.

'Why don't you give her a call now while we're all here together?' suggested Finn, perking up. 'You could put her on speaker, and then we could all join in if it seems like the call is going well.'

'Great idea.' George beamed and they all cheered up a bit at the thought of sorting things out.

Valerie took out her phone and clicked on Olivia's phone number. She pressed the speaker button and they all waited with bated breath.

'Hello? Valerie, is that you?'

'Yes, Olivia, it's me. How are you?'

There was a pause followed by the sound of a door closing.

'I'm okay, but not at my best to be honest.'

Finn's face fell at the sadness he detected in Olivia's voice. Not for the first time, he regretted not taking Olivia with him when he went to collect the boys. At least he could have tried to persuade her to stay. He gripped the edge of the table, waiting to hear what she would say next.

———

'Your dad told me about your decision to go and work for Damian Carter. How's it going so far?'

Olivia was grateful to Valerie for calling, and touched that she was concerned for her welfare. She was one of the few people she could tell how she felt right now.

'It's awful. I've hated every minute of it so far. Working with both Rupert and Damian is just about the worst combination ever in a work role. The minute I walked through the doors, I knew I'd never fit back into this corporate life. I miss Lynford and the bistro so much. And I can't even begin to tell you how I feel without Finn by my side.' She let out a long sigh.

'Have they said anything more about the sale of the bistro? You know Finn has the money to buy it now, I presume?'

'Oh yes, that was the best bit of news since I left Devon. I'm so pleased for him and grateful to Mr Stephens for all his help.' Her voice had brightened for a moment but the reality of her situation soon crept back in. 'I've been pressing Damian for a schedule for the sale, but he's proving elusive. I'm going to have to come up with some-thing to force his hand soon if he doesn't get the ball rolling, but I have no idea what that could be. Is Dad with you, Valerie? I could use his advice.'

'I'm here, Olivia.' The sound of her dad's voice brought tears to her eyes.

'Oh, Dad, it's so good to hear your voice. I'm sorry I was short with you the other day. Are you still in Bristol? Shall I come round this evening?'

'No, we're in Devon now, sweetheart.'

'In... in Devon. Why?'

'We came down to see Finn to see if there's anything we can do to sort this situation out,' said Valerie.

'What do you mean? There's nothing for you to sort out. I'm going to do everything at this end, providing Damian doesn't go back on his word.'

Valerie fell silent, and Olivia regretted her sharp tone at once. She and her dad were only trying to help. She heard whispers at the other end and imagined they were working out what to say next, much as she was.

'Olivia, it's Finn. Please don't hang up.'

'Finn? Hang on, who else is there?' It was so good to hear his voice but now she realised she must have been set up.

'Mr Stephens is here too. Everyone came to see me to talk over what's happened and to see what we can do. If I'd known you were going to leave, Olivia, I would never have gone off without you. I want you here with me, otherwise having the bistro means nothing.'

Then the tears did fall. She swiped them away, not wanting anyone to see how upset she was.

'Oh, Finn. I'm so sorry. I thought I could sort everything out on my own and all I've done is make a complete mess of things.'

'Don't say that, sweetheart. You did it for all the right reasons. We just need to work together now to make it right again.'

'It's too late for that, Finn. For better or worse, I'm stuck here now.'

'Listen, we have an idea that might work, as long as Carter sticks to his original promise.'

'But how can I make him do that?' She groaned. None of them seemed to understand how difficult it was.

A knock at the door interrupted their conversation, and Damian appeared.

'Olivia, I need to talk to you.' He walked briskly to the chair on the other side of her desk, unbuttoned his suit jacket and sat down facing her, quite ignorant of the fact that she was on the phone. He put the sheaf of papers he was holding on the desk in front of her, but she couldn't see what they were from where she was sitting.

'Of course, Damian,' she said smoothly, hoping the others could still hear her. 'I can make this call later.' She slid her phone into her bag under her desk and away from Damian's line of sight, leaving it resting on top of her book.

'I know you want to press on with the sale of that bistro in Devon, and that's fine. You have the authority now to liaise with the Sales and Acquisitions team. As agreed, you can sell it back to that chef for the same price your father paid for it. But I expect you to recoup the loss we're going to make there with the sales of all the other independent restaurants. Is that clear?'

'I'll do my best.' She tried to keep calm and not rise to his bait. She could have challenged him on the so-called loss, but it wasn't worth wasting time on it. All she wanted to do was to sell the bistro back to Finn as soon as possible.

'I want those other restaurants sold off quickly, too.'

He stood up and Olivia hoped that was all he had to say. He didn't leave though, and she held her breath, wondering what other demands he had yet to make. He picked up the papers and thrust them towards her.

She released her breath as her curiosity got the better of her. 'What's this?' she asked.

'That's your contract. Read it through – it's all fairly standard – sign it and give it back to my PA as soon as you can.'

With that, he turned on his heel and left the room, closing the door quietly behind him. She waited to make sure the coast was clear before retrieving her phone from her bag.

'Hello? Are you still there?' she whispered, afraid someone else might come in if they heard her.

'Yes, we're here,' her father said. 'Olivia, whatever you do, don't sign that contract before we have a look at it. It's important you know what you're signing up for before you give it back to him.'

'Did you hear everything else he said?' she asked.

'Yes, we all heard it. I don't trust him, Olivia. I want to see what's in that contract before you sign it in case there are any hidden clauses you're not prepared for.'

Olivia surveyed her bedroom for what would probably be the last time. She'd spent the previous day at home packing up her things. A suitcase with everything she was going to take with her stood in the corner by the door, next to a bag of stuff to throw away and another to recycle. She was pleased with the job she'd done of sorting through everything.

Having been home so recently, her emotions weren't quite as raw this time. Her dad had packed the things she wanted to keep into a smaller bag, and he'd also boxed up some kitchen equipment for Finn to use. She'd been touched by that. It pained her to know she wouldn't be able to see Finn using it, but at least a small part of her would still be with him. Her dad had also offered to take everything down to him once the house was all sorted. Olivia was going to take all her stuff with her today back to the hotel she was staying in.

In between packing, she'd spent time talking to her dad about her contract with Damian Carter and what she was going to do about it, but she still hadn't been able to make a final decision. It was one thing her dad saying there was nothing in her contract to make her stay, but another to actually make it happen. She would have to stand up to Damian Carter and that wasn't a prospect she relished at all. Her dad had also told her Finn wanted her to come back and work by his side. She just couldn't believe that after the way she'd let him down so badly.

Now she was all dressed and ready to go downstairs for breakfast, but still trying to decide what to do. She hoped her dad could give her one more piece of advice.

'Good morning, Olivia. Did you sleep well?' Her dad looked like he'd been awake for ages, and yet he was full of beans.

'I did thanks, Dad. How about you?' She kissed him on the cheek before studying the breakfast options on the kitchen counter. In the end, she decided against having anything to eat. Her stomach was churning again, which was becoming a regular occurrence in the mornings, and the thought of food only made it worse.

'I always wake early, so I don't get as many hours' sleep as I'd like, but I do sleep well. It's another aspect of my age, I suppose.' He chuckled, and Olivia thought once again how much he'd changed since leaving the company and getting together with Valerie. She smiled at him and sat down at the breakfast table to pour herself a cup of coffee.

'Do you miss going into the office?' she asked, as she sipped at her drink.

'No, I don't. I've had enough of all the backstabbing and the stress, but it took leaving for me to realise that. Finally being able to be with Valerie has also made a huge difference to my wellbeing.'

'I was thinking how much more relaxed you look.'

'Have you thought any more about what you're going to do?'

'I've thought about nothing else. I'm worried about how Damian's going to react if I leave as soon as the sale of the bistro goes through. He'll feel tricked and I know that will infuriate him. And I can't help wondering why the contract doesn't say anything about me staying for a minimum length of time. It's not like him or Rupert to miss something so important. It all makes me uneasy.'

'I understand how you feel, Olivia, but you have to be strong enough to hold your nerve for a bit longer. Just think about what's waiting for you at the other end. You can go back to Devon and run the restaurant with Finn.' Her father smiled kindly at her and she envied him his optimism.

'Be honest, Dad, if Valerie had betrayed you like I've betrayed Finn, would you welcome her back with open arms?'

'That's just it. I don't think you have betrayed Finn, and nor does he. You've made the ultimate sacrifice by leaving him when you love him so much. You want him to have the restaurant back and this was a way for you to achieve that for him. By doing that, you've shown him just how much you love him.'

'I do love him so much and I know the bistro means everything to him. And if he understands that, I'm glad. I miss him terribly, and if there had been any other way to do this, I would have done it, I promise.'

Her father stood then and so did she. He took her hands in his and looked down at her. 'So if you love him, you have a few more things to do before you can go and spend the rest of your lives together. I'm confident you can do it, sweetheart, I really am.'

Olivia wasn't so sure, but she knew she would have to try. She would sign the contract and then get on with organising the sale of the bistro back to Finn. Once that was all in place, she would worry about how she was going to persuade Finn to take her back.

CHAPTER EIGHTEEN

Finn's first job of the day was to ring Amy to confirm the details for her hen do meal that evening. It would be more straight forward than Esme's exhibition, because it was a meal for ten people in the restaurant. All he needed to confirm with Amy was the start time and the menu.

He was glad they were still so busy, because it gave him plenty to do to take his mind off how much he was missing Olivia. It was still odd without her at the bistro. After only a few months, she seemed to belong here. George had let him know she'd been more receptive to their idea once they'd talked it over. Finn just hoped George's powers of persuasion were enough to make Olivia come back. He knew she would do her bit in making sure the bistro was sold back to him, but Finn wanted them to own it together. He was just going to have to trust her to follow her heart.

Finn had planned a relatively simple menu for Amy's hen party and was looking forward to cooking for her. He'd struck lucky with not having to collect his samphire this time, because Jamie had now passed his driving test – after three goes at it – and he'd offered to go with Harry. Finn had paid them a bit extra and was grateful to them. It meant he could make a head start while they were foraging.

Gavin, the journalist and photographer from the *Gazette*, was interested in doing a feature on the bistro for the paper, and Finn was keen to emphasise their use of local samphire. He'd been practising lots of different recipes with it and had taken some photos for Gavin to consider for his piece. Tonight, he would pair it with fillets of sea bream as the main course. He was sure everyone would love it. He set to filleting his fish as his first job and tried not to think too much about Olivia.

It was about time he started to believe in himself and got on with managing things on his own. He'd asked Harry to help Zoe front of house, to see if he was up to the job. If he managed it, as Finn was sure he would, he could work future events, too.

He carried on prepping till lunch-time. By that time the boys were back from their foraging and Zoe had arrived to start work on the dining room. He made them all an early lunch of bacon rolls and then they all split off to take care of their separate tasks. While Jamie and Harry got busy in the kitchen, Finn went into the dining area to chat with Zoe.

'Have you got everything you need for tonight?' he asked, pulling up one of the chairs to sit on.

'Yes, I think so. Amy has given me some balloons and some confetti to put on the tables, and I have some bunting to string up. Other than that, it's the usual setting up to do. It shouldn't take me too long, but as they're coming at five, I want to make sure everything's done in plenty of time.'

'Great. And how's everything with you otherwise?'

'What do you mean?' Zoe looked up sharply, confirming he had hit on something.

'You have a look about you, Zoe, as if you got up to no good this weekend.'

'If I did get up to something, I wouldn't tell you about it.' She rolled her eyes and turned away.

'Well, I want all the details, and you and Ed are keeping every-thing close to your chest. So is it official with you two? Are you an item?'

Zoe let out a gasp. 'It's none of your business.' She pursed her lips and carried on polishing glasses within an inch of their lives.

'Why not? I'm friends with you both and I want to be happy for you. Surely that's not too much to ask?'

'Not everybody's looking for love, you know.' She was on the defensive and that only made Finn more eager to find out why.

'There's a lot to be said for love,' he replied with a laugh. Then he stood up, realising he wasn't going to get anywhere. 'I guess I'll just have to speak to Ed and get his side of the story.'

Zoe made a huffing sound and went off to the cupboard to get out the hoover, signalling the end of their conversation.

Not long afterwards, Amy and her best friend arrived, and when Finn showed them through to the dining room, the transformation was magical. Zoe had decorated all the tables with balloons, flower arrangements and confetti. Amy took one look and her eyes filled with tears.

'Don't you cry now,' her friend advised. 'You'll set us all off.'

Amy was wearing a small tiara and a sash saying 'Team Bride', but apart from that, she was a low-profile 'hen', and Finn was relieved about that. Soon afterwards, her guests started arriving. Harry, now in a white shirt and black trousers switched roles to serve welcoming drinks. Meanwhile, Zoe passed round the appetisers Finn and Jamie had prepared earlier. Finn had used some of the same recipes from Esme's art exhibition, at Amy's request, and they went down a treat once again.

When they were all seated, Zoe and Harry began serving the starter – a salmon mousse served in a glass teacup, topped with a tiny piece of salmon and dill. This was accompanied by a basket of sour-dough bread, fresh from Rosie's bakery. Rosie had agreed to try working in partnership again, and so far it was going well.

Zoe and Harry were kept constantly busy serving food and

topping up the white wine, a crisp Sauvignon Blanc, and everyone seemed happy. After the first course, Amy's guests moved seats to talk with other people. Once they were settled, Zoe and Harry began to deliver the sea bream.

'Yes, freshly gathered this morning from the coast that samphire is. It tastes a bit like asparagus so I'm sure you'll like it.' Harry chatted to the guests up and down his side of the table and they responded well to his background details.

When everyone had been served, Zoe led him to the kitchen and called Finn over.

'Harry was just doing a great job of selling the samphire, and the bistro too, you know, Finn.' She smiled as Harry blushed at her comments. Finn gave him a thumbs up.

After the main course, the guests played a quiz game of 'Mr and Mrs', much to the bride-to-be's delight, and then they were able to move on and serve the dessert, a light lemon tart with a fruity raspberry coulis on the side and a single raspberry on the top. Zoe and Harry brought out pots of coffee and tea for the guests to serve themselves and retired to the kitchen for a well-earned break.

It had been another long but successful day. Finn only wished Olivia had been there to see the result of all her hard work.

Olivia had been up until the early hours of the morning re-reading the contract one last time to make sure there was nothing in the small print to catch her out. Relieved she hadn't found anything, she wanted to get on with the job in hand as quickly as possible. After snatching a few hours' sleep, she was up early to get ready. She was just making her way to the bathroom when she was overcome with the need to be sick. Making it there just in time, she admitted to herself that this had been happening once too often, and when she tried to think back to the date of her last period, she couldn't remember. With a groan, she pushed herself up and forced herself to continue getting ready.

She took a cab to the office, giving herself time to stop in at the chemist's on the way. Then, with superhuman effort, she put all thoughts of what might be happening to her body aside and focused on the task before her. She was determined to get to work immediately on selling the bistro back to Finn, as well as handing in her contract. She emerged from the lift into the executive suite and made her way straight to Damian's office. His PA looked up as she came to a stop in front of her desk.

'Good morning. Is Damian here yet, please?'

The PA peered over her glasses at her with a look of disdain. '*Mr Carter* is out on business today. He told me you might be dropping off your contract, however, and said for you to leave it with me.' She thrust her hand out, but Olivia wasn't comfortable with that idea.

'I'd prefer to give it to him directly. When will he be back?'

The PA tutted. 'Tomorrow. There isn't an issue with you leaving it with me. I'll make sure he gets it.'

Olivia stared at her for a moment before making up her mind and handing the letter over. 'Thank you.'

She turned on her heel, away from the PA's disapproving looks, and set off for her own office further along the corridor. She only took a second to deposit her things before setting off again for the Sales and Acquisitions team. She entered the office to find Rupert talking to some of his team in the corner. She'd begun making her way towards him when she realised he was with the vultures: Ryan, Marcus and Jake. She groaned inwardly, berating herself for having forgotten that she would see them sooner or later. Why had she ever thought it would be a good idea to come and work for Damian? Rupert turned, sensing her arrival. There was no sign now of his broken leg or any after effects.

'Olivia, how lovely to see you this Monday morning.' His oily voice grated on her now but she worked hard not to let it show. She needed him to make the sale of the bistro go through smoothly.

'Rupert. Do you have a minute, please?'

'Of course, of course. Come into my office.'

She followed him without so much as a glance at her former colleagues. She'd been promoted to the same level as Rupert now, so they'd better watch their step.

'Take a seat, Olivia. Now, what did you want to talk to me about?'

She ignored his obsequious smile and ploughed on with her request, without sitting down. 'As you'll know, Damian has given me authority to press ahead with the sale of the Devon bistro back to Finn Anderson. I'd like to get the ball rolling with that today, so I need to know who is handling it in your office.'

'Well, I... ah... I haven't actually assigned anyone to it yet. I wasn't aware Damian had given the go-ahead, but if you say he has, then I can get on to that today.'

'Can you tell me who to speak to about it? I don't want to drag this out for any longer than I have to. Damian is keen to recoup his losses on these independent restaurants as soon as possible, and I think he would look unfavourably on anyone causing any unnecessary delays.' She had to stop herself from smiling at the almost imperceptible rise of his eyebrows. *Yes, Rupert, I've changed*, she thought to herself, *and you'd better get used to this new version of me.*

'Right then. Let me think.' For the first time ever, Rupert looked flustered.

'What about Ryan?' Olivia went on. 'We know each other and I think he's reasonably competent.'

'Yes, of course. I'll get him to come in.'

Rupert stood up and went to the door to call Ryan in. The whole office fell silent as he hurried over to join them.

'Ryan, the bistro in Devon is to be sold back to the chef there. You will liaise with Miss Fuller to ensure this happens as soon as possible.' It had only taken a second for Rupert to switch back to his normal arrogant self.

Ryan swallowed nervously and nodded.

Rupert gave Olivia a smug look. 'I assume the chef now has the funds for the purchase?'

Olivia stood up. 'You leave me to worry about the details, Rupert. Ryan, come with me.'

She left Rupert's office and walked briskly back to her own, knowing only from the shuffling behind her that Ryan was following. Once back at her office, she closed the door.

'Please take a seat, Ryan.' He did as he was told, and, she was pleased to see, waited for her to speak. 'I know the bank that organised the original sale of the bistro to my father has the funds in place for the re-purchase. We're going to have a conference call with Mr Stephens now, and from here on, you will keep me updated every step of the way to make sure this sale happens quickly and smoothly. Do you understand?'

Again, Ryan nodded. Olivia picked up the phone to make her call, and a few seconds later, she was put through to Mr Stephens.

'Miss Fuller, what a wonderful surprise!'

She wanted desperately to chat with him as she would normally have done, but this call was all about putting on a front for Ryan. She hoped the bank manager would understand what she was doing and not take offence.

'Good morning, Mr Stephens. I have my colleague, Ryan, here with me, from our Sales and Acquisitions team. You may remember him from when he came to the bistro. Ryan's going to organise the sale of the bistro back to Mr Anderson from this end. We're just ringing to confirm the funds of £50,000 are available at your end.'

'Yes, of course. I can transfer the funds as soon as the paperwork is in hand. How soon can you send the documents over?'

Olivia looked pointedly at Ryan. 'Can you get that sorted today, Ryan?'

'I should be able to, yes,' he mumbled.

'Make sure you do, and if there are any problems, you are to come directly to me. Could you confirm to me when you receive the paperwork, Mr Stephens, please?'

'Yes, of course. I look forward to hearing from you later today.'

They said their goodbyes, and Olivia turned to Ryan. 'We're keen to sell these restaurants off quickly, Ryan, and a lot is riding on it. So make sure you get this done and copy me in on any emails you send.'

Ryan nodded and left the office, clearly eager to get started.

Olivia let out a long sigh of relief and crossed her fingers that she'd done enough to make this work for Finn.

Finn had heard nothing from Olivia since the conference call nearly two weeks ago. Mr Stephens contacted him to tell him about their call, though, and he was heartened to know she was moving ahead with the plan they'd discussed then. He just had no idea how long it was all going to take. He was missing Olivia more than he would have thought possible. He'd carried on running the business using the principles she'd taught him, and he'd called Harry in to help Zoe front of house in Olivia's absence. For now, he was rising to the challenge on his own, and marvelling at how he was able to do just that.

He was planning a catch-up day in the kitchen today and had already made a start on his stock when his phone rang. Wiping his hands on his apron, he quickly swiped to accept the call.

'Mr Stephens, hi,' he said, just in time before it went to voicemail.

'Hello, Finn. I'm calling to let you know our payment has gone through to Café Express and they've acknowledged receipt. We can now confirm everything is in order. I gave Olivia a quick call this morning and she's hopeful everything can be signed over from them to you today. If you could be on standby to pop over here later, you can sign the paperwork here, too.'

'That's brilliant news, Mr Stephens. Thank you. Just let me know when you need me.'

'Olivia's waiting for it all to be confirmed, of course, before she hands in her notice.'

'Does George know what's been happening?'

'I haven't called him myself, but Olivia may have done. I'll be in touch again later today.'

Finn decided to send a quick text to Olivia. Even if she didn't respond, he wanted to thank her.

'*Thank you for all you've done. It means so much to me...*' He stared at his words for a while before starting again. He didn't want to imply the bistro meant more to him than she did.

'*Thank you for all you've done. I miss you xx*' He stared at the second version for ages as well, before clicking send and crossing his fingers everything would work out.

Before he could call her father, his phone rang again. George had beaten him to it.

'Finn, how are you? Have you heard the latest? I haven't been able to get hold of Olivia.'

Finn filled George in on everything Mr Stephens had told him. 'So it's possible I could be the new legal owner of the bistro today.'

'I'm pleased to hear that, Finn. Olivia has done a marvellous job of holding her nerve. I wish I could have spoken to her to give her moral support.'

'I sent her a text just now to say thank you. You could always text her?'

'I prefer to speak to her, but yes, that's an option, I suppose.'

'How's everything going with the house sale?'

'Valerie has already exchanged contracts on her house and I'm due to do the same on mine today. We've both sorted out our furniture and put what we want to keep into storage. So we're ready for a new adventure now, which will start with us coming down to Devon again. I expect Olivia will be travelling south within a few days, too.'

Finn wished he had George's confidence about Olivia's plans once the sale of the bistro had gone through, but he didn't say anything. He desperately wanted to talk to her, but he didn't want to push her. He hoped she would call eventually.

'Well, you know you're always welcome here.' He said goodbye and returned to prepping his fish stock. It was going to be a long day waiting for Mr Stephens to call, and he would need to keep himself busy.

At three o'clock his phone rang again. He was so eager to answer it, he didn't look to see who was calling.

'Mr Stephens, hello? What's the news?'

'Finn, it's me.' Olivia's soft voice was like a slam to his soul.

'Olivia, hi, I'm sorry. I've been waiting to hear how things have gone. How are you?' He was rambling and sounded stupid. These weren't the things he wanted to say to her.

'I'm okay, Finn. I miss you too, though.'

Finn's heart soared with possibilities. 'How have things gone today? Are you okay?' He longed to see her face and to touch her again.

'The sale has gone through and all the paperwork has been signed. So the bistro belongs to you again.' She sounded pleased and he was so grateful for her sacrifice, but he wanted her to come home.

'The bistro will always belong to you, as well as me. I couldn't have done any of this without you. I hope you know that.'

'It meant a lot to me to help you, Finn, and I'm so proud you've got the bistro back. It's the least you deserve. I... I just want you to be happy.'

'You make me happy, Olivia. All I want is for you to be by my side at the bistro and in my life.' Finn closed his eyes and prayed she would accept what he was saying. The line was silent for a long moment.

'Could you really forgive me, Finn, after all the hurt I've caused you?' Her voice was almost a whisper.

'There's nothing to forgive. I wish you hadn't gone, but I know you did it for the right reasons, and I love you even more for it.'

'I have to go now, Finn, but I love you too.'

And with that declaration she was gone. Finn didn't know whether to be full of hope or despair. Had he done enough to get her to come back, or was she gone forever?

Today was the day Olivia had decided to face Damian. She hadn't seen him for several days, and she would need to be strong. The sale of the bistro back to Finn had now been concluded, all the monies transferred, and all the paperwork signed. Olivia had asked her father's former lawyer to confirm she could now hand in her notice at Café Express with no repercussions for Finn, and that was what she intended to do. She was dreading it, of course, but she was also looking forward to relieving herself of this terrible burden. She'd done what she set out to do, and this was the final step in her plan.

She didn't bother going to her office when she emerged from the lift on to the executive floor, she just went straight to Damian's. Once again, she found herself face to face with his intimidating PA. She'd seen the woman's name on her desk this time and wondered if using it might soften her up a little.

'Is Damian here yet please, Janet? I'd like to see him.' She had her resignation letter in her bag, and this time she wanted to hand it to Damian himself.

'He is. Is he expecting you?' Janet was still haughty but not as hostile as she had been the previous time, so maybe her strategy had worked.

'No, but I only need a few minutes.'

The PA stood and knocked softly on Damian's door before slipping inside. Olivia waited with bated breath, crossing her fingers he would agree to see her.

Janet returned a minute later. 'He can see you now.'

Olivia smiled her thanks and went towards the open door.

'Good morning, Olivia,' Damian said. 'What can I do for you? Well done for sorting out the sale of that bistro so quickly, by the way. The money will be a welcome boost for our cash flow.'

Olivia reached into her bag and extracted the letter she'd prepared the previous night. She handed it to him without a word. He opened it and read its short contents.

'What the...? You can't do this.' He stood up, sneering.

'I can, and I am doing it. I never wanted to work here, Damian, and you can't seriously believe I fit in here either. Now, would you like me to stay and work out my week's notice or would you rather I went straight away?' She smiled sweetly, daring him to challenge her.

His face turned a beetroot colour. 'If you think you're going to get away with this, you're wrong. Rupert assured me the contract has a clause—'

'That's where you're the one who's wrong,' she interrupted him, secretly pleased Rupert would get hell for this mistake. 'I took the time to read the document through word by word, and I also had it double-checked by a lawyer. There's nothing to stop me handing in my notice, and it's only a week because I'm on probation.'

He picked up the phone. 'Get me security at once.' His eyes met Olivia's, cold with fury. 'You will leave this office accompanied by a security guard so you can't do any more damage and I never want to see you again. Do you hear? And don't expect any pay for your time here either.'

The guard arrived. 'Go with her while she clears her desk and then see her off the premises.' He threw one last venomous look at Olivia as she left the room, closely followed by the guard.

As Olivia had cleared her desk and office the previous week, the guard took her straight out of the building. She stood on the pavement outside the building and inhaled a deep breath of fresh air. Then she burst out laughing. It was probably part nervous reaction, part absolute joy at having got one over on the supercilious Damian Carter. Her dad would be so proud!

Now it was time for part two of her plan. Since finding out she was pregnant, she'd known she must go back to Devon to tell Finn the news. She wasn't quite as confident about doing this bit, but she had to try. She made her way to the station, pausing to make a quick phone call before she caught her train. Now she had to hope this part of the plan would also be successful.

When she came out into the station foyer, Finn was there waiting for her, as Zoe had promised he would be. He opened his arms, and she ran towards him, desperate to be in his embrace. From the moment she kissed his lips and felt his arms around her, she felt safe. She never wanted to let him go again. He drew away first, stroking her hair and whispering her name. Then he picked up her bag and took her hand to lead her out to the car.

'Come on, we're going to get ourselves some late lunch while we're here, to celebrate being back together.' He put her bag in the boot and they made their way into town, leaving Finn's battered old car in Barnstaple station's car park. They crossed the Long Bridge that would take them into the centre, happy to be together again. They strolled along the main road, past the museum and turned up one of the back streets.

'Thank you for coming, Finn. I wasn't sure you would.'

'I'm just so glad you've come back.' He squeezed her hand and Olivia knew he meant it. She wanted to tell him her news there and then, but it didn't seem the right place or time.

'You seem to know where you're going. What are you up to?' She grinned at him.

'I've heard about this new fish and seafood place and I thought we could check it out. You know, we might pick up some ideas.' He winked at her and within a couple of minutes they were there, and it was like old times. They sat at a table by the window, where they could watch people passing by on their way to the river.

Over their starters – crispy squid for her and crab salad for him – Olivia filled Finn in about the meeting and how vile Damian Carter had been towards her.

'I'm sorry you had to put up with that from him again, but at least he got his comeuppance. And I'm so proud of you for standing up to him and holding your nerve till the end.'

'Thanks. It wasn't easy, but it was worth it.'

Finn closed his eyes in delight as he swallowed another delicious mouthful of local crab. She smiled as she watched him.

'This crab salad is wonderful,' he said, 'I'm definitely going to put one on our menu, but with a few tweaks. How's your starter?'

'It's nice, but the batter's quite heavy. I think the squid would be better lightly pan-fried, rather than weighed down with all this batter and grease.' She pulled a face and Finn laughed.

'It's so good to see you. I was bereft without you, you know.'

'Bereft, huh?'

'Yes, and I'm not ashamed to say it.'

Her eyes sparkled. 'How did Amy's do go on Sunday?'

'It all went off excellently, thanks to your planning, and also Harry was brilliant. We should ask him to work again when we have events. That would also give you the space to oversee everything.'

'Yes, good plan. I'm proud of you for running that whole event on your own. We've both come such a long way over these past few months.'

Olivia had never been happier than she was now, back where she belonged, with Finn in Devon. All she had to do now was to find the right moment to tell him her remaining news, and to hope this was what he wanted too.

CHAPTER NINETEEN

Finn finished his call and put his phone in his pocket before going out to find Olivia.

'All done?' he asked, coming to a stop in front of the bar counter.

'Yes, almost,' she replied. 'You look like you're up to something, Mr Anderson.' Her eyes lit up.

'You'll just have to come with me to find out, won't you?'

Finn took her hand and led her out from behind the bar, guiding her to the back door.

A minute later, they were walking up the high street, away from the bridge, as if they were going out of the village, but just before the end of the street, Finn turned right up a side street. Olivia followed his lead.

'Ooh, this is intriguing. You've never taken me this way before,' she said, looking closely at the residential area around her.

Finn stopped outside a terraced stone cottage. The tiny front garden was bursting with pots planted with all kinds of colourful flowers and herbs, including begonias and geraniums, as well as scented lavender and mint.

'Who lives here?' asked Olivia, turning to face Finn.

'We do, if you like it.'

Olivia's eyes widened and her mouth fell open. 'But how can we...? We can't afford something like this.'

'We'd only be renting, and it's within our budget. I've been sensible about it, I promise. You've taught me well. Why don't we go and have a look inside and you can see what you think?'

She nodded without saying another word, but she was smiling, much to Finn's relief. He fished the keys out of his pocket and led the way up the few steps to the front door.

It was a two-up, two-down house, making it quite cosy but it was definitely bigger than what they had already. The front door opened straight into the lounge, with the stairs off to the right. It was a good size, with a nice little fireplace, as well as space for a dining table. The galley kitchen leading off from the lounge was big enough for the two of them to work in side by side, and the stable door at the end, which led to the courtyard garden, was delightful.

'What do you think so far, then?' Finn asked, as they walked out into the garden to have a look around.

'I love it, Finn. I can't get over how lovely it is and how much space there is. Are you sure we can afford it?'

'I am. It belongs to Rosie's sister, Tilly, and she's got a new job up in London. She doesn't want to sell it until she's sure everything's going to work out up there, which is why she's renting it out. It will also come with all the furniture, and we're getting a special deal because we know Rosie. So we can afford it. Come on, let's go upstairs.'

They poked their heads in to see the downstairs bathroom, which was alongside the kitchen, before going up to the first floor. The main bedroom was a good size and looked over the garden at the back. They could see all the neighbouring gardens, and it looked like most of their neighbours were keen gardeners, too, because they were all very well-kept. Rosie's sister had done a great job of maintaining hers.

'It would be fun to have a garden, wouldn't it? I'd love to try growing some herbs and a few vegetables,' said Olivia. At that point,

Finn was hopeful she would say yes to renting the cottage, and his heart lifted.

They looked into the other bedroom, which faced onto the street, and were once again pleasantly surprised by the available space. Finn watched Olivia as she took in all the details, and wondered what she was thinking.

'Could you see yourself living here?' he asked, as they made their way back downstairs.

'Yes. I like it very much, and it would be good to start out renting rather than having to commit to a mortgage.'

'Shall I say "yes", Miss Fuller? Will this be our first house together?'

She leaned against him and kissed him firmly on the lips by way of an answer.

'When can we move in?' she asked, when they came up for air a few minutes later.

'As soon as we like. Tilly's already taken all the stuff she's going to. And I was thinking we could offer the flat above the bistro to Jamie for free if we're going to give him the job of apprentice. That way, he can get to work quickly and we know he's living somewhere safe, which will stop his parents from worrying about him too.'

'That's an excellent idea. You seem to have thought of everything, Finn.'

'Are you sure? I don't want to push you into it. I want you to be doing it for the right reasons.'

He still had his arms around her waist. She looked up into his eyes.

'I want to be with you forever. We have our own restaurant now – our own successful business, I should say. We love each other and this is the obvious next step.'

They left the cottage shortly afterwards, stopping at the bakery on their return journey.

'Hi, Rosie, how are you?' Olivia asked as they walked in.

'Tired but happy.' She laughed.

'How are the children?'

'They're good, thank you, but we're exhausted. Anyway, have you two been to see the cottage?' She raised her eyebrows.

'We have and we loved it. We just need to ask when we can move in.' Finn smiled at her, unable to contain his excitement.

'How about this weekend, when you've got some time off from the restaurant and can do it all in one go? Would that work?'

'That would work well. We have lots of events coming up in June and we might not get the chance again for weeks otherwise.'

As they returned to the restaurant to prep for the evening service, Finn had never been so happy, and he hoped Olivia felt the same.

Olivia's feet had hardly touched the ground since coming back to Devon. What with the bistro being so busy and their plans for various events, she hadn't had much time to think about the fact that she was now the joint owner of a restaurant. She was delighted at the way everything had turned out, and her relief at not having to worry about it any more was incredible. It had also freed her to follow her heart and stay down in Devon with Finn.

She was looking forward to today's event very much. She went through her checklist for what she hoped would be the final time. Now they had a few events under their belts, it should be getting easier, but Olivia still liked to fuss over the final details. She knew how important these events were to her customers.

The previous weekend they'd hosted Gavin's wedding reception, and she remembered how delighted the couple had been with all the extra little touches they'd added for their pleasure. They'd hired in special linens for the tables and asked Esme's friend, Amy, to design and print out name cards and seating plans. The local florist had made up table decorations in the bride's colours, as well as free-standing displays to place around the bistro itself. Zoe had decorated the whole space with bunting again and had also brought in some colourful balloons. The bride's face had lit up when she'd entered the restaurant, and it had been a wonderful event.

The event they were holding today was to celebrate Olivia and Finn owning the bistro. It would be the first time her dad and Valerie and all their local friends had come together. Zoe and Ed, now finally a couple, had offered to organise all the decorations; Esme and Amy were working together on some special art for the occasion; Rosie and Ewan were baking bread; even their wine supplier had given them a special discount for all the business they had brought his way in the last few months.

'Hello!' Jamie called from the kitchen as he arrived to get started on the menu. Jamie was now a fully-fledged apprentice and he'd volunteered, along with Harry, to make all the food for the event. Finn was supervising, of course but as it was going to be a buffet he could afford to take more of a back seat.

'In here,' Olivia replied.

As Jamie made his way through, the door opened again and she heard Zoe's voice, which meant Ed probably wasn't far behind.

'Morning. How's everything going?' Zoe came in carrying bags and boxes in her arms. There was no sign of Ed.

'Fine, fine. I can't seem to stop double-checking my list, though.'

'Where's Finn? Shouldn't he be giving you a hand?'

'He had to go and collect Dad and Valerie. They should be back soon. Anyway, could you look at my list and help me check it through one last time, please?'

Zoe plonked all the bags and boxes down without mishap and Jamie disappeared again to the kitchen. Within half an hour, they'd gone through the list between them and worked out what was left to do. Harry arrived to help Jamie, so that was the food prep sorted and Zoe started work on the decorations.

'Where's Ed, then?'

'I sent him to the bakery to pick up the bread, and to borrow their stepladder for some of the decorations. That's one thing we need to invest in, since our old one broke. Ed would have brought his one if I'd remembered to ask. Never mind, we'll soon have it all organised.'

'Okay. I think I'll go home and get myself ready, then.'

It was great knowing they had such a good team around them, and that they could trust them to get on with things in their absence. As Olivia wandered up the road towards their cottage, she thought about how far they'd come in such a short time. She never imagined when she came down here to the bistro all those months ago that she would find love, or that she would never want to leave. She'd become attached to the village and its people, as well as the bistro, and now the cottage was the icing on the cake. When Finn had taken her to see it, that's when she knew how committed he was to her and their relationship. She still had to tell him about the baby, but with each passing day, she became more confident he would be happy to hear her news.

Just as she was arriving back home, Finn pulled up with her dad and Valerie. She waited on the pavement while they got out of the car.

'Hello, sweetheart. It's good to see you.' Her dad flung his arms around her and hugged her tight. Olivia was still getting used to this much more tactile version of her father, but she liked it.

'How are you both?' she asked Valerie.

'We're wonderful,' she replied. 'We've completed on both house sales, and all we have to do now is pick up our camper van after the party and we can be off on our travels.'

'That's exciting! Come on in and see the cottage. You'll love it.'

After giving her dad and Valerie the tour and showing them the front bedroom, where they put down their things, Olivia took them downstairs again to the garden, where Finn had prepared some tea.

'We're looking forward to sharing your event with you all tonight,' her dad said, after taking a sip of his tea. 'How many people will be there?'

'About twenty or so, if everyone comes. And everything's in hand, even the cooking.'

'Yes, although I do want to be around in case they need any help.'
Finn chewed his lip, trying not to be too nervous about delegating for
the first time.

'I just need to get changed and then we can go back over. We've
still got all afternoon to make sure everything is ready. Try not to
worry.' Olivia patted his hand and smiled, knowing he would
anyway.

By the time they got back to the bistro, the place was bustling with
activity. Jamie and Harry were hard at work in the kitchen, and Finn
stayed with them.

Olivia continued on into the dining room, where she came to an
abrupt halt. There had been a beautiful transformation in her
absence. She lifted her hands to her face and blinked back her tears.
Zoe was at her side in seconds.

'Do you like it?' she asked, frowning.

Olivia put her hand on her friend's arm. 'Like it? I love it. Thank
you.' They hugged and Olivia had to work even harder to stop her
tears from falling. While she had been gone, Zoe had pinned up large
expanses of pale blue voile on every wall, making the inside of the
dining area look like the sea. She'd found some new bunting in all
different shades of blue, and Ed was just finishing pinning it up. In
between all this, she'd put up hundreds of fairy lights that cast a glow
over the whole room. They looked like little stars.

'It's beautiful, thank you both so much.'

She turned around, trying to take it all in, and caught sight of the
lovely new paintings Esme and Amy had been working on. There
was one of the outside of the bistro that was a marvellous likeness of
it. Finn was going to love it for sure. Each table was covered with soft,
cream linen tablecloths and each place was neatly laid, with its own
name card in front of it. There was also a seating plan by the door.
The florist had obviously been, because all the tables were adorned

with a bunch of sweet-smelling yellow freesias – Olivia's personal favourite.

There was just one more person Olivia was hoping to see, and hopefully, she wouldn't have to wait much longer. 'Thank you, everyone. You've all done a fantastic job,' she called out.

Finn rejoined her at that point, looking as delighted as she was with the sight of the bistro.

'Wow! This looks fabulous. The boys have done a great job in the kitchen, too. I didn't know how dispensable I was,' he added with a grin.

'You'll always be indispensable to me,' she said.

'Shall I check all the drinks are chilled?'

'I'm sure they are, but good idea to check.'

While Finn was gone, Olivia had a last look at her checklist to confirm everything was ready. The next time she looked up, it was to see an older man, who looked like a more mature version of Finn, hovering outside the bistro. She went outside to greet him.

'Mr Anderson? I'm Olivia.'

'Hello, Olivia. It's lovely to meet you.'

She took Finn's dad back inside just as Finn reappeared with some sparkling wine, ready to get the party started. His face lit up and he came straight over.

'Dad! It's great to see you.' Finn drew his dad in for a hug. Their eyes held a sheen of tears when they pulled apart. Finn took Olivia's hand and gave it a squeeze, before grabbing a glass of sparkling wine for them both.

Once everyone had a glass in their hand, Finn called them all into the dining room.

'Thanks to all of you here, we're going to have the best celebration tonight. You guys mean the world to us – all our friends, who have helped us make such a great success of things second time round, and our family, who have united around us when we needed it most. Thank you, and have a wonderful evening.'

Cheers rang out and then it was back to business, pouring drinks and finishing the final food prep before everyone arrived. Rosie and Ewan were the first to arrive, and Olivia and Finn welcomed them warmly.

'We're sorry we haven't been before, but it's never easy to get a babysitter. My mum's doing it for us tonight, so we can relax.'

Olivia passed them both a drink and they went off to mingle. Esme and Amy returned from getting changed. Shortly afterwards, Ed arrived too, beaming at Zoe on his way in, so much so, she blushed.

'Those two have to stop being embarrassed about being together,' said Finn.

'Hello, Mr Stephens. It's wonderful to see you.' Olivia leaned forward and kissed the older man on both cheeks. He looked delighted to be there and very different in his casual clothes. Finn shook his hand, gave him a glass of sparkling wine and pointed him in the direction of her father and Valerie, who were chatting to Finn's dad.

When Gavin, the photographer, arrived with his wife, Beth, Olivia mentally ticked off the final box on her checklist.

'So good to see you both again. I hope the honeymoon went well.'

'Thank you for inviting us,' said Beth.

'Come on in. Let me get you both a drink. I know Finn would like to talk to you about the feature in the paper if you get a minute tonight but if not, you can do it another time.'

When everyone had arrived and had taken their places, the boys started to serve the platters of food to the tables for the guests to help themselves. Zoe put bottles of sparkling wine and juices around the tables and then took her seat next to Ed, knowing everyone would serve themselves with more drinks when needed. Finn nodded at Jamie and Harry to take their places, too, and then Olivia stood.

'Thank you all very much for coming here to celebrate with us tonight. We owe our success to all of you in this room, as friends, as family and as customers.' Everyone laughed. 'Finn and I are so grateful to you all and hope we will continue to be successful for many years to come. Please, raise your glasses.'

'These are hard times to be running a restaurant anywhere in the country but even more so in a small seaside village. It's no wonder Finn Anderson struggled to make a success of his restaurant business the first time round.

Then he got a lucky second chance. Now in business for just over four months, Finn and his new partner, Olivia Fuller, have not only found success on a much bigger scale, they have also found love...'

'What a wonderful piece Gavin has written in the *Gazette*,' said Finn, as he put down the paper. 'The photos look great, too. I hope this will encourage even more customers to come our way.' He smiled at Olivia over his cup of coffee.

'I love that picture of Jamie and Harry foraging for samphire down on the beach. It's a unique selling point for us, isn't it?'

'Yes, I hope so.'

'I can't believe how many new bookings we've had this week for extra events since the article was published. We're going to have to manage our time carefully to make sure we don't take on too much, otherwise we might never get any time off.' Olivia frowned as she considered that prospect.

Finn patted her hand. 'What would you like to do today, since we do have a day off for once?'

'I'd love to go for a walk along the coastal path again, and to take one of your wonderful picnics with us like we did before.'

Half an hour later, they were walking along the stony path away from the village and up above the sea, as they had done all those weeks before when their relationship hadn't even properly started. This time they were holding hands, and they were partners in every sense of the word.

'I've had some more ideas for events we could hold at the bistro in the future, apart from the private parties we've had so far,' Finn revealed, as they made their way towards the Iron Age hill fort.

'Go on,' Olivia said warily.

'Don't look so worried. When I was with the wine supplier the other day, Alex, the owner suggested holding food and wine tastings every now and then, which we could organise together. And I've wondered about an occasional live music event, and even cooking classes for both adults and children.' He paused to let Olivia take in the full extent of what he was saying.

'Those all sound like good ideas, but I do think we're going to have a problem in the longer term between managing the bistro, which is our core source of income, as well as managing these extra events. And as I said earlier, we'll have to be careful not to spend all our time working.'

'I know, that's true, but we have to keep developing, in order to find new customers.' Finn looked at her hoping she would see his point.

Olivia took a deep breath. 'The thing is, Finn, I'm pregnant.'

There was a brief moment of deafening silence, followed by more noise than it was possible to imagine a human being making all on his own. Finn jumped up and gently pulled Olivia to him, whooping with delight.

'I'm so happy to hear that news, I hardly know what to say,' he told her in between numerous kisses. 'I love you so much, Olivia, and now we're going to have a baby!'

'Are you pleased, then? I just thought this news was coming all at the wrong time for us.'

'I am beyond pleased, I'm thrilled to know you're carrying our baby inside you.' He kissed her more softly this time. 'Babies come when they want to and we will manage a new addition. We've got all our friends and family around us, and we'll be okay. And look at Rosie – she runs a business and has a growing family too, so if she can do it, I know we can.'

'I'm glad you feel like that. I've been worrying about it since I found out.'

'Oh, sweetheart, I'm sorry you were worried, but we're in this together, like everything else we've done. And I think a baby is just what we need next. Just think, we'll have someone to pass the bistro on to when they grow up.'

Finn put his arm round Olivia and pulled her close, and they gazed out towards the sea. This was only the beginning of all the wonderful things they were going to do together.

THE END.

Because reviews are vital in spreading the word, please leave a brief review on Amazon if you enjoyed reading *The Bistro by Watersmeet Bridge*. Thank You!

FREE BOOK: The prequel to my début novel, *From Here to Nashville*, is available **FREE** when you sign up to my newsletter. Find out what happened between Rachel and Sam before Jackson arrived on the scene in *Before You*, at **www.julie-stock.co.uk**.

READ AN EXCERPT FROM THE VINEYARD IN ALSACE

Fran

'Here, you can have this back!' I wrenched my engagement ring from my finger and flung it in the general direction of their naked bodies, huddled together under the sheet on the bed. *Our* bed. 'I obviously won't be needing it any more.'

'What the hell, Fran?' The thunderous look on Paul's face as the ring pinged against the metal bed frame almost made me doubt myself. I closed my eyes briefly. *Don't let him control you. You are definitely not the guilty party!*

I took one last look at him and then I turned and ran. I kept on running, as far and as fast as my legs would take me, blood pounding in my ears, my long hair whipping around my face. The whole time my mind raced with thoughts of his double betrayal.

Eventually, my body couldn't take any more and I stopped on the pavement near an underground station, doubled over and panting from the effort. Once I'd got my breath back a bit, I gave Ellie a call. She picked up on the first ring.

'Hey, Fran, how are you?'

That question pushed me over the edge into full-blown sobbing and once I'd started, I couldn't stop.

'What's the matter? Where are you? Is Paul there? Talk to me, please!'

'Hold on a minute,' I managed to choke out, wiping my face on the sleeve of my t-shirt. 'I'm at the Tube station and I need a place to stay. Paul... Paul... well, there is no Paul and me any more.'

I heard her sharp intake of breath before she said, 'Of course you must come here. Will you be okay on your own or do you want me to come and get you?'

'No, I'll be okay. I should be about half an hour. Thanks, Ellie.' I rang off and made my way down into the depths of the Tube, grateful that I would have somewhere to stay so I didn't have to go back home tonight. Afterwards, I couldn't remember finding my way to the platform. I was so distracted by all that had happened and in such a short space of time but the next thing I knew, I was squashed into a seat on a crowded rush-hour carriage, trundling north on the Northern line.

No-one spared me a second glance on the train. It was oddly calming to be sitting among complete strangers in my misery and to know I didn't have to explain myself. I wrapped my arms protectively around my body. *Why on earth had Paul done this to me?* I wracked my brain as the train rattled on, but I could make no sense of it.

When I arrived at Ellie's, she scooped me into her arms at once for a hug, which only made me start crying again. She patted my back comfortingly, and eventually the tears subsided.

'Why don't I get us both a drink and then you can tell me everything that's happened?'

I nodded silently. While Ellie was gone, my phone buzzed with yet another text message. It was from Paul, no doubt trying to find me, but I deleted it along with all the others and set the phone down on the table in front of me. Ellie returned shortly afterwards with two cups of tea. I wouldn't have minded something stronger under the circumstances but it probably wasn't a good idea to get drunk just now. I'd need a clear head for whatever was going to come next.

'So, what the hell has happened?'

And I told her.

'I can't even begin to process it, Ellie. Why would he do that to me in the first place but even worse, why would he do it to me just after we'd got engaged?'

'I don't know what to say, apart from telling you that I never really liked Paul – I'm sorry – and he's proved what a bastard he is by doing this to you. There's no excuse for cheating and you'll never be able to trust him again now.'

I winced at her honesty and at her harsh judgment of Paul.

'In just that one second, my life's been turned upside down. Everything I was planning on – you know, getting married, settling down, starting a family – is now in doubt. I feel like my life is over.' I set down my cup and let the tears roll down my face. My phone buzzed once more with another text. This time, I read it first.

'*Where are you? I just want to know that you're okay. I'm really sorry, I've been incredibly stupid.*'

'Well, at least he realises that much,' said Ellie, her lips tight with anger as I read it out to her.

My fingers hovered over the keypad but in the end, I deleted the message and turned off the phone.

'I'm going to bed, Ellie. I'm exhausted, and I just can't think straight. Hopefully, things will be clearer in the morning.'

Once I'd climbed into the little single bed in Ellie's spare room, sleep just wouldn't come. I tossed and turned restlessly as images of Paul in bed with this other woman invaded my mind. I thought again about what Ellie had said about never really liking Paul. Had I been taken in by him all this time? I covered my eyes with my hands, embarrassed by my foolishness. I lay there for hours, railing against the injustice of the situation and wondering how I would explain all this to my parents. By the time I finally fell asleep the sun was coming up but I had the beginnings of an idea about what I was going to do next.

ALSO BY JULIE STOCK

From Here to You series

Before You (Free prequel) - From Here to You

From Here to Nashville - Book 1 - From Here to You

Over You - Book 2 - From Here to You

Finding You - Book 3 - From Here to You

From Here to You series

Domaine des Montagnes series

The Vineyard in Alsace - Book 1 - Domaine des Montagnes

Starting Over at the Vineyard in Alsace - Book 2 - Domaine des Montagnes

Standalone

Bittersweet - 12 Short Stories for Modern Life

ABOUT THE AUTHOR

Julie Stock writes contemporary feel-good romance from around the world: novels, novellas and short stories.

She published her debut novel, *From Here to Nashville*, in 2015, after starting to write as an escape from the demands of her day job as a teacher. *Starting Over at the Vineyard in Alsace* is her latest book, and the second in the Domaine des Montagnes series set on a vineyard.

Julie is now a full-time author, and loves every minute of her writing life. When not writing, she can be found reading, her favourite past-time, running, a new hobby, or cooking up a storm in the kitchen, glass of wine in hand.

Julie is a member of the Romantic Novelists' Association and The Society of Authors.

Julie is married and lives with her family in Bedfordshire in the UK.

Sign up for Julie's free author newsletter at **www.julie-stock.co.uk.**

facebook.com/JulieStockAuthor

twitter.com/wood_beez48

instagram.com/julie.stockauthor

ACKNOWLEDGMENTS

Many years ago, not long after my husband and I first met, we found out that one of our favourite restaurants was for sale. It was a fish and seafood restaurant located in the Scottish Highlands. We thought really seriously about buying it, but eventually, common sense prevailed, and as we had no experience for the job, except for a love of cooking and eating (!), we decided against it. We've never regretted it because we know how hard it would have been to make a success of it, but there's a little part of each of us that would have loved to do it all the same.

The premise for this story came to me when I saw another restaurant for sale many years later, in Lynmouth, in Devon. I was so excited by the idea that I told my husband and daughters about it straight away, and their enthusiasm for it persuaded me to go ahead and write it. Since that first idea, my husband has spent many hours talking the story over with me to help me get it right, and I'm really grateful to him for his time and patience.

I've dedicated this story to our family friends, Sylvia and John, who I've known for over forty years. Sylvia was a wonderful cook when she was alive, and we spent many hours poring over recipes together, and then enjoying the results when we'd finished cooking. Sylvia instilled a love of cooking in me, and John taught me most of what I know about wine. I'd like to think that Sylvia would enjoy reading this book.

As always, I'd like to thank my writing friends, Kate and Ros, for all their help during the writing process, and their friendship. They're both always there to listen and to help me work things out, and I really do appreciate it. I'm also lucky to have the support of a number of other writing friends, and I'd like to thank the Beta Buddies, and Sam especially for their support.

This past year has been a difficult one as I discovered that I had a benign tumour just about a year ago, and then had to have major surgery to have it taken out. It has been an emotional time but I'm thankful to have come out the other side now and to be mostly recovered. It was while I was on extended sick leave that I finally finished this story, and I'm so glad I had the chance to do it. You never know what's round the corner in life, so it's best to try and make the most of it. Thanks to my friends, Tanya, Julia and Mandie, and to my family for keeping my spirits up when I needed it most.

Made in the USA
Coppell, TX
18 January 2021

48394282R00146